DEVOURING THE DEAD 2

NEMESIS

RUSS WATTS

For my better half.

Time to get your game face on.

PART THREE: AWAKENING

CHAPTER ONE

Leonard silently mixed the tin of cold beans with a fork. He swirled the reddish brown mush around, staring at it vacantly, just stirring it around and around and around. A lone bean made a bid for freedom and plopped over the side of the tin, dribbling down the side until it landed on Leonard's foot.

"Come on, Leonard, I'm hungry," said Billy, drawing his dressing gown closer together. The nights had gotten much colder lately and the attic was not well insulated. Small drafts of cold air managed to find their way through the thin walls and into Billy's bones with annoying regularity.

Leonard grunted and handed the tin to Billy. He picked up another and dug his spoon in. As he raised it to his mouth, he paused. "I hate baked beans, Billy."

"Especially if they're not Heinz," whispered Billy under his breath, shaking his head and eating a huge mouthful of them, tomato juice dribbling down his unshaven chin.

"*Especially* if they're not Heinz. Bloody cheap rubbish," said Leonard. He ate a solitary spoonful and placed the nearly full tin back on the floorboard in front of him.

"Leonard, you've got to eat, come on." Billy continued eating, watching Leonard fold his arms and tuck cold fingers under his armpits. It had gotten worse lately. Leonard's temper could flare up at any moment. Sometimes he refused to eat and he would lash out at Billy. It had gotten worse since they had run out of his pills.

Billy sighed. Maybe it was the light, or maybe it was the lack of fresh air. Up in the attic it was difficult to stretch the legs or the mind. Leonard was struggling. Billy was glad he had the foresight to stock the attic before things went really wrong, before they had been forced to lock themselves away for God knows how long.

Billy finished the beans and stood, which at his age was no easy thing. He pulled himself up using the stepladder and waited a moment for the inevitable head-rush to disappear. Careful not to upset the torch balanced on a box – Leonard didn't like the dark – Billy made his way over to a cardboard box in the far corner. It was cooler there and so they kept the food wrapped up, out of the way, packed up in the corner to keep the insects and mice away.

He began rummaging through the box, ignoring the stiffness in his legs, ignoring the pain running down his arms, and the fuzzy headache that had come over him three weeks ago but steadfastly refused to leave. A month ago, he had been playing whist, enjoying his strolls in the gardens, and three solid meals a day. Now he was living in an attic with Leonard. Nobody else had made it. It was just the two of them left.

"Eureka." Billy found the Bourbon biscuits and took a couple out. He knew if he took the whole packet they would be gone instantly. He didn't trust Leonard, or himself for that matter, to take any more than that and not eat the whole lot. He could still remember rationing from his childhood in the forties and knew how important it was to preserve everything they had for as long as possible.

Billy stood up and banged his head on a low beam. "Bugger it," he muttered, rubbing his sore head and walking back to Leonard. "Here you go, Lenny. That's all we've got for today."

Billy handed him a biscuit, wishing he had some real Bourbon, and put the other one in his mouth. He used to love the sweet, sugary, delicious biscuits. They would only be given them on Sunday afternoons and were one of the few treats they were allowed. Now Billy hated them. They reminded him, not of Sunday roasts or that cheeky nurse who always gave him a wink when she handed him an extra one. No, they reminded him now of Lenny, the attic, the prison they had built for themselves and the shit-hole that was now home.

Leonard took the biscuit and ate it quickly. For a moment, while Leonard was munching his way through the chocolate, Billy forgot he was sharing a room with a seventy year old man. His roommate's face was full of such simple delight it was like looking at a five year old. Billy smiled.

"What's funny?" Leonard let out a loud burp, swiftly followed by an even louder fart.

"Nothing really," said Billy, sitting back down and taking Leonard's beans. Billy knew that Lenny wouldn't eat them now. They had been through this ritual before, so he knew he may as well save them for later. Billy placed them by the torch.

"Remember old nurse Wendy?" asked Leonard.

Billy frowned. "Windy Wendy?"

"Yes! Boy she could fart like a trooper. Always used to blame it on us, didn't she. We knew though." Leonard leant forward until Billy could smell the stale urine on Leonard's pyjamas. "We knew, didn't we? We always knew."

Billy nodded and smiled weakly. He didn't much like talking of the old days. The nurses and doctors who used to look after them were all dead now, some of them only a few feet away. Still there, still shuffling around the corridors of 'Peaceful Valley Rest Home,' still banging into the walls and doors and empty beds.

"Do you think we can go out tomorrow, Billy? I'd love to go look around the garden. It's been ages. Please?" Leonard clasped his wrinkled hands in front of him as if in prayer and looked at Billy with large sagging eyes.

"We'll see, Lenny. I'm not sure. We might have to wait a bit longer, okay?"

"We could ask Bob to come too? He always likes a wander in the mornings before dinner. Wendy can push old Norma in her chair and we'll have a lovely time. I bet the sun will be shining and the roses will be out and..."

"Lenny, we can't. Do you remember what happened? Bob's dead. Norma's dead too. I think Wendy is probably..."

"Yes, yes, all right, I remember," said Lenny. "I just thought..."

They sat in silence. The lantern torch illuminated the attic well enough, although there was not much to see: boxes of food and bottles of water in the corner, six piles of books in the other and two makeshift beds. They had grabbed some blankets and a couple of pillows just before they had to pull up the trapdoor. They'd thought of everything: food, water, entertainment and lighting. Billy had been feeling quite happy until Leonard pointed out he needed to piss. One corner of the attic was now strictly off limits.

There were only two windows up in the attic and as it had never been intended to be used as a living space, they had not been kept in good condition. One had rusted shut completely, so Billy had boarded it up easily. The other window was their only solace, the only link to the outside world they had. A thick green rug had been pinned over it so that it hung down and covered the window entirely. It blocked out prying eyes. In the daytime, they kept the rug there, but on sunny days, chinks of sunlight would sneak through. They both would sit, sometimes for hours, just watching the sunlight creep across the wooden boards. Billy mused if the outside world might have improved since the infection had broken out. After a week had passed, he had opened the trapdoor to take a look downstairs, but old Norma had appeared out of nowhere, her clothes covered in blood, and Billy had quickly pulled the trapdoor up, deciding the outside world could wait.

The truth was, despite being stuck in a cramped room with Leonard for twenty four hours a day, seven days a week, he was lonely. He had enjoyed living here. Everyone was friendly, and he didn't even mind that his family didn't visit much. His only son was always busy with work and his daughter-in-law had never really taken to Billy, so he made friends and enjoyed life for what it was. There was not much point when you got to eighty-one in being bitter and twisted. He had worked that one out a long time ago.

"I wonder if Carol will come tomorrow?" said Lenny, interrupting Billy's thoughts. "I enjoy her visits. She's a teacher, you know. She always comes on Saturdays."

Exasperated, Billy said, "Lenny, she's not coming."

"But it's Saturday, and she always comes on Saturdays." Leonard turned his bottom lip down and hunched over, upset. "Just because *your* family don't visit you, there's no need to be mean."

"Lenny, she's not coming. Just leave it, will you. Look, it's nearly bedtime, why don't you just go lie down and..."

"No. You're always telling me what to do, Billy. Well, I won't, I won't go lie down. I don't want to. I want to wait for Carol." Leonard shifted to turn his back to Billy. Leonard's voice was rising and Billy couldn't take any risks. He had to make Leonard keep quiet. Every day, Billy had to tell Leonard what to do and he was sick of it. He didn't enjoy being the boss, but he had to get through to Leonard somehow.

"For God's sake, Lenny, she's dead. Your precious fucking daughter is dead. You already know this. I'm sorry, it's just, you...you can't keep on like this. Three weeks we've been stuck up here. Just for one night, can't you keep your mouth shut about sodding Carol and Wendy and...just bloody everything!"

Billy was angry, but instantly regretted shouting at Leonard. He had a temper as a child and through his adult life had tried to control it, sometimes successfully, sometimes not. Since they had run out of pills, Leonard's condition had become worse. Every day they did a little dance. Sometimes Billy would pretend nothing was wrong and they were just playing a joke on the nurses, hiding up in the attic where they couldn't be found. Today though, he couldn't take it anymore. Today he had to let off some steam and get Leonard to understand.

"When Carol comes I'm going to tell her what you said, you know?" said Leonard. "In fact," he said suddenly standing up, "I'm going to ring her right now. I shouldn't be treated like this."

"Lenny, you sit down right now and shut up," said Billy alarmed.

Leonard walked over to the trapdoor. His purple dressing gown flapped behind him and Billy noticed how thin he looked. They hadn't eaten properly in three weeks, so it was hardly surprising they were losing weight. How much longer could they keep going like this?

"Lenny, you know we can't go down there. You *know* this." Billy got up. He hadn't had to physically restrain Leonard yet, but today might be the first time. He looked over at his friend, the torchlight casting him in strange shadows. Leonard's pale face was drawn, his lips pursed together, his hands clenched together around his tattered robe, and he was looking at Billy with scorn.

"You're a fool, Billy Johnson, a goddamned fool. I am not your pet. I am not your child. I am a *man*. So help me, God, I am going downstairs right now and you are not going to stop me."

The hairs on Billy's arms tingled as Leonard reached for the latch to the trapdoor and he felt his bladder weaken. He took a step back. No, he couldn't succumb to fear now. Leonard didn't know what he was doing. It wasn't his fault. It was just the way things were now, the way Leonard's mind worked, or didn't work.

Billy strode over to Leonard. "Lenny, listen to me, please. I'm sorry about earlier. I was out of line, but you have to do me one favour, okay? Don't open that door." Billy put a hand gently on Leonard's right arm.

"Get lost," growled Leonard and he pushed Billy away. Leonard was a lot stronger than his seventy year old frame suggested, and he pushed Billy away with enough force that Billy was caught off guard. Leonard had lashed out before, but never truly struck his friend. Surprised by Leonard's violent reaction, Billy tripped backward.

Leonard pulled open the trapdoor as Billy tumbled over a discarded copy of 'Catcher in the Rye' that had been left half read on the floor. As Billy fell, he saw Leonard's face suddenly illuminated by a square shaft of glorious English sunlight that leapt up through the trapdoor opening.

"No!" Billy managed to scream as he fell onto the hard wooden floorboards. He fell flat on his back and his head smashed back, cracking on the old boards, sending mushrooming clouds of dust up into the air above him. His left arm broke just above the elbow, a tiny crack in the brittle bone sending blinding pain throughout his old body. Billy broke two fingers on his right hand as he tried to stop his fall and bursts of silver stars cascaded across his vision briefly before he passed out.

Leonard looked down through the open trapdoor in wonder and horror as Norma struggled to clamber up. The last time he had seen her, she was sitting in her wheelchair asleep having eaten too much supper. She was standing now, something he had never seen her do, and her face was a bloody mess. Something had eaten her eyes and from the dark empty sockets, something grew, small shoots of something strangely looking like moss. Looking closer, Leonard could see the dark green moss was moving, waving around like a jellyfish waving its tentacles in the ocean, as if searching for something. Her mouth was open, but no sounds came out. He could see down her throat. Her teeth had long since rotted away, and he noticed that she had no tongue, just a blackened stump where it used to be. Presumably she had swallowed it – or someone else had.

Leonard recoiled as she jumped up, trying to reach him. Beneath her, on the beige carpet that he had walked across for so many years, lay pools of faeces and entrails. Norma was caked in blood, some of it her own, most of it not. Beside her stood a tall, naked man with a gaunt haunted face who was nudging against her, arms outstretched too, reaching up as if Leonard was some kind of god to be worshipped. The man had thick white hair and a pointy nose matching his lanky frame. Long gangly legs held the body upright while bony arms stuck out from the man's side. Leonard tried not to look at the shrivelled penis that was only just hidden beneath a thin forest of white pubic hair. Leonard vaguely recognised the man as Bob's roommate, Ted or Fred or something, but he was dead, wasn't he? Leonard distinctly remembered Billy telling him *before* they had come up to the attic. Bob's roommate had suffered a heart attack and...

Another figure suddenly appeared, knocking Norma over. A large naked woman with huge, sagging veined breasts swaying violently stopped directly beneath the opening of the trapdoor and cried out. Leonard couldn't tell what she was trying to say, as she only made short guttural noises, like the insistent grunts of pigs fucking. Over and over she grunted, all the time jumping up and down trying to get up into the attic. Her dirty black hair was wrapped around a grimy pudgy face and Leonard only then noticed that she had one arm. Her left shoulder bone was exposed and shreds of flesh and muscle hung off it loosely, whipping around and around as the fat woman danced up and down desperately. Her fingers kept brushing against the lip of the attic access.

"What are you doing? Go away," he said. Leonard took another step back into the attic, unable to pull his eyes away from the horror below. "I just need to...I need...oh Carol..."

As the familiar, fetid stench of death reached up to Leonard, he put his hand up to his mouth, but it was too late. Reeling, he threw up, the little amount of food he had eaten in the last day mixing with viscid bile and projecting itself out of his mouth, down through the trapdoor onto the dead below. Leonard watched as his vomit splattered over the dead fat lady and the tall man. They didn't flinch, didn't recoil from the rejected warm contents of his stomach. In fact, the fat woman licked her lips as the chunky puke dribbled over her face. With her only hand, she scooped as much of it as she could from her face and thrust it into her mouth, sucking greedily on her hand, enjoying the warmth; the taste of the living.

With their appetites further aroused, the three dead below resumed jumping and stretching, trying to reach up to the ceiling, to reach Leonard. Norma was struggling to get back up off the floor as the fat woman, as full of energy as a rabbit in heat, repeatedly knocked her down. As Leonard took a step back, the tall man took a step forward, and trod on Norma's back. A small bone in her fragile spine snapped, but still, she struggled on the floor.

Aided by the extra height he had, the tall man surged forward and pushed himself up. He clasped the lip of the attic trapdoor with his dead fingers. His hands grabbed a supporting beam nearby and he slowly hauled himself up, pulling his long nude body over the lip of the trapdoor. The tall man's eyes never left Leonard.

"Billy? Billy?" hissed Leonard, staring at the man who was coming at him, now crawling across the wooden floor of the attic.

Not getting an answer, Leonard turned around to see Billy on the floor, unconscious.

"Billy, get up!"

The tall man had succeeded in getting his legs up over the trapdoor ledge and was beginning to stand. A nail, protruding from the floorboards stuck into the dead man's side, and as he stood up, it tore into the man's skin. Leonard's mouth fell open as the man ignored the deep cut widening from his hip to his knee and continued walking toward him. No blood fell from the man's leg and now, the lantern shining over the man, Leonard could see his terrible skin, mottled with magenta bruises, purple and green welts that blossomed into bright red blisters. Pus oozed from the sores on the man's chest and a violet coloured fungus seemed to wrap its way around his chest like a bloodied tourniquet. The deceased man's skin was thin and black lumps of clotted blood seemed to shift beneath it, oozing out of the open gash on his leg onto the dusty floorboards.

Leonard raced to Billy. He knelt over him and shook him.

"Billy, get up, quick!"

Billy lay still, unmoving, breathing, and not responding to Leonard.

Leonard's heart was racing and he could feel an uncomfortable sweat breaking out over his body. He pulled off his purple robe and threw it aside, dressed now only in the flannelette pyjamas he had been wearing three weeks ago when he and Billy had come up here together. He could sense the tall man behind him and Leonard shouted.

"Get away, get away! Leave us alone!" He shoved the tall man in the chest and the dead man stumbled backward. Leonard wiped the slime from his hands and watched the tall man attack again. The man's teeth were clacking together, but otherwise, he made no sound. Leonard could hear wailing and moaning from below, but the tall man was silent.

Leonard ran to the corner of the attic and for a moment, the tall man seemed confused, unsure of whether to follow him or jump on Billy who was prostrate on the floor only four feet away. There was a small pile of unused wooden planks and floorboards, and Leonard grasped one. It was about three feet long but solid, the same type they had used to board up one of the attic windows. Leonard charged at the tall man, swinging the plank and bringing it crashing down onto the man's head.

Again, the tall man stumbled, but did not fall down. Leonard was sure he had struck the man firmly and sure enough, when he lowered the plank, he saw the man's head cocked to one side, his jaw broken. Still, the man kept coming.

"I told you to leave us alone!" shouted Leonard running toward the tall man. He kept the plank horizontal, levelled out in front of him so that one end was nestled in the cradle of his shoulder, the other stuck out in front of him like a battering ram. The plank sliced into the tall man's chest, crunching through the rib cage and locking itself with the man's body. Leonard shoved with all his strength and the tall man wheeled away, unable to stop as Leonard propelled him back toward the trapdoor.

Finally, Leonard let go of the plank as the tall man dropped out of sight, down through the attic opening into the corridor of the rest home below. Leonard dropped to his knees, exhausted. His fingers were sore from gripping the plank but he was relieved and grateful that he and Billy were alone again, safe.

"Billy?"

Leonard walked over to his unconscious friend, ignoring the moaning sounds that were echoing up into the attic from the growing dead beneath them. He shook Billy once again, and this time, he stirred. Billy coughed and Leonard helped him sit up.

"Are you all right?"

Billy coughed again and winced as he felt the pain in his broken arm return. "My arm – I think I broke it." He looked at Leonard who was sweating profusely. "Lenny, what happened? Are you..?"

Leonard shook his head. "I'm okay, Billy. I'm sorry, I just wanted to see Carol. I didn't know about...I mean I forgot...one of them got up, but I got rid of him. He's gone now."

Billy saw Leonard smile and forgot all about the argument earlier. Maybe he had underestimated him. If he had fought off one of the dead, then maybe Leonard still had a few marbles left.

There were worryingly loud noises now from below them. Moaning sounds, horrible slithering sounds, and they seemed to be increasing. He looked over Leonard's shoulder and saw the shadows dancing on the attic roof, arms and hands, heads, bodies, jostling below. Suddenly, an arm appeared and a hand reached up, finally settling on a beam. The hand grabbed it.

"Lenny, we have to get out of here, it's not safe anymore," said Billy, struggling to get to his feet. "They know we're here now, so we can't stay."

"But where are we going?" asked Leonard following Billy over to the window and the green rug. "You said this was the safest place to be. You said we just had to be quiet and still and they wouldn't find us. You said..."

"I know, Lenny, I'm sorry, but...look behind you." Billy pointed toward the trapdoor and Leonard saw Norma struggling to pull herself up into the attic. She was half in, half out and another arm was scratching at her back, trying to use her as a springboard into the attic. Norma's face looked hideous in the half lit attic, her mouth seemingly locked in a ferocious sneer exposing her teeth.

Billy pulled aside the green rug and opened the window. He kept his broken arm as still as possible, but the pain was sending throbbing waves around his brain and it was difficult to move without the pain intensifying. He looked out at the evening, across the rooftops of the neighbouring houses and wondered what they were going to do now. The town seemed quiet, but he knew that was a false security. The dead were everywhere and they didn't sleep. Leonard was right. They had nowhere to go, certainly nowhere safe, but they couldn't stay here. Even if they could get the trapdoor shut again, the dead knew they were here. The two men would be trapped in there forever until their food and water ran out. Then what?

"Lenny, we're going outside. We're going out the window right now, do you understand? The roof outside is flat and we'll find somewhere else to stay. Don't worry, just follow me." Billy was scared, but he didn't want Lenny to see. He wasn't sure how he would react.

Billy went through the window and crouched down low on the roof as Leonard followed him. The green rug flapped down behind him and Billy hoped it might buy them some time before the dead realised where they had gone.

"Come on, Lenny, this way." Billy kept low on the roof. The streets were deserted, but he still didn't like being out in the open, so exposed and vulnerable.

He led them over to the front of the building and peered over the edge into the car park. Luckily, there was a car parked right beneath them. There was no ladder or stairway so he told Leonard to follow him and then he sat down on the ledge. With a broken arm, he was worried that when he landed he might hit it and pass out again. Leonard sat down beside him.

"Lenny, we're going to jump down onto that car, okay? As soon as we land, you need to run as fast as you can. See over there, that alleyway? Run down there. It leads into Victoria Street. It's empty right now, but I don't know for how long. You need to find somewhere to hide: a house, a shed, a garage - anything you can."

"You're coming with me, aren't you, Billy?" said Leonard frowning.

"Yes but...I'm slower than you, so don't wait for me, just run, okay Lenny? I'll find you."

Leonard nodded. "I'm sorry, Billy." He put his arm across his friend's shoulder gently, careful not to touch the broken arm.

"It's all right, Lenny. I'll be right behind you." Billy gave Leonard a wink and smiled. "Come on then, old man."

Billy dropped off the roof onto the blue car below, and unable to use his arms as balance, slipped straight off it onto the tarmac. Leonard followed him, but landed with ease and slid of the car's bonnet before softly planting his feet on the cold ground. He heard Billy scream in pain and hesitated.

"Go on, Lenny, run!" Billy's vision was swimming and he felt dizzy, but he knew he had to urge Leonard on. Billy got to his feet and saw Leonard running down the alleyway as he had been told to do. Billy started after him and from the corner of his eye, saw the dead. They were streaming out of the rest home. The older ones like Norma and Bob were slow, but some of the nurses and doctors were fast. Billy ran and made it to the alley just in time to see Leonard leaving at the other end. He knew the dead were close behind him and if he tried to run the length of the alley, they would catch him there. He began running down it as fast as he could, but he was already breathless. You're only as old as you feel, he told himself. A voice in his head told him he felt like he was a hundred years old. He was only halfway down the alley and any moment now the dead would be too. He wouldn't be able to outrun them or reach the street in time. He would be trapped.

There was a skip on one shadowy side of the alley. Graffiti covered much of it, hiding the yellow scratched paint, and Billy peered over the edge. It was full of black bags and rubbish, discarded plastic bottles and decayed food. He hauled himself painfully up, standing on a wooden pallet and looked closer. It smelt foul, but that could be to his advantage. If they couldn't see him, or smell him, maybe they would run past. He could catch up to Leonard when they had gone.

Billy straddled the rusty lip of the huge skip and sank down into it. His velvet slippers fell off as he lowered himself down the sloping walls and his bare feet touched the black bags. He half expected a rat to shoot out and dart up his leg, but nothing moved. Billy held his breath as the disgusting smell of week's old rotten food billowed up into the air. Finally, he sank into the skip, trying to ignore the slimy objects underfoot. He could hear footsteps in the alley now. The dead were running, coming for him, getting closer every second.

He lay down out of sight and drew a few bags across him. Surely, he would be safe? He tried to not picture what he was lying in. A cool liquid from the bottom of the skip was soaking into his pyjamas and his head was resting on something sticky that felt worryingly like a dead animal of some sort. Billy could practically feel its dead furry tail wrapping itself around his neck, but he knew he was letting his imagination run away with him. He kept quiet and still, forcing himself to take shallow breaths.

A pair of footsteps suddenly ran past the skip. He could tell from their echo that they hadn't paused or stopped. The sound carried on to his right, to the other end of the alley. It was working! If Leonard had managed to find somewhere to hide, they would be all right. He just had to wait them out, give it a couple of minutes and they would be gone. The dead weren't intelligent. They didn't know that their prey could hide right under their noses. He might smell like the back end of a horse, but he would be alive at least.

Billy waited as the multitude of footsteps diminished and then began to sit up. It had only been one minute, two at the most, and he heard nothing. There were no shouts or screams, which was good. He hoped that meant Leonard had found somewhere to hide.

He pulled himself up to the edge of the skip and looked out. The alleyway was dark and empty. Billy felt such relief that he felt like crying. He let his head touch the cold metal of the skip and waited for his emotions to settle down. He would need a cool head out there to find Leonard.

He wasn't paying attention to the skip anymore, feeling safe, and one of the black bags he had kicked to a corner moved. Just a little at first, a small movement so slight it wouldn't have been noticeable to anyone who wasn't looking for it. Suddenly, it began to jostle back and forth. Billy heard rustling behind him and whirled around to see a hand thrust out from beneath the bag. It reached around and Billy kept out of reach of it. He had seen so many things in the last few weeks he was not surprised. He was shocked that anything could be in here though. There wasn't room for anyone else but him, and he would've noticed if he had lain on another body.

Billy inched his way slowly toward the side where he could clamber out and back onto the pallet to escape. The lone hand waved around in the air and then grabbed hold of a rotten piece of wood. It grabbed it and Billy watched in horror as the hand pulled the rest of its body up. A pale arm appeared, followed by a shoulder and finally a head. The dead woman must have been dead a long time, as she looked more like a skeleton. Only thin strips of skin hung on her face and Billy could clearly see her ribcage. The dead woman hauled herself up and Billy noticed that beneath the ribcage there was nothing but emptiness. With nothing else to hold her up, her skeletal body rested against the side of the skip. The lower half of her body was somewhere else, decapitated long ago and eaten.

Billy jumped for the pallet resting against the skip's side, but the woman sprang forward at the same time. He felt fingers grab around his ankle and he fell backward into the rubbish once more. He writhed around in the sludge and the dirt as the dead woman sank her decayed teeth into his leg. Billy tried to kick the dead woman off, but she held on to him and continued tearing her way through his leg. He tried to sit up, but he could not get hold of anything substantial and the pain was overwhelming. His broken arm was useless and he tried to hit the woman's head with his one free arm. Black bags kept falling on him as he screamed and shouted for help. He was aware of a warm wet liquid spreading down his legs and saw it was his own blood. The dead woman, still gripping him, had gnawed through to his bone.

He hoped Leonard had found somewhere safe. Billy could take no more and closed his eyes. He wished he could see him one more time. He wished he could have lived longer to help his friend. As the dead woman literally tore the last slices of life from Billy, his heart gave up and he died, wishing he could go back to the attic and stay with Lenny forever.

CHAPTER TWO

Heidi screwed her eyes up and then stretched out, extending her arms and legs, and arching her back. Yawning, she glanced at the clock on the wall. Her electric bedside clock had died, but the reliable battery-powered Swiss clock on the wall still ticked without fail, every second of every turgid, tedious day. It would never die. Only 8:25 P.M., Heidi was bored and frustrated. She shook her head as if to shake herself awake and picked up the book she was trying to read. It was some romantic historical novel her mother had recommended, but in truth, she had only read fifty pages and was bored already with its predictable characters and storyline. The light was poor anyway and the effort to read was making her eyes ache.

She threw the paperback onto her bed and got up, her long legs sliding off the bed with ease. She wore a pair of comfortable cotton shorts and a red vest top. Her wavy blonde hair just reached the top of her smooth shoulders. She looked in the long mirror and frowned at herself. Her hair was greasy and it looked like her face was having a breakout of spots. She looked closer and squeezed a small pimple on her cheek.

"Nineteen years old and this is all I have to look forward to, squeezing spots? Fucking hell."

Heidi ambled about her room, picking things up that were once so important to her: fashionable jeans, make-up, magazines and DVD's of trendy bands. She put them all back down, bored. It wasn't fair. Her parents had lived their lives, and had their youth, so why shouldn't she have hers? She went over to the window and slowly pulled the curtains apart. Her father would kill her if he knew she was doing it, but she couldn't take much more of being cooped up here like a battery hen.

As usual, the street was empty, and she wondered if her father might let her go out today. Just for five minutes, just to feel the fresh air, just for something to do. The end of the world was boring as hell. The houses on the opposite side of the road were quiet, empty, and dark. A few broken windows, some front doors open, but no people: living or dead.

Heidi closed the curtains again and sat down at her desk, pulling a diary out of the drawer. She opened it to today's date and began writing. Just enough light came through the thick curtains for her to write by. It was one of the few things she had to do now that reminded her she was still alive and not just like one of those zombies out there.

She wrote about how she longed for something to happen, for someone to do something, for the world to come back, for her friends to come back. She wrote about how she actually missed college now, how she had been wrong to think it was stupid to carry on her education after school. Her career as a veterinarian seemed a long way off from happening right now. She wrote about how she loved her mother and father, but being locked away with them for twenty four hours a day, not knowing when they could leave, was driving her insane. It was probably driving her parents insane too, admittedly. They had no customers now, probably wouldn't have again, yet her mother kept up the pretence, cleaning and tidying the bedrooms every day, 'just in case.'

It had been over three weeks since anyone had stayed at the small bed and breakfast her parents, Glenda and Daniel Cooper, ran in the equally small village of Longrock. They had been three very long weeks. The first week hadn't been boring, although it had been scary. The infection had broken out and spread across the country quickly. Her mother had wanted to go back to Austria, but her father had refused, and said they would be better off waiting, it wouldn't get any worse, it would be contained, and the British government would sort it out, just as they always did. Well, they had watched the news go off the air, the electricity die, and finally the water. They had watched the streets fill up with dead people, attacking and eating the living who in turn rose up to repeat the process. Finally, they had barricaded themselves in. Her father had stocked up on as much food and water as he could and so they waited.

Heidi continued scribbling, lost in her thoughts until she heard a small knocking on her bedroom door.

"Heidi?"

"Hi, Mum," she said, watching her mother come in with a candle in each hand. Glenda placed one candle carefully beside Heidi's bed and then walked over to her daughter, giving her a kiss on the head. Her mother looked tired, very tired. She was nearing retirement age and Heidi had suggested they retire last year, but her parents couldn't bear to part with the home and business they had built up over the last thirty years. Now, with little else to do, Glenda spent her days cleaning and trying to make edible meals from tins, boxes and packets of dried food. She wore the same thing every day: a long dark grey skirt, a practical black t-shirt and she tied her dirty blonde hair up in a ponytail.

"No bookings today then?" said Heidi, unable to resist a dig.

"No, Heidi, not today." Glenda looked inquisitively over Heidi's shoulder at the diary and her daughter snapped it shut.

"Your father wants to see you, downstairs. Do you mind?" Glenda spoke softly as if she might wake the whole town up if she spoke any louder. "Only for a minute, then you can do what you like. Well, you know what I mean. You can come back up here. The candle will last an hour or so if you want to read."

"Yeah, sure." Heidi took her mother's hand and followed her. As they walked through the house, Heidi looked into each guest room at the immaculately made beds, each one made up with crisply folded sheets and not a speck of dust to be seen.

They went downstairs in the gloom, the house only lit by candlelight, and Heidi followed her mother into the kitchen. The lounge was not safe as it had huge bay windows that looked out onto the road. They had nothing to board the windows up with and if anyone, or *anything,* saw them inside...Heidi shivered, not wanting to dwell on her thoughts.

In the kitchen, she found her father sitting at the table, reading a cricket magazine that he must have read twenty times already. There was a candle in the middle of the table and two empty glasses. The window was covered by a sheet and the door to the driveway obscured by towels which had been tacked up crudely, her father's attempt at learning DIY having failed long ago. He looked up expectantly, his eyes peering over the rim of his reading glasses as they entered.

"How are you, Heidi?" he said.

"I'm fine," she said sighing, giving him a peck as they sat down at the table together. "Don't suppose there's anything else to eat?"

The evening meal earlier had consisted of a tin of tuna each on dry, stale ryebread crackers, followed by a packet of cheese and onion crisps and two squares of plain chocolate. Heidi's stomach growled as she remembered the chocolate and she wished her father had gotten something rich, luxurious and milky instead of the supermarket own brand which tasted more like cardboard than chocolate.

"Sorry, Heidi, you know the rules," he said taking off his glasses. He was a strict man, but he wasn't an over the top disciplinarian. He was quite jovial and generous when he wanted to be, and his daughter and wife loved him dearly.

"That's what we wanted to talk to you about, honey," said Glenda.

"What's wrong?" asked Heidi, feeling guilty even though she had done nothing wrong. There was something about sitting at the kitchen table with her parents looking at her in the dark that made her feel nervous. When she was ten years old, she had sat in this very spot where her parents had made her confess. She had taken a five pound note from the register to buy sweets and she had confessed it all in one blubbery dreadful evening. Her parents had sent her to bed without any supper and she was that timid ten year old girl all over again.

"Well, nothing has changed out there as far as we know," began Daniel. "I've been keeping a look out from upstairs, but there's no sign of life. I haven't seen a soul. I've only seen...them...sometimes just one, but sometimes a group of them."

"No cavalry on the horizon yet then, Dad?" asked Heidi.

"No, I'm afraid not," he said, missing his daughter's sarcasm, unable to see her expression clearly in the gloomy room. "The thing is we've been here for nearly a month and well...well, our supplies, the food, is running a bit low."

"What do you mean 'a bit low'?" asked Heidi worried. "I thought you'd stocked up? You said we could sit it out, wait here...have we got enough for tomorrow even?"

"Settle down, Heidi," said Glenda hearing the rising pitch in her daughter's voice.

"Yes, yes, we've got enough for tomorrow, but after that..." Daniel trailed off and fidgeted with his glasses, tapping them on the desk.

Heidi felt guilty again. She had let her parents keep things organised, settling quickly into the old routine once she had come home from college, and let them sort things out while she had done what? She could feel panic rising within her, her heart beating a little bit faster and she took in a deep breath. She let it out slowly and the candle flickered as her breath blew over it gently.

"So what are we going to do?" Heidi asked. "Should we leave? Maybe try for Penzance like we said?"

"No," Daniel said assertively. "The car's pretty much empty and we'd never make it on foot. No, we need to stay here and wait this thing out. We can probably find food in the neighbours' houses, but we're going to have to be careful out there. I will..."

"Dad, you keep saying wait this out, but what are we waiting for? You said yourself you've seen nothing out there. Nobody's coming, Dad. We have to leave, we can't stay here forever, we..."

"Listen to your father, honey," said Glenda, the eternal peacemaker between a stubborn father and a headstrong daughter. "I know your friends were in Penzance, but you remember the news, don't you? There's nobody there now, your friends will have left or are..." Glenda trailed off unable to think of the right thing to say.

"Dead? You mean they're all dead?" said Heidi getting angry.

"All right, Heidi, don't take this out on your mother," said Daniel.

"Well, they are, aren't they? They're very likely dead or wandering around looking for people like us to eat. Fucking corpses, that's what they are now."

"Enough!" Daniel slapped his palm down on the table and Heidi was quiet. Glenda looked down at her lap. "I will not have that language at my table in my house."

Heidi could tell he was glaring at her and she muttered a quiet sorry.

"I'm not stupid, Heidi. I know we can't stay here forever. Look, when we go next door, we can look for some more food, but we can check their car too. If we can find one that's got a full tank, and we can find the keys, then I'll listen to you. Maybe we will leave, but right now, we need to focus on staying here where it's safe."

Heidi sighed. "All right, Dad, I suppose so."

Glenda smiled at her. "We'll figure this out in the morning. Do you feel like getting the water, honey? I'm parched."

"Sure, Mum." Heidi got up and peeled back the towels hanging over the door.

"Be careful," said her father watching her.

"Don't worry, Dad, I know what I'm doing." Heidi unlocked the door and stepped outside, letting the door close behind her. She stood in the garage letting her eyes adjust to the darkness. She could see the garage door still firmly closed and sensed nothing outside. She manoeuvred her way around her father's car, an old silver Rover that he refused to trade in, and to the back door that led to the rear garden. She paused again, listening for noises on the other side. It was highly unlikely that anything could get into the garden, but it didn't hurt to check. Better safe than sorry and wind up as dinner for a walking corpse.

She unlocked the door and pushed it open. There in the garden, illuminated by the moon, were the buckets, the pots and pans, the tubs, jars and containers, all laid out to catch as much rainwater as possible. The garden was fully enclosed by a six foot high wooden fence her father had erected years ago, only one small gate on the far side that led to a small side street. The gate hadn't been used in years, so Heidi was surprised to see it open. She was even more surprised to see an old man pushing it closed quietly. The gate squeaked shut and he turned around. She saw a wrinkly old face and a frail body wearing nothing but pyjamas, and she screamed.

* * * *

"Hey, Tom, did you hear something?" asked Laurent quietly. "Sounded like a woman screaming, eh?"

Tom stopped and listened. They were in a stranger's house, rifling through cupboards and he had his hands in a toiletry bag. He gently dropped the ointments and plasters he was holding into the sink and listened. Tom looked at Laurent and shook his head. "I thought I did, but it's stopped now. I can't hear anything. You?"

Laurent held a finger up. "Oui...there, shouting, I hear shouting."

Tom listened and then he heard it too, faintly, but distinctly, the sound of people shouting. "Shit, we need to move. Grab what you can, let's go."

Laurent stuffed the medicine and toothpaste he had found into his backpack and tried not to think about what the screaming meant. The last time he had heard a woman screaming like that it had been his wife being pulled out of their family car by the dead. The screaming had ended as quickly as it had begun, his wife's throat torn out as she was gobbled up by the zombies. Laurent had been powerless to save her at the time and still her screams haunted him, obliterating all emotions bar one: guilt.

Tom ran his hands across the medicine cabinet and shoved everything into the backpack regardless of whether it was of any use or not. They had no time to dwell, only time to move. He had spent days on the road, moving from place to place, and learnt that if you hesitated, it invariably led to problems or death. He had to get back to the others, and get the supplies back. He and Laurent could not afford to stay here or worse still get stuck in this stranger's house where they were exposed to danger.

"Laurent, you ready?" Tom put his arms through the straps and the rucksack nestled onto his back. The moon illuminated the small bathroom and he could see Laurent zipping up his bag.

"Oui. Ready." He looked at Tom and knew they were in danger. Since they had been together, they had survived on the road, running, hiding, learning how to live in this strange world. It had been a long and difficult journey, but Laurent recognised the look on Tom's face. His features were set, locked in determination and Laurent knew the situation was serious. They had not seen or heard anyone living for six days. The dead did not scream or shout.

Laurent followed Tom out of the bathroom, down the hallway, and back to the front door of the house they had broken into. Tom opened the door and they crouched down, scanning the street. Laurent saw only deserted houses, no lights or movement. "What do you think? Is it safe?"

Tom waited and looked. It appeared quiet, but he couldn't afford to take any risks. On more than one occasion they had been startled in the past by losing focus, not checking where they had been going. The dead were quiet creatures, always lurking in corners, hiding in shadows, waiting to pounce like a cat stalking a bird. The small van they had come in was still sat at the end of the path, which led to the front door. They had coasted up quietly and parked it without being seen. The screams and shouts though might have drawn attention. It didn't seem like the sounds were very far away and sure enough, just as Tom was preparing to tell Laurent the path was clear, a zombie shuffled past the van. It failed to notice Tom or Laurent crouched down in the doorway and continued on its path down the road, drawn to the noise.

"We're going to have to run for the van and do a loop," said Tom. "Whatever's going on is away to our right. I'll turn the van around and do a circuit. Hopefully, the road will be clear and we can get...home." He didn't know what else to call it, but it was their home for now. It varied from day to day, but for now it was theirs. "Okay, let's go."

Tom sprinted down the path to the van with Laurent right behind him. They didn't run into any more zombies and got into the van easily. As Laurent ran around onto the road to get in the passenger side, he heard glass breaking and paused. Looking up the road he could see a crowd of around a dozen of the dead, all heading into one house. The crowd had broken through the huge bay windows and were scrambling through the window frame. Laurent got into the van as Tom started the engine.

"Tom..." began Laurent.

"I know what you're going to say Laurent, but we can't. We *can't*. You know how dangerous it would be and we don't even know if they're still alive. We need to get this stuff back to Caterina."

With the engine purring they sat for a moment and Laurent stared straight ahead saying nothing. Looking at the growing swarm of zombies ahead he felt safe in the van. Looking through the windshield it was like watching it on television and he felt disconnected from it all. That scream though was definitely a woman's. What if she was in trouble? No, Tom was right they couldn't risk it when they didn't even know if there was anyone to rescue. Still, that nagging feeling of guilt was a difficult one to shed. This time there was nothing stopping him, nothing barring his way from the screaming woman.

The van lurched forward, but instead of doing a U-turn Tom sped up. "Put your seatbelt on, Laurent."

Laurent looked at Tom, puzzled, but did as he was told. Tom had been right about many things and instinctively Laurent knew he was right now. As the seatbelt clicked in, so too did Tom's plan click in Laurent's mind. He braced himself.

Tom kept his foot on the accelerator as he ploughed into the zombies outside the house. Several bodies were obliterated; arms, hands and heads bounced off the van onto the pavement. The van lurched as Tom drove over the fallen bodies, but he kept it straight and Laurent looked in the wing mirror to see Tom had cleared a path through the dead. Many of the zombies who were trying to get into the house had stopped and were following the sound of the van now. Tom screeched to a halt. "Do you trust me Laurent?"

"Of course but..."

"Then get out."

Laurent unclipped his seatbelt and put his hand on the door handle. "And?"

"The ones that can still stand are coming this way. Run straight ahead, lead them away, down the road and away from here. When you've drawn them away, I'll reverse up to the house and see if there's anyone there. When you get to the end of the road, take a right and there's a car park. I saw it on the way in. Hug the right hand side of it, run around it back to the street. I'll pick you up in five minutes, no more."

Laurent thought for a moment, fingering the knife in his pocket. Then he slid the backpack off and put it in the footwell. "Okay. Five minutes."

Tom nodded and Laurent got out of the van. Tom kept the engine running, but ducked down out of sight. He heard Laurent shouting.

"Hey, over here, you fuckers! Come and get some! Fresh meat, you dirty fucking bastards!"

Tom heard Laurent running away and then he heard the dead. They clattered past the van, banging against it, but following Laurent's voice. In a moment, they were gone and Tom was left alone. He sat up and looked in the mirrors. He could see no dead behind him. He prayed that he would have no trouble at the house. He knew he was risking not just Laurent's life, but all those who were depending on him too: Caterina, Christina and the others. It didn't occur to him that he was risking his own life too.

Tom reversed the van quickly, but quietly, to the house where they had seen the commotion and heard the shouting. Leaving the engine running, Tom got out. The pavement was scattered with pieces of meat, limbs that he had decapitated minutes earlier, arms and legs still twitching, yet unable to move. He walked past them to the window and looked through into an empty room.

It looked like so many other houses they had been in: a television set in the corner, books, ornaments, a black leather sofa and armchairs. There was an open doorway in the corner and Tom carefully headed toward it, aware he could no longer hear any noises. He passed through the doorway into a carpeted hallway. There was a side table on the floor and a telephone and papers next to it. Something had gotten in and knocked it over. He could hear noises now. Somebody was crying, whimpering. He pulled the knife from his belt, a large kitchen knife he always kept with him and had saved his life on more than one occasion.

Holding the knife in his right hand, he pushed open the door at the end of the hallway slowly. It was a kitchen, illuminated by candlelight. There was a large wooden table in the middle covered in blood. In one corner of the room were two women, hugging each other, crying and consoling each other. One looked old, the other young, although they both had the same blonde hair. Probably mother and daughter, thought Tom. In the other corner, a man, covered in blood and wearing glasses, was staring at the table. Beneath it was one of the dead. It had fallen there after Daniel had killed it, severing its head with a carving knife. Daniel was shaking, his hands trembling and when Tom walked in, he dropped the knife. He opened his mouth to speak and looked at Tom in horror.

"They were coming, they were coming in and we had to...we had to...oh God." Daniel pushed his glasses up his nose, smearing them with blood.

Tom kept his knife held aloft, ears sensitive to any noise in case one of the dead decided to attack again, perhaps hiding upstairs or behind the door. "Are you hurt? Are any of you hurt?" He looked around the room and could not see anyone else. The two women were scared, but appeared unharmed. He knew from experience though that a single bite was all it took. Teeth could bite through clothing and sometimes those infected didn't realise it until it was too late. His friend Parker had died the same way. A single bite was all it had took to take him away from Tom. He hadn't been the only one.

"I said are any of you hurt?" Tom strode into the room and kicked the zombie on the floor. It didn't move. Its head rolled away from the body as Tom kicked it and came to rest at Daniel's feet.

"No, we're okay, just a bit...I'm sorry, who are you?" asked Heidi. She stepped forward still holding onto her mother's hand.

"Tom. Look, if you're not hurt then you need to come with me. It's not safe here now. The noise will bring more of these." Tom kicked the lifeless body on the floor again. "There's not time to pack or think, just come with me. I have friends. We can help you."

Tom looked at the girl who had spoken to him. She was pretty, but thin. She looked like she hadn't eaten well and had probably lost weight over the last few weeks. Her greasy blonde hair hung like tangled spider webs around her face and her skin seemed unnaturally pale. Probably hasn't left the house since it started, he thought. Her eyes looked at him with a curiosity, and if this was a different world he would've liked to carry on a conversation with her. But the world didn't have time for that any more.

"Dad, he's right, we should go," said Heidi.

Daniel just nodded and walked slowly over to his wife and daughter. Glenda let go of Heidi and embraced her husband.

"Oh, Dan, what are we going to do?" said Glenda sobbing into her husband's shoulders.

"What's your name?" said Tom to the girl standing before him.

"Heidi." Her thin arms hung by her sides and she felt cold. The cool night air was coming in from outside now and the candle was flickering, about to extinguish and leave them in darkness. She didn't want to be in the dark, not with that thing in here with them. She had never seen her father be violent once, yet he had fought off that person, that dead *thing*, and killed it in front of her.

Now here was this strange man standing in front of her with a knife and she didn't know what to do.

Tom could see that the girl was about to break down. He didn't have time for tears or hysterics, much less anyone going into shock. They had to go get Laurent. "All of you, come with me. I've a van outside. I can get you out of here, but we *must* go now." He put the knife back in his pocket and held out a hand.

Carefully, Heidi took it, sliding her fingers into Tom's. His hand was warm and strong and she let him lead her out of the kitchen, out of their house. Daniel and Glenda followed.

"Oh, my God," said Heidi outside, looking at the carnage right at their front door. She trod carefully over to the van, not wanting to step on anything organic, and Tom pulled back the van door. He ushered Heidi and her parents inside. The street was still empty, but he didn't know for how long.

"We're going to pick my friend up, okay? Then we'll go somewhere safe." Tom put his hand on the door to close it, but Heidi stopped him.

"We can't go, not yet," she said looking at Tom. Her eyes implored Tom to listen to her and he waited.

"Why? I already said, there's no time to pack, we have to..." Heidi cut Tom off.

"The old man. We can't leave him. He's in the garage."

"What? There's someone else in there?" asked Tom.

"Yes," said Daniel. "There...there was an old man in the garden. He just appeared out of nowhere and frightened Heidi. She screamed and I guess that's what brought those things to us. I locked him in the garage. I didn't know what else to do."

"Is he alive, infected? Who is he?" said Tom impatiently. He looked up and down the dark street. He still couldn't hear anything, but trusted his senses that this was not a safe place to be hanging around right now.

"He's alive, but we don't know anything about him. Like I said, he just appeared."

"Shit. How do I get in the garage?" asked Tom.

"Through the kitchen," explained Heidi. "The key's in the door."

Tom thought for a moment. He really didn't have time to go back again. Laurent was waiting for him, relying on him. But knowing there was someone back there, he couldn't give up on them and leave them to certain death, or a fate worse than death.

"Wait here," said Tom and he slung the door shut leaving Heidi, Daniel and Glenda in the back of the van. He ran back inside, into the kitchen and saw the door. The candle had nearly gone out completely, but it still had a faint trace of life left in it. Tom pulled the towels down and knocked on the door to the garage.

"Hey, you in there, are you okay? I'm here to help." Tom heard a banging noise and then feet slowly shuffling across the concrete floor. It's just one of the dead, thought Tom. Those bloody idiots are going to get me and Laurent killed for nothing. A zombie accidentally wound up in their garden and they freaked out. Tom sighed, annoyed that he had wasted his time. Every second wasted was another second jeopardising Laurent's life. Tom turned around ready to run back to the van when he heard a voice.

"Please, can you help? I can't find Billy."

It was a man's voice and the shuffling had stopped.

"Are you hurt? Answer me or I'm leaving right now. Are you hurt?" demanded Tom.

"No, I'm fine, I just got lost and I can't find Billy," came the pleading response.

Tom unlocked the door, and just as Heidi had said, an old man was there in the shadows, snot running down his nose. He had been crying and he wore pyjamas and slippers. Tom was taken aback at how thin the man looked. If he hadn't known better he would've thought he was already dead. Tom motioned for the man to come out.

Leonard walked hesitantly into the kitchen. "Do you know where Billy is?" he asked Tom.

"I'm sorry I don't, but we can try to find him later. Can you walk? It's not very safe in here, Mr..?"

"Gentle. Leonard Gentle."

"Well, Leonard, we need to go now, I'm going to get you somewhere a bit warmer and safer, okay?"

Leonard looked at the body on the floor and the head. "Okay, yes, let's go. Billy said he'd find me."

Tom took hold of Leonard's arm and almost dragged him out of the house. Knowing how he had spooked the family earlier, he didn't want to cause any more unnecessary screaming, so he took Leonard to the passenger seat. Leonard got in and Tom buckled the seatbelt around him. He heard murmurs coming from the back seats and ignored them.

Tom got in and started the engine. He turned around to face the back. "Listen, me and my friend Laurent have risked our lives to help you, so I need your help now. My friend is waiting for us around the corner. We're not going to have time to stop for a coffee or a chat, so when we see him, someone needs to pull that door open and yank him in. I'll only be able to slow the van down for a moment. Got that?"

Daniel and Glenda kept hold of each other and Heidi leant forward. "I'll do it," she said. Tom nodded at her and turned back. He glanced at her in the mirror and saw she was looking at him. Feeling awkward, he turned back to the road.

"Leonard, just stay there, you'll be okay."

The van roared off leaving Longrock's last remaining bed and breakfast empty. Tom hoped that Laurent had managed to fend off the dead. They would find out sure enough in about two minutes.

CHAPTER THREE

"Keep listening," said Lazarus walking away. "If you hear anything you come get me at once, understood?"

"Yes sir," said Tim. He knew when his boss wanted a discussion and when to be quiet. This was *not* the time for a discussion. He sat at the radio controls and put the headphones over his ears. He kept adjusting the frequency, just slightly, trying to tune back in. They had heard nothing except static, but last night, he had finally heard something: just a faint conversation, too quiet to be able to be heard properly. There were two distinct voices. One was a British accent, the other American. Tim had only heard the odd word now again: 'Tomorrow...nowhere...captured...Admiral...help.' At one point, he thought he heard the words 'Abraham Lincoln,' but he couldn't be sure. He had tried to lock onto the signal, but it had drifted away, back into the static. The radio they had was old and struggled with long-range frequencies. Tim was no expert either. They had found the equipment and managed to get it working, but they didn't know what they were doing, not really, not even Lazarus.

Tim stared as Lazarus slammed the door shut, leaving Tim alone. The room was cold and bare. Hell, the whole *house* was cold and bare. He wasn't upset though. If Lazarus hadn't helped him, he would certainly be dead by now. Tim had been stuck in his car for three days, surrounded by the dead. Three solid days with no food or water, pissing and shitting on the back seat, unable to move. It was three long days of dead bodies slamming themselves against his car as they tried to get at him. In an attempt to escape his home town, he had crashed into a police car going the other way and got jammed in. The car refused to start and Tim found himself a prisoner.

It was lucky Lazarus had found him when he did. Tim had reasoned he was going to either starve to death or eventually they would get in and he would be so weak he would be unable to fight them off. He was going to be eaten alive.

Much as the way the static clung to his ears now, Tim had only heard a buzzing grey noise when Lazarus had rescued him. His senses were hazy and without nutrition, water or much sleep he wasn't far from death. It had been so quick he hadn't comprehended it at the time. Lazarus and his men had swiftly executed the zombies, freeing Tim from his motorised coffin, and brought him back here to 'The Mount.' Tim had been unconscious for most of it, so he wasn't entirely sure where 'The Mount' actually was, or how he got here. It didn't matter. He was here and he was alive, thanks to Lazarus. He and his men had nurtured Tim back to health, and so here he was, a loyal follower, his life in debt to another man. His old life, as a grocer, seemed like a dream now. The mundane life he had inhabited before was gone. Tim turned the volume up higher on the radio and listened, desperate to hear another voice, to know he hadn't imagined it, that someone was still out there.

* * * *

Lazarus strode out of the small house and let the wind whistle around him. Tim was decent and honest. He wouldn't have imagined it or lied about it. If he said he had heard talking then he heard it all right. But damn it, he should've reported it immediately. Lazarus still bristled at the thought they might have missed their chance, missed out on hearing from the big bad world; missed hearing what was going on out there.

He looked around at the small houses that were in a small circle, all eight of them made of solid stone, created centuries before Lazarus had been born. Heating was an issue. They had little to burn, so fire was restricted to the main castle, and only on the coldest of nights. He also didn't want people running around lighting fires whenever they felt like it. Apart from the obvious inherent dangers, the smoke could attract unwanted attention. Water was not a problem, however. There was a spring on the island which served them with all the fresh water they needed. Lazarus walked past the houses, aware the occupants were probably watching him. His gait was confident and long, and he pushed his hands deeper into his long black coat. His collar was turned up, but still the cold wind blew around his body, sneaking its way past his coat, sending shivers down his spine. To the onlookers, it appeared as if he was entirely black. His long, jet black hair fell to his shoulders and the coat sucked on it, merging with it. Approaching forty, he felt lucky not to have gone bald like his father. He felt less lucky to have been blessed with such a name as only a Professor of Classics would bestow upon a first child.

Lazarus walked on, past the houses and the pub from wherein he heard music and laughter. It was after nine and the men often congregated there, regaling each other with stories of their exploits and adventures, their spoils and their finds. Today had been easy. He had sent four of his men out. They had been looking for nothing in particular, as it was a quick trip, there and back, just to see what was what. They had enough food and drink to last months, but it kept the men occupied. If he let them get lethargic they would soon get bored. Boredom could lead to thinking and too much thinking led to grandiose ideas; ideas that might mean his autocracy challenged. It was best to keep the men on a leash, just long enough to let them have a little fun, but not too long that they would stray. Occasionally, if one got out of hand, he would put one down like a dog.

Ignoring the laughter carried to him on the howling wind, he trudged on, up the rocky slope to the castle. His feet found hold on the tough terrain, avoiding the slate and granite rocks, his boots crunching down the grass underfoot. The grass would spring back. It was strong and undeterred by centuries of gales, storms and floods. The feet of invaders and soldiers had trod this path many times before and Lazarus knew he was not the first. He may be the last though. The era of man seemed to be coming to an end. On their excursions to the mainland, they found less and less survivors, and none at all in the last five days. The infection had taken nearly everyone. Here, on the island, there were twenty two people and one dog.

Lazarus wondered if this was how it had come about before man. The dinosaurs had been wiped out by a meteor or an explosion that killed all life on Earth, that's what his father had taught him. What if the meteor had been carrying an infection; one that turned all of those prehistoric creatures into cannibals and carnivores, even after death? Lazarus grinned as he thought of a resurrected dinosaur trying to eat another. It was absurd to think that an infection could bring down a T-rex. No, this must be something new.

As Lazarus climbed higher, he looked over to the mainland a mere four hundred yards away, but he could see precious little. Blooming storm clouds obscured his view and he could see torrential rain would be heading their way very soon. The tide was high and they would be safe tonight. Nothing would reach them. He might even give whoever was on watch tonight a break. There was only an hour before curfew and the entertainment only worked well in shifts. Honok, Christopher, Grayson and Edward were on watch tonight. He would send Walker to relieve them later and they could then 'relieve' themselves. Lazarus chuckled. He might have to relieve himself too shortly.

He strode up to the castle and walked through the gateway, casting a slight nod at the guard, Grayson. Lazarus continued through the yard and into the castle, through the main doors. Inside, he threw his black coat off and over an axe hanging on the wall. His clash with Tim forgotten, Lazarus walked up the huge stairway. The stone walls of the castle were adorned with relics of a bygone age: axes, swords, flags and pennants. Each one could tell a story of the past, of battles they had seen, grand victories and glorious failures. Lazarus wasn't interested in the past anymore, only the future. He began whistling as he walked up the stairway, the soft red carpet underneath his boots soiled with dirt and earth from outside. He let his hands drift over the banister, feeling the smooth polished oak beneath his rough, calloused fingers.

Upon reaching the top level, he headed down a long corridor to his room. Outside was a chair and Walker was sitting upright in it, alert as ever. As Lazarus approached, Walker stood up. As usual, Walker's hand flinched as he stopped himself from saluting. Lazarus inwardly smiled, knowing it was an old habit he found hard to stop. Walker smoothed out his creased white shirt as best he could and stood to attention. Lazarus stopped whistling.

"Everything okay, Walker?" Lazarus asked lightly.

"Absolutely. All quiet on the western front, sir. Any news on the radio? Some of the men have heard and were wondering what the deal is?"

Lazarus looked at Walker's blue eyes and Walker found himself being scrutinised. He glanced away, reluctant to look into

Lazarus' eyes. They were a deep dark brown, almost black like his thick hair. Lazarus was a few inches taller than him, at least six foot six, and a simple stare from him could stop you in your tracks.

Lazarus contemplated his answer briefly. "Tim heard something that's for sure, but nothing tangible. You can tell the men we are listening and *when* there is news, I will announce it. In the meantime, try to not let the men gossip. Remember, Walker, *when rumours are rife...*"

"...you risk your life," said Walker. He knew the saying that Lazarus had introduced to them a couple of weeks ago. They had been twenty three then.

Ricardo had been a good man, ex-army, strong, colourful, but he had started spreading rumours about Lazarus, about how he kept the best finds for himself and didn't share with the men. Unrest had grown and Walker had informed his boss of the uneasiness spreading throughout their makeshift village. He knew it couldn't be true. If Lazarus was hiding anything he would know about it. Lazarus had called a meeting in the village square and everyone had been present. There were no scouting parties that day, no entertainment. Lazarus had told everyone quite clearly that he wouldn't listen to illicit lies or rumours spread by mutinous factions within their community. They survived together because they worked together. Yes, Lazarus was in charge, but without him there would be no order, just chaos, anarchy and death. He had suddenly grabbed Ricardo and with the help of Walker, they had put him in the stocks. Lazarus made an example of Ricardo there and then. Everyone knew it was him that had started the gossip, but no one was prepared for what came next.

Lazarus had brought a steak knife with him and with Ricardo locked in the stocks he casually sliced our Ricardo's tongue. Walker had seen blood before, plenty of it, but some of the men had not. Until a few weeks ago, they had been postmen, lorry drivers, the unemployed. Blood spewed from Ricardo's mouth as Lazarus held the man's tongue aloft.

"Hear this. When rumours are rife, you risk your life. If anyone wants to question my judgement or my character, then you should come to me. I am fair. I have helped you all, have I not?"

There were mutterings from the crowd of mostly men, a few ayes, and then Lazarus threw the tongue down in the dirt. He stomped on it, squashing it and grinding it into the hard ground. He turned back to Ricardo, blood dribbling down his chin. Lazarus raised the steak knife and stabbed it into both of Ricardo's eyes, blinding him instantly. Ricardo had screamed and screamed. He had tried to get out of the stocks, but there was no way. Lazarus then lopped off both of Ricardo' ears and threw them to the ground too. He turned to the twenty two men and women still gathered around, and spoke.

"Mizaru, kikazaru, iwazaru. See no evil, speak no evil, hear no evil. What Ricardo has done is not to question me, but you. He has effectively branded you all as cowards. If anyone questions me, then they question all of us. We are in this together. We have to stick together because we will only survive this as a team. Do we all understand now?"

With the knife glistening in his hand, blood dripping down and soaking into the ground, the gathered men answered Lazarus with approval. Walker started clapping and before long, they all were. Lazarus smiled.

"Right, back to work everyone." He drew the knife across Ricardo's throat and let the man bleed out, his life draining away into the hard cracked ground beneath the stocks. Ricardo's body shook violently as bright red blood spurted from his throat and cascaded out of his body.

"You cannot make a revolution with silk gloves. Throw that piece of garbage away, will you?" Lazarus said, passing Walker on his way back to the castle. The crowd dispersed, leaving Walker to take away Ricardo's dead, mangled body. Nobody ever forgot that lesson.

"There'll be no gossiping on my watch, sir." Walker stood upright once more and dared a look at Lazarus.

"Good man," said Lazarus and he opened the door to his room. "Give me a few minutes, will you? Then you can go and relieve whoever is on watch in the parapets. I think it might be Ed. There's no need for a look out tonight. There's a storm coming in and the tides up, so we'll be safe enough. Go and take the men down for the entertainment, yourself too. Leave Tim though, he's working."

Walker breathed an audible sigh of relief when the door closed and he walked off down the corridor, leaving Lazarus alone. Lazarus knew Walker could do with some fun now and again and the man practically had to be ordered to relax. Lazarus knew Walker respected him, but he was intimidated too and was always on edge when around him. Lazarus smiled again and sat down on the bed. He began pulling off his heavy work boots. It was a large four poster bed, which was added to the castle in the eighties to add some character for the tourists. Now it was only used for what it was intended: sleeping and fucking. Lazarus stretched out behind him and felt a leg, the skin smooth and soft. Smiling, he turned around and saw her there, sleeping. The bruising had gone down around her arms a little, but he could see where the ropes still chafed her wrists and ankles.

He nudged her and she stirred. He nudged her again, harder, and she woke. She looked around the room and tugged at the binding that held her to the bed, naked and spread-eagled over the quilt.

"Did you get a good rest, Keisha?" said Lazarus undressing.

"Please let me go, I...I..." She felt too tired to cry. She was too exhausted to even plea for her life anymore. She knew he wasn't going to release her. He had kept her here for three days, only untying the ropes so she could go to the bathroom, and even then, it was under armed guard. She watched him undress and felt the nausea creep over her. He was a big man; muscled, stocky, swarthy, and he was already aroused.

Lazarus climbed onto the bed and held his face above hers. "Keisha, my dear," he said, stroking her exquisite light brown skin, "I hope you rested, because I do not intend for you to get much sleep tonight."

She turned her face away as he looked at her, his dark brown eyes only inches from hers. She could smell the stale sweat on him, and his long black hair dangled down, brushing her shoulders. She tensed as she felt his hardness on her belly. How much longer would he keep her a prisoner here?

"Don't worry, my dear, I shall free you soon." Lazarus pushed himself inside the young girl and clamped his hand over her mouth to drown out the screams.

* * * *

Walker wound his way through the castle, passing the battlements until he reached the tower. As he went out, he could smell the sea air and he felt like he was living out a fantasy, living the life of a soldier in this castle, just living off the land. He was almost surprised there wasn't a pirate ship anchored in the bay.

Ed threw his cigarette quickly over the tower ledge when he saw Walker approach. "Evening, Walker."

"Ed. Anything?" Walker stood beside him. Ed was an athletic man, popular with the rest of the men on The Mount. He had been an unexpected guest, but a welcome one. They found him by accident, but he joined them with no quarrels. The others still sometimes took the piss out of his Australian accent. He had been on a working holiday when the infection had started, doing odd jobs for cash, living the surfer's lifestyle.

"Some sweet waves, but otherwise no, all good, mate. It's quiet as fuck out here. Getting cold too." Ed hoped Walker hadn't seen the cigarette he had been smoking from his private stash. They were worth more than money now.

Walker nodded. "Boss says you can head in now if you like. Head on down to the dungeons. Entertainment's on tonight, apparently."

"Fucking A," said Ed rubbing his hands together. "You coming?"

"In a minute. Just need to clear my head first." Walker leaned over the parapet and looked at the beach below. Waves were washing over the rocks at the tower's base and there was no doubt the swell was increasing. A storm was definitely coming in.

"Right you are, mate," said Ed. "Hanging around the boss too long would give anyone a headache. I don't know how you do it. I mean fair play he's got us sorted, but he's a bit, you know, *off*, eh?"

Walker eyeballed Ed. "Be careful what you say. The walls have ears, you know. I would hate to hear of any *rumours* that you were...doubting him."

The inference was clear and Ed knew what Walker was alluding to. He had been present when Ricardo was murdered. He hadn't totally agreed with it, but he knew why it had to be done. The world had changed since he had left Melbourne and his family behind. He missed his brother Evan and his niece and nephew. With any luck, Australia had escaped this terrible infection, but he didn't know. There was certainly no way back now. The world of politicians and policemen was gone. This was a time for leaders and men. Lazarus was a born leader, Ed could see that.

"Yes sir." Ed left Walker alone and made his way down to the dungeons. He ignored the faint screams coming from the master bedroom upstairs. He knew Lazarus kept one for himself and it was best not to question it.

Ignoring the historical flags and pennants on the walls, Ed passed through doorways, treading carefully over the raised stone lip in each, until he found himself at the dungeon's entrance. There were three cells, each one small and damp. It was cold, since there was no natural sunlight and as he walked in, he felt the temperature drop almost instantly.

"G'day, Norm," said Ed as he walked in. "Boss says it's on tonight."

"How's it going, Ed? Yeah, well lucky you, you're the first here so make the most of it. Once the others get here it'll be carnage, you know how it goes."

Ed laughed as Norm got up and handed him a set of keys to the cells. Norm was not the brightest of men, but was well suited to prison guard. He was a huge man, at least six feet high and almost as wide. Ed guessed that when he got the chance he probably helped himself to the entertainment. It would be easy, because nobody guarded the guard.

Ed took the keys and looked into the first cell. Cowering in a dark corner was a girl, dressed in jeans and a blue top. She was curled into a ball and whimpering. She was caked in filth and dirt, and he could smell the shit on her.

"For crying out loud, Norm, can't you at least keep 'em clean?"

Norm didn't answer, just sat back down on the chair provided for him and watched Ed walk down to the second cell. There was another woman, this time much older, perhaps in her fifties. She was lying on a mattress and she looked like she was asleep. She was naked and in good shape. Ed thought about it, but decided not to. This one was in a very deep sleep and if he woke her, she would be liable to scream the place down. By the time he'd calmed her down, the others would be here and then she'd be shared around before he even got a look in.

Ed moved onto the final cell. A woman stood gripping the bars and spat in Ed's face.

"You fucking sadistic degenerate!" She drew back to spit at him again, but Ed ducked to the side and her saliva dribbled down the cold stone wall behind him.

Ed smiled as he wiped his cheek. "All right then, darling, having fun are we?"

"Fuck you, you pig, fuck all of you. What the fuck are you doing? How can you treat us like this? How can you lock us up?"

Ed looked the woman up and down. He had screwed her yesterday, but she had been so out of it, she probably didn't even recognise him. Sometimes they had to supply the entertainment with drugs to keep them going, that and to stop them topping themselves.

The woman stood back from the bars when she realised Ed wasn't scared of her. He liked her. She was slim, in her late twenties, had glorious blonde hair, and plenty of character. She reminded him of the girls at home and he felt a pang of homesickness. She only had a blanket and held it around her as if it might protect her.

He dangled the keys in front of her. "Just shut up, will you? Now you know how this works er...Sal?"

"You don't even know my name, do you? I'm just a piece of meat to you, nothing more than that, isn't that true? Where are your morals? Eh? What would your family think of what you're doing?"

"My family? My family is on the other side of the world, probably dead. Don't try it on with me. You want to talk about morals?" Ed's laughter echoed around the small dungeon. "They're part of the old world now, darling." He stepped up to the bars and stared at her. "Now are you gonna be a good girl, or do I have to get my friend Norm to help me out?"

Sally was quiet and her spirit sank. She knew she couldn't fight them. Two days ago, they had captured her and she had lost count of the number of times she had been raped since. The woman in the cell next to her, Eve, had been here a week and had tried to kill herself last night. Norm had caught her trying to slit her own wrists with a small stone that had crumbled from the wall.

He'd taken the stone, swept her cell, and left her without food and water since.

"I'll be good," whispered Sally. She watched as Ed unlocked her cell and he stood in the doorway looking at her. She dropped the blanket to the floor and tried to fight back the fear that threatened to engulf her. Trembling, she sat down on the dirty mattress as Ed walked over to her.

As he raped her, she wondered if her friend Keisha was still alive. She wondered if her parents were still alive. And she wondered if she would ever get out of here alive. When she heard the footsteps and laughter of the other men approach, she tuned out completely, praying that someone would come and rescue her from this never-ending nightmare.

CHAPTER FOUR

Harry's stomach growled and he decided this would be the last one for tonight. They had been going from door to door all afternoon and achieved little. Ignoring his hunger, he looked up at the sky. The sun was low and soon the light was going to be too small to see by safely. From his hiding place behind the low-hanging branches of an apple tree he motioned for Moira to come over to him. He watched as she cast a quick glance around the garden before scampering over.

They had followed the usual process which had kept them safe so far. Always watch before entering a new property, whether it was a house, a shop, or a garage. Always look and listen first. The previous house had looked empty, but they had waited, and sure enough, after a few minutes, they had seen a figure pass by a window. Five minutes later and it had stumbled right up against the glass. They could see it was dead, trapped inside and unable to free itself. They moved on.

"What do you reckon?" whispered Moira crouching down beside Harry.

"I reckon this is a good one. This is the last one though. We need to get back before it gets dark. You set?" Harry felt his stomach muscles tighten. It wasn't hunger anymore, it was fear.

Moira nodded. "Set." She let Harry take the lead and he walked up to the back door. They had been waiting in the garden for around thirty minutes and saw no evidence of there being anyone inside. The tall hedge around the garden kept them well hidden from the street, but they were still cautious. The dead could appear from anywhere and it only took a second. Even when you felt safe you had to keep your guard up.

Harry discreetly wrapped a cloth around a large stone he found and smashed the window. He brushed aside the broken glass and reached through to open the door. It opened easily and nodding for Moira to follow him, he disappeared inside the house.

Moira's deep orange hair flashed brilliantly in the low evening sunlight as she crept across the garden, her pale skin almost shining. The rucksack on her back weighed down on her thin frame, but she was content. She knew she carried important things they needed to survive: food, matches, and even a few little extras for treats. She stood up as she neared the house and went through the open doorway after Harry.

"I'll go upstairs, check out the medicine cabinet. You look around down here, see what you can find, all right?" said Harry, disappearing through another doorway not waiting for a reply. They had done this so many times it almost didn't need saying. Invariably Harry would take the upstairs floor and look for medicine first. They needed vitamins, creams, tablets; anything that would help Caterina both now and later. Moira's main task was to search for food. Her rucksack currently contained six tins of sliced pears, three tins of rice pudding and one sweet corn, plus a packet of crackers and two slabs of dark chocolate. Just thinking about it made her mouth salivate and she was already thinking about getting back to the others so they could eat.

This was the fifth house they had broken into today. Together with Harry, she had managed to gather a few supplies and she knew he had found some useful things for Caterina. They hadn't ventured too far from the others, from home as it currently was. They were still on the same street, just a few doors down. The back gardens made for a difficult path between the houses. Often they had to climb over fences or through thick hedges, but it was safer than the other option. The first day out together, they had tried to take the road, but had instantly drawn an unwelcome following of zombies and had soon abandoned that idea. So, they stealthily crept through undergrowth, accruing scratches on their hands and arms, but still alive.

Moira heard Harry's footsteps above her, and looked around. They had come directly into a dining room. She saw a large table with six high-backed chairs around it in the centre, various cupboards and shelves around it against the walls. The window at the far end looked out onto the road and the curtains were not drawn, so she kept low and scuttled over to them, pulling the curtains shut quickly. Standing up again, she could now look around easier. On one shelf she noticed a stack of books and reading the titles found one she liked the look of.

"*The Shawshank Redemption*," she said aloud. She stuffed it into her bag. Just because it was the end of the world didn't mean she had to give up reading. She still pined for her days at the library, but they would never return, so now she took the opportunity to read whenever she could. Such peaceful times were rare.

Past the stairs, she saw the kitchen through an open doorway and made straight for the cupboards. Most were empty. It was a common occurrence which was extremely annoying. Moira reckoned that a lot of people had left, trying to escape the infection, and had probably taken most of their food with them, leaving only perishables behind. Moira found nothing of use, only mouldy biscuits and a cereal box that had fed a mouse or a rat until it was used up. There was nothing she could add to her collection of tin cans, so she tried the fridge. Moira found something green and mouldy growing at the back, and a carton of milk that smelt very off. Yet again, she had drawn a blank and found nothing edible.

The kitchen was proving to be useless. The sink was full of dirty dishes and cutlery, cups and mugs, idling in stagnant water. The plants on the kitchen sill were covered in mildew and cobwebs hung from every corner. She peered through the peephole in the doorway and looked out onto the street outside. It seemed deserted and they wanted to keep it that way. She thought she might go upstairs to help Harry when she noticed another doorway at the back of the kitchen and she pushed it open. The room was quite dark, just a small amount of light coming through a tiny oblong window which was open and letting in a cool draft. It was actually pleasant, much better than the stale air in the kitchen.

Moira looked around the utility room: a washing machine, a basket of wooden pegs, a shelf full of cloths, polish and bleach. Against one wall was a chest freezer. A pool of water surrounded it on the flat concrete floor. Moira noticed on the lid a photograph in a small six by four silver frame. Approaching it, she saw the picture was of a young boy eating a chocolate ice-cream, his hair blowing in his face, and a sunny beach in the background. Against all the darkness the boy's smile was radiant and Moira smiled herself.

Either side of the frame were two candles that had burned themselves down to nothing but stumps. Low blackened wicks stood proudly in pools of dried wax. On the freezer lid rested a bouquet of flowers that had long since wilted and withered away. Moira picked them up and felt them crumble in her hands, the brown crusty petals tumbling to the floor, brittle stalks snapping easily in her fingers. The freezer suddenly jolted, and surprised, Moira dropped the flowers at her feet.

She looked at the socket on the wall. The freezer was still plugged in, but she knew it couldn't be on as all power had gone off weeks ago. The freezer jolted again, as if it was trying to spring back into life. The frame wobbled and then toppled over, the boy on the beach falling face down into the candle wax. Moira reached out, her fingers touching the freezer's handle, when another hand clamped itself on hers.

She retracted her hand and spun around to see Harry behind her. Moira let out a long sigh, unaware she had been holding her breath. "Shit, Harry, you made me jump."

"Let's go, Moira, you ready?" In the dim light Moira saw the tiredness on his face. It wasn't just the hunger or the fatigue of surviving; he was still grieving.

"Yeah I just..."

"No, Moira. We don't need to know what – or who – is in there. Best to leave it be," Harry said, lifting his hand to her shoulder.

Moira tugged on the straps over her shoulders, tightening them so the backpack nestled closely against her spine. She whispered to Harry. "What if they're all right. What if someone's hiding in there? I think a little boy lived here and..."

"Moira, listen to me. Whoever is in that freezer is not alive. If it was someone hiding when we came in then how did they put the things back on the lid? If it was someone put in there for safe keeping then I'm afraid they would be long dead. That's airtight and judging by how long those flowers have been dead, they would have suffocated days ago at least. I'm sorry, Moira, but no good can come from opening that lid."

Moira remembered the smile on the boy's face. He was so happy. She wanted a part of that, a part of his happiness, to know he was still happy. Deep down though she knew Harry was right. There was no way the boy could still be alive, not now.

"You're right, I know. Let's get home." Moira gave Harry the best smile she could manage.

Harry led the way back out of the house and Moira looked behind her as she left the utility room, the freezer bouncing on its feet one last time. Maybe one day she would see and experience real happiness instead of having to read about it in books.

* * * *

As Caterina dozed, Christina flicked though a wedding album she found buried in amongst a shoebox full of photos in the oak bureaux. The bride and groom were currently being showered in confetti and looked deliriously happy. In fact, everyone looked happy. As she turned the pages, she saw more smiling faces: women and men, old and young. She wondered if the people who had lived here were the wedding couple. The bedroom she shared with Cat offered no clues. There were no other photos on the walls or shelves, there was no wedding dress hanging in the closet, and no wedding rings at the bedside.

Glancing at her watch, Christina saw it was getting late. The others would be back soon. They had decided they would eat as a group, and share out equal portions. The more they shared, the closer they felt. They chanced upon this house three days back and Christina managed to sleep well here. They had been on the road for days. Sleeping and resting was never easy with one eye open. She looked over at the silent Caterina, someone who seemed to have no problem sleeping. Even though Christina was no relative and only met Cat a few weeks ago, she felt proud. Cat was so young, but so strong to be going through all of this while nearly six months pregnant.

Christina sat on the end of the bed waiting for Cat to wake and for the others to return, and turned another page of the album. The photo was of the bride and groom again, this time on the church steps with the priest in the middle, grinning foolishly as the sun bounced off his bald head. Christina remembered her own wedding only vaguely now. She thought at the time that she would never be happier, but her marriage only lasted a year. The wedding was at a small church, much like the one in the photo, but she didn't remember confetti. She could still picture her husband, Karl, looking at her with such love as she walked down the aisle. What she would give to see him again.

They had met and married within a year, even talked of having children. Karl had been eager to settle down, but Christina

44

focussed on her investment company. It was still in its infancy back then and she dedicated herself to building it up. She wanted it to grow bigger and better than all of the others. Unfortunately, she spent so much time on it that she neglected her marriage. She still felt bitter the way it had ended; how quickly she had divorced the only man she had ever loved and how quickly she immersed herself in the business world instead, telling herself it was for the best. She convinced herself of that for many years.

She was powerless to stop the wry grin on her face from spreading as an image of her yacht popped into her mind. Was it still anchored or had it been stolen, torn down, drifting away unattended? Both her homes would be empty or burnt down. Her bank balance was most likely still intact, but it may as well be on Mars. A packet of matches was worth more now than a few million pounds in the bank. Would she trade the millions in her bank for a family like this in the album? She looked again at the happy couple. Hindsight is a wonderful thing, she thought. If she had settled down and had children back then with Karl then she wouldn't be the person she is now. Who knows what would have happened.

She looked over at Cat, still sleeping. They had forged a bond, no doubt about it. The natural maternal instincts must have been there, buried deep within her and squashed under a pile of banknotes and paperwork. Why had she given up so easily on Karl? Was she scared, ambitious? Did she succumb to peer pressure? No, the truth was it was just greed. Christina looked at a stylish photograph of the wedding cake, a white tower of sugary sweetness. She couldn't deny the past, couldn't change it. It was there no matter how you looked at, there for all to see in black and white. Only the future can be changed. She listed to Cat's peaceful breathing and knew she still had a chance to forge a better future, for both herself and others.

Christina turned a page and the bride was sitting in the middle of a park, huge trees towering above her with bright green grass beneath her feet. An array of colourful flowers adorned the garden's edge: roses, hyacinths, rhododendrons and even more that Christina couldn't name. She began to wonder what would happen to them. No doubt they were now overgrown, the gardener most likely dead or undead. Would the infection leave them alone, let the grass and the trees grown? Would it spread through the animal kingdom, leaving the flora alone? Perhaps the Earth would return to normal, to a more natural state, a world without men or beasts. Her thoughts were interrupted when Caterina stirred and sat up on the bed.

"What's the time?" yawned Cat.

"Nearly suppertime, honey. How're you feeling?" said Christina closing the album.

"Not bad actually. I just needed a bit of a snooze, you know?"

"Well, the others will be back any minute, I expect. We should get ready, see what's to eat. You get dressed. I'm going to speak to Jackson, all right?"

Caterina got out of bed and began dressing as Christina silently left the room to go find Jackson. She was worried that it was getting dark and the others weren't back yet. It was not like them to be late. No sooner had she stepped out onto the hallway than she heard a rap at the door downstairs. Somebody was here.

* * * *

Jessica blinked her eyes, but it was difficult trying to figure out the best route. She was not used to reading maps.

"Rosa, stop it, I can't concentrate" giggled Jessica, pushing Rosa gently away.

"Stop kissing you? Never," said Rosa leaning back.

They were lying on the bed together, trying to work out the best way from Longrock to Penzance. They needed to avoid the main roads and towns, but still wanted the most direct route they could. As Jessica traced her finger along a small line, a railroad, Rosa nuzzled her lips against the back of Jessica's neck.

"Seriously, quit it!" Jessica laughed and sat up, taking the map with her and resting it on her lap.

"Okay, okay, it's just boring, is all," said Rosa. "And lying here with you makes me...you know..."

"I know, but we've got to figure this out, Rosa. There'll be plenty of time for hanky-panky later," said Jessica.

"Hanky-panky?" sniggered Rosa. "How quaint!" She traced her fingers across Jessica's arm, up to her shoulders before entwining them in her long brown hair. She stroked Jessica's head and the map slipped onto the floor. Jessica gave up trying to read it and ignore Rosa, and turned over to face her. She pulled Rosa to her and they kissed longingly. Rosa's hands ran over Jessica's dress until they came to rest on her bare legs.

"You know I can't resist you," whispered Jessica. She kissed Rosa on the tip of her nose. "So are you going to tell me now?"

"What?" asked Rosa. She stared into Jessica's light brown eyes innocently.

"What we were talking about earlier? You know what." Jessica pulled her dress down, aware the others would be back soon and that hanky-panky truly would have to wait until later.

Rosa sighed and licked her lips. "I don't see why it matters."

"It doesn't *matter* as such. It's just...I want to know about you," said Jessica. "You know about me. You know I go both ways, you know who I've dated, who I've slept with, what my parents did, where I went to school; everything." She took Rosa's hand in hers.

"Okay well, no I haven't. So now you know," said Rosa sitting up in bed. She let go of Jessica's hand.

"Not even a kiss? Never been tempted?" said Jessica sitting up too.

"Nope," said Rosa plainly. "I'm not attracted to men, never have been, never will be."

"Well, that's fine, who cares right? I mean I don't know why you have to be so defensive about it." Jessica tried to look at Rosa, but she was looking the other way through the net curtains to the street below.

"I'm not defensive. I just don't like to talk about it. I lost a lot of friends when I came out, and my parents, well...I guess I'm not really used to talking about it. It's like you're testing me or something. I know you like men. I've seen the way you look at Tom." Rosa got off the bed and picked the map up. "We should finish looking at this and..."

"Hey," said Jessica, "forget the bloody map will you? I'm bi, but I don't look at Tom like anything! You're imagining things, Rosa."

"Am I? Whatever. I remember him telling me that he thought you were 'quite something.' The way he looks at you it's pretty obvious he loves you."

Jessica got off the bed and cupped Rosa's face forcing Rosa to look at her. "Maybe so, but I don't love him. I love *you*." She leant forward and they kissed.

Rosa dropped the map. "I love you too," she said. "But I don't know what the hell is going on with me." Rosa sat back down on the bed, "I didn't mean to get snappy with you, I'm just tired. Actually, that's not quite true - I'm not tired. I sleep reasonably well. I wake up most nights, yes, but not for too long. I'm just weary. I wish things were normal. I'm fed up of being on the go all the time, having to watch our backs, having to eat out of cans. I'm fed up of not knowing where we're going to be from one day to the next. This is the longest time we've spent in one place and it's only the third night we've slept here. Who knows, tomorrow we could be sleeping on a concrete floor again and then..." Rosa's shoulders visibly sank.

"Look around you, Rosa," said Jessica. "Go on, I mean it, look. See those photos over there on the bookcase? Well, those people are dead. That canvas over there on the wall of the tropical island and the palm trees? We'll never go there. You see that diary beside you? It'll never be written in again. Normal is what this is. I'm just fucking glad to be alive. And to be with you."

Rosa smiled, but her face looked tired. Jessica could see the strain was starting to show. Rosa had looked so young and vivacious when they had met last month. She could still vividly remember their first kiss in a church of all places. She hadn't changed much, but she was right. She looked weary. The last month had taken its toll on them. Rosa was younger than everyone else and a couple of years younger than Jessica. She was struggling to adjust to life on the run. Jessica opened her mouth to speak when there was a short knock on the door.

"Jessie? Rosa? Harry's back with Moira." It was Christina's voice.

Jessica got up and opened the door. "Hey, Christina, did they find much?"

"Um, yeah a bit." Christina looked worried.

"What is it, what's wrong?" said Jessica. Suddenly, she forgot all about Rosa's insecurities and worries. A vision ran through her mind of Harry being bitten by one of the dead. "Is it Harry, oh please tell me he's not..."

"No, no he's fine," said Christina. "It's Tom and Laurent. They're not back yet. There's no sign of them."

CHAPTER FIVE

"Dad, Dad, there they are again!"

"Shush, Jimmy, keep it down. We don't want to get spotted, do we? We don't know *who* they are or *what* they want. We're safe enough in here, lad, just quiet down now."

David Ireland was sweating, hoping his son would keep his cool. They had been holed up at their house since the outbreak had started and David did not intend to let anyone destroy their refuge now. He had sworn to the boy's mother he would protect their son from the lunatics outside; from the looters, thieves and murderers. There were worse things patrolling the streets of Longrock than zombies. By God, he had done so for, what, nearly a month? Well he wasn't about to make a mistake now.

"But Dad, I think they're okay. Look, I can see there's two men in the front and at least two in the back. I can't really count how many, it's too dark though." Jimmy tried to see into the van, but the rain was coming down and without streetlights, it was getting hard to see far beyond his window. He only had a narrow strip to see through. Wood had been nailed over the window except for an inch at the side.

"Jimmy, get away from that damn window this second, you hear me, lad?"

Jimmy sank back and pulled the drape across the window obscuring the outside world from view. He knew if he pushed it any further he was likely to feel the back of his father's hand. He sat at the table opposite his father and took a swig of lemonade. David could tell from the look on his son's face that trouble was brewing.

"Dad, we can't stay in here forever. Mum's gone. Fuck, the neighbours are gone, the whole country's gone."

"Watch your language," said David, pointing a thick finger at Jimmy.

"Sorry, Dad, but come on, how long are we supposed to live like this?" He began picking at the dirt under his fingernails and scrutinised the table, too scared to look up at his father's face.

"You want to go back to Belfast, is that it? You think it's any better over there, lad? You don't know anything. No, it's safer here. Your mother - God rest her soul - and I brought you here for a better life. I know things have turned to custard, but there's nowhere to go, son. Listen to me, Jimmy, we are as safe here as anywhere. We've got enough supplies to last us months. Why would you even want to leave?" David had been sharpening a knife and laid it down on the table. There was a solitary candle between the two of them and he was amazed at how old his son looked. He was only fifteen, but in the last month, he seemed to have grown up a lot. Jimmy could probably pass for twenty now, ever since his mother died. That had been tough on him. His mother tried to help a friend, a neighbour, and look where that had got her. A bite on the arm and hours later, she was dead. David had implored her not to go out, but she wouldn't listen. She had to help, she'd said, she couldn't just sit around, *waiting*. Jimmy was just like her.

"Dad," said Jimmy calmly, "all I'm saying is think about it. Please. I agree there are psychos out there. The infection didn't just kill the nasty people as we both know, but those people out there looked good. They weren't shooting off guns and the two men in that van stopped to help those others. They could've driven off, but they didn't. Hell, if it wasn't for them that house would've burned down with them still in it. And what did we do, Dad? Eh? We just sat here and watched.

"I saw where they went, you know. We could probably find them. They took a right down Richardson Avenue, then up Patterson Street. They can't have gone much further than that, there's nothing there. You know that street leads out to the crop fields. They had a van, Dad, they could help us...maybe they have somewhere safe to go, maybe...?"

"All right, lad, that's enough." David toyed with the knife on the table, twirling the handle around with the sharp point embedded in the table's wooden surface. "I'll think about it, but we're not doing anything tonight. There's a storm coming in, I can tell. It's already raining hard and we don't ever go out at night, right? We'll sleep on it and talk about it in the morning, right enough?"

"Okay, Dad." Jimmy got up, knowing there was no way he was going to be able to convince his father they should leave their home. Any offer to talk about it in the morning meant the matter was closed. There would be no talking and there would be no leaving.

"I think I'll turn in. Good night, Dad." Jimmy left the kitchen and his father behind, and went into his bedroom. It was too early to sleep and his mind was blazing with plans of how they could leave this prison they had built themselves. The hardest part would be changing his father's mind. He lay down on his bed in the cool darkness. There was a faint flickering on the ceiling as the flames across the street danced their way through the house, through the curtains to his room. The house would burn down to be sure. There was nobody to stop that now. It was on the other side of the road though, so they were in no danger for now.

He saw the dead burning, walking around, and chasing after those strangers. He knew the infection was unstoppable. It had taken his mother, his friends. If they stayed here at home, it would inevitably take them too. Damn, his father was stubborn. Why could he not see it? So what if they had food enough to last them for months, or years even. You couldn't live your life in a box. And when the food ran out, then what? Venture outside only to find six million zombies waiting for you? No, those people were good, he knew it. He had to find a way to convince his father, but talking wasn't going to work. When David Ireland's mind was made up, it was made up for good.

Jimmy decided as he lay there that his father might need a prod, just a little nudge in the right direction to make him see that they weren't invincible. Jimmy lay on his bed watching the orange light on the ceiling above flicker and an idea grew in his head. His father was right, a storm was coming. Perhaps the rain would put the fire out? The wind was picking up too. In the morning, he would do it. His father was not an early riser. Jimmy would be up first, he would make sure of it. He would sneak downstairs and open the door. He could prise out the nails. He knew where the tools were kept (under the sink where David thought they were hidden.) He would leave the door ajar and call out, just so one of the dead, not many, would come. His father would see they weren't safe. Then they would *have* to leave. Yes, first thing in the morning.

Jimmy lay there dreaming of his plans and scheming, whilst his father drank another six bottles of cider alone at the kitchen table, wondering how he was going to be able to keep protecting his son in these conditions. Later, before David fell into his bed, he prayed for his son.

The wind whirled around the house as the storm intensified. By sunrise father and son would be separated, and one of them would be dead.

* * * *

Tim carefully laid the headphones down on the desk and stood up slowly. He didn't want to risk losing the frequency he found. If he lost contact, he knew what Lazarus would do to him. He also knew that he had to report this straight away, never mind that it was approaching midnight.

He had scribbled down a few notes, but he remembered most of the conversation he heard. He couldn't believe it. Finally, after hours of listening to nothing but static, he chanced upon it, the transmitter picking up some garbled conversation. With a bit of fine tuning, Tim had managed to hone in on it and heard the conversation perfectly clearly. Tim was under no illusions as to its importance. He had to tell Lazarus about it, right now.

He opened the door and immediately the raindrops slapped into his face like ice cold pins. He closed the door and began the trudge up the hill toward the castle. The houses were dark and quiet. Everyone would be asleep now. He knew someone would be watching him though. There was always someone on watch at the castle.

Tim picked his way carefully up the steep slope, not wanting to fall down and twist an ankle on the rocks, or worse still, break his neck. If he was right, then Lazarus would be pleased. Maybe he would be allowed some entertainment instead of being stuck in a cold damp house all day and night listening to a sodding radio.

Tim tripped on a wet rock and fell into the mud. He held onto the hillside, clutching clumps of grass as the howling wind tore at him. The rain pelted his face and dribbled down his neck. He got up and walked faster to the castle, as eager to be out of the storm as to be standing before Lazarus with some good news.

When he reached the castle door, one of Lazarus' henchmen let him in, a stout surly man by the name of Honok. He had been a labourer before the infection. Now he was a sort of bodyguard, entrusted with the keys to the castle, literally. Honok disliked Tim, thinking he was weak and cowardly.

"What do you want, *Timmy*, you should be working," asked Honok curtly.

Tim shook himself dry in the grand entrance, shedding his sodden jumper and using it to dry his face and hair. "Need to see Lazarus. Now. Important news. Very important." Tim spoke in quick short sentences, practically hopping from foot to foot so keen was he to see Lazarus before he forgot the radio conversation.

Honok raised one eyebrow. "At this time of night? I think it'll wait, don't you? Get back to work." He folded his arms and stood before the main stairway that Tim knew led up to Lazarus' room.

Tim took a step toward Honok. "I said *it's important*. Do you think I don't know what'll happen to me if I disturb him and it's not. Let me up there or face Lazarus in the morning. Your call."

Honk thought for a moment, and then stood aside. "Fine." He cracked his hairy knuckles. "I'll be waiting down here for you, *Timmy*."

Tim bounded up the stairs two at a time and raced toward Lazarus' room. He almost burst straight in, but then thought better of it and knocked on the door. He waited a moment then knocked again. He heard grunting sounds inside and began to doubt himself. Perhaps he should've waited until morning. Waking his boss up in the middle of the night wasn't the best idea he had lately. Before he could slink away, the door was thrown open and Lazarus stood before him wearing an unbuttoned black shirt and jeans.

"Tim? What is it?" Lazarus was clearly surprised to see him. "You look terrible."

Tim looked over Lazarus' shoulder and saw the figure of a woman on the bed. He heard a faint groan before Lazarus took a step into the corridor and shut the bedroom door.

"I heard something, sir, on the radio, just now."

"Well, I hope it was something important, Tim, for your sake. I don't like to be interrupted when I'm...busy." Lazarus's lips curled into a half smile, but his dark eyes never left Tim's.

"It was a naval boat, sir," Tim went on. He thrust out a handful of soggy papers. "I made a few notes for you. It's nearly all there. I wrote down what I could. It was the British Navy, sir, they're here!"

Lazarus motioned for Tim to sit down as he scanned the wet pulp in his hands. "Go on and tell me what you heard," he demanded, frowning.

Tim had expected Lazarus to be pleased. He hadn't imagined he would be jumping up and down with joy, but he had thought what he had heard was a good thing. Lazarus' grave demeanour caught Tim off guard. "Well, I came upon it by luck more than anything. I thought I'd tried the CNR bands and at first I got nothing, but then...It was the HMS Daring. They're somewhere south of here by the sounds of it. I heard an Admiral McCulloch talking. He was corresponding with a Henry Samson, a Captain, I think. It was hard to tell - sometimes the frequency distorted what they were saying. This Henry Samson bloke was definitely American, sir. I'm sure he said he was stationed on the USS Abraham Lincoln."

"And you heard this, just now?" asked Lazarus.

"Absolutely, and the things they were saying..." Tim's mouth was open, still in shock at what he had heard.

"Well, go on then, Tim," said Lazarus, his patience growing thin.

"This Henry Samson was talking to the Brit, the Admiral McCulloch. He said they were on a rendezvous with the USS Gerald Ford in the Caribbean. Apparently, both ships were on naval duties in the Atlantic, some kind of war-games or something, when the infection broke out. They were ordered to patrol the US coastline, but a week after the infection started, they had received no further orders or contact from the mainland. They had been in touch with each other and remained out at sea, unsure if they should try to dock or keep their last ordered positions.

"Samson said he'd been trying various frequencies to get in touch with command, but hadn't been able to raise anyone. From the sounds of the conversation, I'd say they had only just begun talking with each other, sir. McCulloch had told a pretty similar story. He told the yanks about the evacuation of Britain, but that it largely failed, as there was nowhere to go to. The infection was worldwide. Too many of the evacuation ships the navy used unwittingly took on infected people and were eventually overrun. He said there was only themselves, the HMS Daring and one other ship he had maintained contact with, the HMS Illustrious. Both are somewhere close, I think, but he didn't say where exactly."

Lazarus let out a long sigh and drew up another chair to sit down beside Tim. "Why where they so open with each other? I mean I know we're long-time allies, but still, these are...tense times to say the least. They must be on a war footing. How come they were so...*trusting*?"

"That's what I thought at first too, sir. McCulloch told Samson that effectively the chain of command had broken down. With the governments collapsed and the military broken, then the infrastructure of their operations was compromised. He said normal protocol would be for radio silence, but and I quote, 'This is war. Fuck protocols. We are leaderless. Britain is under attack and we have to act before she is lost.'

"Samson said they would stand side to side with McCulloch and they started to talk about formulating some sort of plan, some way of attacking the infection and killing the dead. They began to suggest meeting somewhere, perhaps in the Caribbean where they could replenish stocks from a small military base and meet. Then the reception started to die out and I came here to tell you."

Lazarus looked at Tim's scribbled notes. "Did they say anything about what the infection is or *how* they might fight back?"

"No, not that I heard, sir."

They sat in silence for five minutes and Tim began to wonder if he should leave before Lazarus spoke again.

"Tim, I assume you haven't told anyone else about this?" Lazarus swept his hands through his thick black hair.

Tim shook his head. "Nobody, not even Walker."

"Good. I'll fill Walker in. You've done well, Tim. Don't tell anyone else about this though. If rumours start going around the Mount about the US Navy riding into town, we'll have anarchy. No, we need to keep this under our hat for now and get organised.

I want you to rest tonight. Go get Ed, will you? He can take over radio duties from you for the rest of the night.

"We're going to need some things from town. We'll send a scouting party out in the morning. You can be a part of it if you like, Tim. You've done well and I know you wanted to get out 'in the field,' so to speak. I'll send Walker to wake you at 0700, all right?"

"Yes sir, absolutely." Tim left the castle, excited about the prospect of going onto the mainland tomorrow.

Lazarus returned to his bedroom in deep thought. Keisha lay on the bed groaning. A huge overhead candelabrum lit the room.

"Shut up, I need to think," he said casting Tim's notes onto a desk. He rested against the desk, pondering how best to use this information. So they weren't alone. Some remnants of the old world still lived; a throwback to the good old days, when the Empire ruled the waves and man would die for King and Country. It was quite amazing. He had not expected to hear such news, especially so long after the infection. There was no doubt, who ruled the kingdom now and that was the zombies, apart from *Lazarus'* kingdom, that is.

"Let me go, let me go!" Keisha began to shout and tug on the ropes causing the bed to shake and creak.

"Very well," said Lazarus. "I'm sick of you now anyway. I have far more important things to consider."

He pulled a knife from the desk drawer and strode over to Keisha. She smiled at him as he held the knife over her, pleased he was finally going to cut the ties that bound her to the bed. He was human after all. After so much humiliation and degradation, she never thought he would finally let her go. Tears welled up in her eyes as she thought about freedom.

Lazarus plunged the knife into her throat and blood spurted out over his face and shirt. Keisha's body struggled, but as her bright blood spread over the stained sheets, she was helpless as she began to die, choking on her own blood, unable to draw one more breath. When she was dead, Lazarus cut the ropes from her arms and picked her up. He scooped up her body and carried it over to a window. He put her down for a moment while he opened it. Rain and wind forced the windows back against the outside wall and he picked her up. With casual ease, he threw her from the window and watched satisfactorily as her lifeless body flailed through the storm onto the rocks below. Her body smashed onto the granite boulders below the castle and into the roaring waves of the ocean, drifting quickly out of sight beneath the churning water and white foam.

* * * *

Jackson stood in the master bedroom, peering through the curtains carefully. It had the largest windows and he shared it with Harry. It offered a view over the whole street. The house sat up on a slight ridge and therefore elevated above the others on the street. Behind it were fields of crops, now growing abundantly, unharvested and untouched by human hand or by mechanical intervention.

They found the house by chance a few days ago, looking for somewhere to stay. Its occupants had clearly left and it was unusual in that it had no doors at street level. The only access was down a gated driveway from the main street and into a garage which had internal access to the building. They had been able to come and go with relative ease. The few zombies that managed to follow the van to the garage could not get to the house and over the night eventually stumbled away. They could not see, smell or sense the living and so lost interest.

The house had four bedrooms and plenty of space. Christina and Cat shared one room, Jess and Rosa another, Tom and Laurent the third, and Jackson and Harry the master bedroom. Moira was happy with the sofa and preferred the privacy it gave her. Despite the protestations of the others, she would not relinquish her solitude for a night in a shared bed with anyone.

Harry entered the room. "Jackson, what's going on, I hear Tom's not back yet?"

It was dark outside now, approaching nine thirty. They had all reluctantly eaten Harry and Moira's bounty upon their return. Jess wanted to wait, to go looking for Tom and Laurent, but had agreed it was better to eat than wait indefinitely. She had eaten only half the amount the others had.

"I'm trying not to worry for now," said Jackson. "On the plus side, there's nothing else out there. The street's empty."

Harry took a look. Aside from a few cars parked up by the side of the road, it was all quiet. They knew all the houses might not be empty, but they didn't risk going where they didn't need to. The road was wet and shiny from the rain and the wind was blowing a gale.

"Jess suggested we go looking for them, but I think we're better off waiting," said Jackson to Harry.

"It could be nothing more than a bit of engine trouble. No need to panic yet," said Harry.

Jackson left the window and sat down on a chest full of clothes left behind by the home owners. "How did you go today?"

"Not bad. Moira found some grub as you know and I just handed over all the medicinal stuff I could find to Christina. I think some of it will be useful, especially for Cat. She's looking more and more tired these days."

"Poor girl, carrying a baby around with her is hard work. She's not really eating the right stuff, but what can we do?"

Harry sat down on the bed opposite Jackson. They hadn't bothered lighting any candles or torches, preferring to save them as much as possible. They sat in the gloomy room together and talked.

"Moira still handling herself well?" asked Jackson.

"Sure is. We have to remember she kept herself alive out there for a long time before we bumped into her. She can handle herself."

"And you? How are you doing, Harry?"

"I'm fine, why wouldn't I be?"

"Well, given the circumstances and with Benzo passing, you know, no one would blame you if you needed to take it easy. I can go out there and do the runs with Moira if you want me to. You can stay inside and just keep watch, help the girls," said Jackson.

"Seriously, Jackson, thanks, but no. I'm better off out there, doing something. I never was one for sitting on my laurels. I think about Benzo a lot. I'm glad I got to say goodbye to him, that's more than most can say. I think about all my family, but there's no point dwelling on it too much. We've all lost someone."

"True," said Jackson playing with his wedding band, "Very true."

Suddenly, the room was lit up with a bright white light.

"That's the van!" shouted Harry jumping up. He and Jackson peered through the curtains and sure enough the van was hurtling down the driveway at high speed. They could see Tom driving, but the figure next to him looked strange, not like Laurent. There were people in the backseat too, although how many they couldn't tell.

"Looks like Tom's brought visitors," said Jackson. "Come on, we'd better get down there."

Harry and Jackson ran out of the bedroom and downstairs into the lounge. The others were all sitting together, looking at an A-Z of the area they had found.

"Tom's back," said Harry. He and Jackson continued running through another doorway and down the stairwell to the garage.

Jess jumped up. "Is he okay? Is Laurent with him?"

"I'm sure they'll both be fine," said Christina. "Tom's got us through quite a few scrapes just fine, hasn't he? He knows what he's doing, Jess."

Rosa had gone over to the lounge window and opened a chink in the middle. She looked out over the driveway as the van drove into the garage.

"Oh fuck," she said quietly.

Behind the van the driveway was filling up with the dead. Hundreds and hundreds of zombies were running after the van, lurching violently against one another like a cresting wave, pouring and fighting over each other to get ahead and reach the van.

"Holy fuck-a-doodle-do," said Rosa as the garage door swung shut. A horde of zombies immediately piled up against it, hammering at it, trying to break it down and force their way in. More and more of them kept coming, filling the driveway completely. Some at the back were burning, despite the rain, and the wind carried the smell of burning flesh to her.

CHAPTER SIX

Glenda looked around the strange new house, clutching her husband's hand tightly. There was a calendar on the wall, hanging from a hook beside a corkboard full of curled up postcards and faded business cards. A date was marked on the calendar, circled in big red ink: 'Jack's 21st.' A post it note had been tacked onto the board beneath it, upon which someone had scribbled: 'Buy Jack a BIG present!' followed by a smiley face. The rest of the room was dark. They had blown out the candles in an attempt to hide, hoping the zombies that followed them would dissipate. They hadn't.

She wondered who Jack was and what he would think of them sitting on their sofa and drinking their wine. She had drunk a large glass already and was still worried about their new situation. Their home and business of thirty years had gone up in smoke and they were forced to leave everything behind. She had the clothes on her back and that was all. The man, who had saved them, Tom, was currently in discussion with two older men in the corner, whispering in the shadows. She didn't like it. She didn't know these men. What if they weren't as friendly as they seemed or what if they were plotting against her, Daniel, and Heidi?

"Did you hear that, Glenda?" asked Daniel.

"Sorry, love, I was, um...what did you say?" Glenda took a large gulp of cool wine and tried to relax. There were four women sitting across from her and Daniel, and she had already forgotten their names.

"Christina here says Cat is pregnant. Nearly six months, would you believe? That's why they were out in the van, looking for a hospital. It's lucky they came across us, don't you think? My goodness."

"Very lucky from what I hear," said Christina. "Glenda, are you sure you're okay? You're quite safe here."

Glenda cast a look at the window, but of course, she couldn't see anything through the thick red curtains. Christina could sense the woman's understandable concern. Her husband, Daniel, seemed less worried, understanding they were in as good a position as they could be for the time being. Glenda had said almost nothing since arriving. Daniel however had hung on Christina's every word. It had been quite some time since they had met anyone else living.

"What about..?" Glenda paused. "What about them? The dead ones? What if they get in here...what if..?"

"They won't." A tall pale woman came downstairs. Through the curtains a sliver of moonlight shone and Glenda saw a flash of red hair. "I've been watching from upstairs. They can't get in. Not for a good while anyway. It'll take them forever to batter down that door. Even then, they have to get through another two doors to get up here."

"And you are?" asked Daniel.

The red headed woman strode past them into the kitchen and came back a moment later with a drink. She ignored everyone and went straight to the curtains where she parted them slightly with lean fingers. She remained there, watching the dead outside funnel down the driveway, some still burning. From the faint light, Daniel could see her face was set tight, her eyes locked rigidly on whatever she was watching outside. Her thin lips were pursed together and she took only small sips from whatever drink she had made herself.

"Is she all right?" asked Daniel quietly.

"Moira's just fine," said Christina. "She's quiet, but..."

"I'm not much of a storyteller," said Moira sitting down quietly on a chair by the window. She seemed absent, as though her thoughts were elsewhere. She sat with her hands clasped in front of her and refused to be drawn any further.

"She's fine," said Jessica, making sure Moira wasn't listening. "Look, I know she takes a bit of getting used to. Moira's an introvert, but you'll soon find that reassuring. She keeps herself to herself, but if you're in a corner, you'd be glad to have her on your side. We picked her up a couple of weeks ago."

"Do you mind if we ask how? I mean, how do you all know each other?" said Heidi. She was sat beside her parents and could not contain her curiosity any longer. Occasionally, she would glance over at Tom, but he seemed deep in conversation with some other men. The old man who had been in their garden, Leonard, was asleep upstairs.

Caterina yawned loudly. "Sorry, but I'm beat. I'm going up. We are safe here tonight, aren't we, Christina?"

"Good night," Christina said giving Caterina a quick kiss. "We'll be fine. I'll be up soon."

"I might go too," said Rosa. The room was getting fuller by the minute and she didn't want to be around for the introductions, or having to face explaining her relationship with Jessica to someone new. "See you all in the morning."

As she disappeared up the stairs, Jessica turned around and patted Rosa on the arm as she passed. "I'll be up in a sec, Rosa."

Glenda caught her husband's disapproving eye. She doubted that he would say anything, but she also knew how he would be feeling. He grew up in a very traditional household with a stay at home mother, 2.4 children, and attended Sunday school without fail every week. He cleared his throat and Glenda worried that he might make a scene. She had to hear who these people were before Daniel said something that might get them thrown back out onto the street. The wine gave her the confidence to speak and she took a large gulp.

"Christina, tell me, what's going on? Who are you all?"

"Well, myself, Jessica here, Rosa, Caterina, Tom, Harry and Jackson all met some time ago. Moira only joined us recently. We bumped into her in a house, what, a week ago?"

"Yeah," continued Jessica. "We literally bumped into her. This was somewhere near the edge of Southampton, I think. Me and Rosa were looking for food and we went into a house that we thought was empty. We were lucky really. We didn't check it out properly first and if there had been one of the infected in there...well, we'd have been in big trouble. We just walked into this big house. The front door was open and there she was. She nearly took my head off. She had a crowbar and swung for me thinking I was one of the dead. I screamed and she missed, thankfully, taking out a chunk of plaster on the wall instead of me. That was it really. My screaming brought the real dead though so we scarpered. We couldn't just leave her on her own, so she came with us."

Moira gave up on the window and came over to Jessica's side. "I'm not all that bad, am I? I'm still pretty handy with a crowbar."

Christina laughed. "When you haven't got your head buried in a book!"

"Oh, that reminds me, I found a new one today I haven't read before. I think I might go to bed and read for a bit." She put her glass down on the coffee table and Glenda noticed it was only water.

"Well, pleased to meet you, Moira," Glenda said.

"You too. Glenda and Daniel, right? Try to rest up tonight. And, er, Heidi? You too."

They expected her to go upstairs, but Moira went back to the window and lay on the floor beneath it. She took a paperback out from a bag and let it sit just beneath the curtains so she could read from the light outside.

Jessica could see that Heidi kept glancing over at Tom when she thought nobody was looking and wondered what her situation was. Heidi was certainly good looking. A typical 'Saturday night' girl was what her friends would have described her as. Heidi was slim, blonde and young. She must've had a lot of attention before the end of the world. Her eyes were large and inquisitive and her light blonde hair draped over her shoulders. She had not said much yet, but from her looks and voice, Jessica guessed she must be about eighteen or nineteen. She had obviously not been wearing many clothes when Tom rescued her and her family. Heidi wore a small pair of shorts and a red vest top with thin straps that showed off smooth skin.

"Heidi, I'm going up to bed in a minute, but in the morning, I'll sort you out with some clothes, okay?" Jessica wasn't sure what reaction she would get, and was trying hard not to shoehorn her into a type or category before she had even talked to her.

"Hmm? Oh yeah, thanks. We didn't get chance to pack or anything, you know, it was all so...fast. I haven't even got a hairbrush with me."

Jessica nodded and then took a step toward her bedroom. She hesitated on the stairs as Daniel spoke.

"So where do we all stay tonight? I'm guessing there aren't enough beds to go around?"

"You'll find some blankets in the cupboard over there. I'm afraid you're going to have to bunk down in here for tonight. We'll reassess in the morning I'm sure," said Christina.

"Thanks, thank you very much," said Glenda yawning. "Daniel, do you think we can try to sleep tonight? I'm exhausted."

"All right, love," he said kissing her head. "Thank you, Christina." He held out his hand and they shook.

Christina tried not to laugh at the formality of it all. Daniel and Glenda proceeded to the linen cupboard and made themselves a bed in a corner of the room. As they lay down, Christina could hear them whispering to themselves and she hoped they would sleep. In the last few hours, they had seen their home burnt down and been attacked by zombies. Now they were in a strange house full of strangers. It would be a miracle if they slept at all.

"So," said Heidi who was still sitting on the sofa opposite Christina, "I guess I'll be sleeping on the couch tonight. S'all right, I've slept in worse places." She realised that actually made it sound as if she slept around and blushed.

"Say, where is your mother from, I mean, originally? I thought she had a bit of an accent, but I couldn't place it?" asked Christina.

"Salzburg. She moved over here years ago with Dad. He was on holiday there and they got married and ended up moving over here. I think she's been here longer now than Austria."

"Wow, I love Austria," said Laurent. He appeared out of the darkness and Heidi jumped. "Pardon, I didn't mean to startle you. I couldn't help but overhear you. I'm Laurent."

"Of course, I remember from the van. Where are you from, Laurent? You don't sound like you're from around here."

"The city of love, of course, Paris. Have you been?" Laurent sat down beside Heidi.

"Um, no, not yet." Laurent seemed like a nice man. He was dressed in jeans and a polo shirt. He had curly hair and a pointy nose. He seemed very enthusiastic when he spoke, which Heidi found a little odd under the circumstances. In the van on the way here there had been no time for anything apart from getting to safety as fast as possible.

Jessica had been standing on the stairway the whole time and something about Heidi irritated her. "Not yet?" said Jessica to Heidi. "When do you think you're going to go? I don't think you'll be going anytime soon. I think you've left it a bit late now."

Heidi missed the sarcastic tone in Jessica's voice.

"Oui, Paris is my home, but I do not think that I shall be seeing her again soon," said Laurent wistfully.

"Why not?" asked Heidi glancing over at Tom. He and the other men had stopped talking and were coming over to the sofa. "One day, maybe, when this gets sorted out, they'll get the trains back up and running. We could go together, all of us. The Eurostar is super-fast, like…"

"Heidi, how aware *are* you of what's going on in the world?" said Jessica leaning forward over the bannister. "Have you been living under a rock? Have you just spent the last three weeks reading 'Bimbo' magazine or something?" Jessica stared at her and Heidi felt like she was being scrutinised. She blushed again.

"Okay, okay," said Laurent, "let's remember, Jess, that this is a very unique situation here. If you hadn't run into me, you wouldn't know any better either, would you?"

Jessica shrugged and stood up. "I'm tired. See you tomorrow, Laurent." She trudged off upstairs and Heidi looked at Laurent.

"I don't think she likes me."

Laurent drew in breath and let it exhale slowly. "Heidi, don't worry, she is just worried. I'm sure it's nothing personal. There are lots of things to think about now. With you and your parents joining us our food and water supplies are going to be strained. We don't have enough beds as it is. And now we have to contend with those monsters outside."

Harry sat down beside Laurent. Tom and Jackson plonked themselves down opposite on cushions they had arranged on the floor around the sofa.

"We haven't seen them in such large numbers since we left the city," said Harry. "I'm not sure they'll be gone before sunrise this time. A few we can handle. They disperse, they thin out, and we can take care of them. But this many? It's dangerous."

"I think we might have to come up with a new plan," said Tom. "Since we left London we've managed, just, but we're running out of time."

"You were in London?" Heidi was amazed. "But…but I had a friend there who said London was destroyed, and that no one got out. She was in Epsom and said the infection basically just swept through London so fast that no one got out. I'm not sure if she got out. I haven't heard from her since. I suppose there's no way of knowing, is there? Did you really all come from London?"

"Yep we sure did," said Jackson. "We worked together. Well sort of. Tom and Caterina were in the same office as me, Christina and Jessica were in the same building. For a few days, we were trapped there in the city with a lot of our other colleagues. The city was overrun, that's true, but we managed to escape. None of our other colleagues did. We met Rosa on the way and Harry here we met at the airport. His son, Benzo, was with us, but he didn't make it either. We lost a lot of good friends, good people, to this thing."

"I'm sorry," said Heidi. "So you got to an airport? How come you didn't get away, get out of here?"

"We were too late," said Tom. "By the time we'd managed to get through the city, England was quarantined. There was no rescue or help waiting for us. We realised we were on our own and had to make our own way out. At that point, we didn't quite realise how bad this infection had gotten. We figured we would head for France, use the tunnel you know? We couldn't fly a plane or sail a boat, none of us knew how. So we thought we'd leave all this shit behind and get to France."

"That's how we met Laurent," said Jackson.

"What these guys didn't know was that I was doing the same thing," Laurent said quietly. "Paris was hit by the infection too. Hell, the whole of France was. Is. I was an engineer on the tunnel trains and me and a friend decided to get out. It wasn't hard. There was a few of us to begin with. When it all kicked off, we couldn't get back to our homes, so we stayed at work. There was a workshop and some small warehouses that were inside the tunnel perimeter so they were well protected. There was a tall fence running around it, designed to stop illegal immigrants from getting onto the trains into England. It turned out to be quite effective at stopping the zombies too.

"Anyway, we heard sporadic reports of what was happening in Paris and then the news just died out. The television, the radio, the phones; everything stopped working. The land outside the working yard was flat and we could see them. The dead were everywhere. I could not believe it to start with. There were women and infants. Some really young infants, just babies, you know? I can see their faces now, pressed up against the fence. My God, it was terrible.

"After, I think five or six days, we began to run out of food. There was a canteen at work, but it was small. I managed to keep in contact with my wife for a while. She was at home, thankfully. I implored her to stay there, and stay hidden, but…

"Me and two of my colleagues decided to try our luck in England. Without any news, we weren't sure if the virus had spread there, but there seemed no point in staying. We would just starve to death. We knew how to drive the trains, and the power lines were still operating. We didn't know for how long, so we decided to leave. I told my wife to come with us. I told her to drive to work and I would get her in somehow. My God, I was an idiot. She made it to my depot, but there were so many…so many.

"I don't know what happened to my friends I left behind. If they didn't starve to death, then they would have had to go outside to find food. I don't think they would get very far. I was travelling with Pierre and Patrice. They were good men. We managed to get the train through the tunnel okay. Officially, it was sealed off. The government ordered it closed as soon as the trouble started. In reality, it was just a few empty carriages blocking the entrance. We shunted them out of the way and hoped we would get out the other end. The tunnel was deserted, and we found nothing stopping us once we got to England. We were through in a couple of hours and everything looked fine. The fields looked so green I was sure we were safe. Pierre kept shouting, 'We've made it!' I didn't feel like celebrating with him, not with how I left my wife. It was my fault she died. I should have told her to stay where she was. If she had…

"Anyway, we never made it to London. When the train was approaching Ebbsfleet, we slowed down and thought we would get off and look for help. We pulled into the station, and I don't know, something didn't seem quite right. It was deserted. It was the middle of the day, so I thought there would be someone around, even if it was just the station manager or someone. We got off and began wandering around the station, but there was not a soul anywhere. The waiting room, café, car park, and the road to the station were all empty. Pierre said we should carry on into London, because there was no way London would be deserted too. We were about to leave when Patrice suddenly saw them. There was a young couple walking down the road toward us. We were so relieved, I can't begin to tell you.

"Patrice ran up to meet them, but...you can guess they were not so friendly. They pounced on him and he would've been dead quite quickly I think. Me and Pierre turned and ran. We had seen the infection in France and recognised it straight away. I was so shocked and Pierre too. He was so quiet. We made it back onto the train and were about to pull away when we saw Tom and Harry. They were walking down the tracks toward us, rifles in front of them and they were shouting at us. Inside the train, we couldn't hear them or what they were saying, so we thought they were going to shoot us.

"We jumped out of the cab, and well, Tom and Harry dragged us away into a sidecar. There we met the others and we waited until the zombies, the two who had killed Patrice, moved on. We waited for a few hours and finally it was quiet enough for us to leave. We talked and they told me what had happened to England. That's how I ended up with them. Tom was taking everyone to Paris, but they did not get very far."

"Holy smoke and where is Pierre? Is he upstairs?" Heidi asked.

"Non. He is dead too. Unfortunately, he didn't make it with me. We have been on the road for weeks, Heidi. He got bitten. We were rushing from one place to the next and we got sloppy. Once you get the infection, you're dead. There was nothing we could do for him."

The room was silent and Heidi became aware that her parents had stopped whispering. She knew they were still awake and must be listening to the story. Moira had heard it before, but put her book down all the same.

Tom knew how hard it was for Laurent to talk about his wife. He took up the story, letting Laurent gather himself. "It was odd at first, wandering around other people's houses, expecting them to suddenly appear and shout at you. Tell you to get out before they call the police. It was probably a week before I got used to it. I guess you just adapt, change to what the situation demands. I guess you just stop thinking about it in the end.

"We didn't know what to do. Our plan had been to get to France. Laurent's was to get to England. We scuttled around from house to house, living off whatever we could find, hiding from the zombies, moving at dawn or dusk only, staying out of sight. It was draining.

"I got a cold and it spread around to everyone pretty quickly. We weren't eating properly so our immune system was weak. We started looking for vitamins then, medicine, anything that would help us survive. We needed clean clothes, rest, decent food and most of all, clean water.

"The first time I put a clean shirt on, I turned around only to see a photo of the man who used to wear it. I felt shameful, stealing a dead man's clothes. That was a while ago now, mind you. I have no such qualms now. It's all about surviving. The things that have been left behind by the dead, the things that they used to live with, their vehicles, their clothes, their stocks of food and shelter is what we use, what we have to do now to live. We have no choice but to take them, grab every little thing we can and devour it. If we don't, we'll soon be infected, or end up as zombies.

"We came across an army barricade, I forget where. It was some small satellite town south of London, and there was a good stock of weapons and medicine. Whilst we grabbed it, Harry tried the radio. One of the trucks had an impressive set up; transponders, receivers, freaking digital everything. Harry had the best idea out of any of us how to use it as he was in the force."

"It was more luck than judgment," said Harry. "It was way more complicated stuff than I was used to in the force, but I managed to find a signal. It was a pre-recorded message on loop. We've no idea how long it'd been playing or even if it's still playing now. We couldn't lug the radio equipment with us as we just didn't have the means. So I listened to the message a few times and memorised it.

"It was the British Navy. They said a final rescue attempt would be made for any UK citizens still alive, uninfected, and residing in Britain. All military personnel were ordered to fall back to the nearest retrieval point. Navy ships would be sent to selected places along the UK coastline for extraction: Southampton, Liverpool, Penzance, and Middlesbrough. That was it. Only four rescue points for the whole country." Harry held up four fingers shaking his head.

"I guess they didn't expect to find many still alive. They said avoid major conurbations and cities due to excessive resistance and the unrestrained outbreak of the infection. Any attempts to leave the UK other than on official certified rescue ships will result in death. The UN ordered all infected countries to be quarantined immediately and indefinitely. The message said rumours of an outbreak in the US are *unconfirmed* at this stage. The British government will not confirm any rumours surrounding the death and reanimation of the UN Security Council leader Darren Collins. We repeat, head immediately to your nearest extrapolation point. Naval ships will be in those ports on October first and fifteenth. After this point, Britain, along with many of its allies, will be restricted areas and any attempt to leave will be met with lethal force."

Heidi's mind was reeling from all the new information. Her hands were gripping the side of the sofa and she felt cold. A shiver ran over her and she felt queasy.

"What's the date today? It's..."

"...October thirteenth," said Tom. He leant forward and took her hand. "Heidi, we are going to try to get out of here and meet that ship. We tried to get to Southampton for the first but it was impossible. There were too many of them. We couldn't even get close to the city. The dead were everywhere." Tom looked over and saw Daniel and Glenda cradled in each other's arms fast asleep. "Talk to your parents in the morning. Come with us. In two days we could be out of here."

Heidi looked at Tom and felt worried, but reassured at the same time. He saved them earlier when she and her parents would surely have died. Should she trust him now? Should she trust all of them?

Heidi nodded. "I can't believe what is happening. I...I need to get some rest. Thank you, Tom. Thank you for coming back for us earlier." She squeezed his hand and was grateful for the darkness covering up her blushes.

Looking dazed, Heidi walked over to her parents and curled up beside her father. She lifted the blanket and crept in close to his warmth, something she had not done since she was a toddler.

"Let's all turn in," said Tom. "We'll need clear heads in the morning."

Jackson and Laurent went upstairs and Tom paused at the foot of the stairs. He put his arm on Harry's shoulder. "You know we have to leave in the morning, right?"

"I know. Those things out there aren't going to leave. I'd hoped we could stay here for another day, but it's not going to work. They'll get in eventually, they always do."

"We're going to have to find someplace else to stay until the ship comes. I don't want to go to Penzance too early. It's highly populated and could be dangerous. We don't want a repeat of what happened in Southampton. We nearly didn't get away from there in time."

Harry nodded. "Let's get some sleep. Let the storm pass, see what's what in the morning. We'll have to find a way out of here then."

They went upstairs and the house was silent. Moira sat up and peered through the curtains again. Under the moon, rain and wind, the zombies were still there, hundreds of them. She lay down, clutching her book, hoping she would be able to sleep tonight and not suffer the usual nightmares. Reality was scary enough without her terrible dreams of what horror lay in store for them the next morning.

CHAPTER SEVEN

Jessica opened her eyes and realised it was still dark. She didn't know what had awoken her. The house was silent and the gale force winds outside seemed to have calmed down. She rolled over underneath the bedcovers and felt a warm spot where Rosa should be.

"Rosa?" Jessica sat upright quickly, fearful that something had happened.

"I'm here."

Jessica saw Rosa sitting on a chair by the window. She wore a white t-shirt, one they had found yesterday. It was too big for her, but comfortable to sleep in. Her legs and feet were bare and Jessica guessed what she was doing. It wasn't unusual for Rosa to wake in the middle of the night.

"I couldn't sleep. They're still out there, you know? They're not going this time."

"Rosa, come back to bed. You're not going to solve anything staring out the window at them." Jessica flung the covers back and felt the cool night air fall over her like a light blanket.

Rosa left the chair and clambered back into bed. Jessica gave her a kiss and took her hands. They were cold and Jessica wondered how long Rosa had been sitting there. Her feet felt like ice blocks.

"You've got to try to get some sleep. You'll be exhausted tomorrow if you don't."

"I miss them, Jess, I miss my family. I miss normal life. I miss so many things I just can't switch my brain off. As soon as I fall asleep, I start dreaming about random things: music and bands I used to like, my dog, my mum, my desk at work and the horrible chair I used to sit on. I miss the kids who used to come into the bank and give me a pound to put in their bank accounts to save for a comic. I miss the bakery I used to walk to on the way home and the smell of it. I can smell it now. I used to love getting fresh bread on the way home. I miss Eastenders, going out and getting pissed. I miss my own clothes."

"When I was a kid, probably seven or eight," said Jessica, rubbing some warmth back into Rosa's hands, "I saw Willy Wonka and The Chocolate Factory. I used to dream of living on chocolate. Didn't matter what sort, I loved it all: dark, white, mint, anything. I even used to like those crappy cheap Easter eggs that tasted like shit, the ones that seemed as if they'd never been anywhere near a chocolate factory. Now I hate it. I would love a meal that didn't involve a chocolate bar, but something green and fresh that had actually grown instead of manufactured, processed and sealed up to preserve it. Mind you, I suppose we'd all be starving right now if man hadn't made so much processed crap and stuck it in a metal can.

"Rosa, there's a lot more to *not* miss, than miss. Understand? It's no good keeping on thinking about all the good things that are gone. Remember the fake plastic smiles you would get every time you walked into some snobby shop or the post office or any place that wanted your money? Remember how *boring* shopping actually was? Remember all that chart music that was so bland and false and utterly pointless that you couldn't wait for it to end? Remember the soulless towns and vacuous shopping centres, overcrowded trains, expensive bills, fake friendliness that you encountered almost every day when somebody wanted something from you. Remember how much of a waste of time it all was?"

"I suppose so, but I can't forget the past and I don't want to forget my family."

"You don't have to, Rosa, but you do have to move on. You can't live in constant fear, or wallow in nostalgia. Look at what we've got now. There's a chance we could be out of here in two days. You've got a roof over your head, which is a lot more than anyone else in this godforsaken country right now. And you've got me."

Jessica kissed Rosa again and they embraced. Rosa had warmed up and she rubbed her feet up and down Jessica's smooth legs. Rosa sat up, pushing the duvet off.

"You're not getting up again, are you?" asked Jessica.

Rosa looked at Jessica and smiled. She pulled the large t-shirt over her head and threw it on the floor. Jessica could see Rosa's small breasts and erect nipples. She wanted her so badly.

Rosa lay down and Jessica began kissing her neck. She traced her tongue down to Rosa's chest and slid over her.

"I love you, Jess," said Rosa.

"I love you too. Now shush," said Jessica as she continued kissing Rosa.

Rosa propped herself up and looked down as Jessica slid between her legs and continued stroking her, kissing her body, her waist and her thighs. Later, only when they were both tired, exhausted from love-making, would they sleep restfully.

* * * *

Lazarus slept little that stormy night. He poured over the notes that Tim had made for him. Lazarus had thought the world was at death's door. There was no stopping the infection that was for sure. It had toppled governments and dictators far more quickly than any elections or coups ever had. Could it be that there were more survivors than he thought? It made sense in a way. Those at sea, away from land and the spread of infection would be safe. If they stayed away from the land, then they would live for as long as they could eat and drink. If they kept away from Lazarus and the Mount, then there would be no problem. But what if they did not? How did the navy plan to fight back? What if they commandeered his men? What if they wanted to use the Mount as a base? It was in an excellent strategic position, as it had been for centuries. That was exactly why Lazarus had claimed it, just as Henry Pomeroy had claimed it in the fifteenth century. It was surrounded by water which the dead could not cross. Sure, sometimes they got washed up on shore, but they couldn't swim or even drift with any kind of aim.

The Mount was close to the mainland, but far enough away so that the dead could not reach them. Even if anyone tried to attack them, they were well defended. Any attacking force would have to climb the steep granite hill to the castle and his men were armed. They had axes, swords, and knives, and they would use them.

Lazarus did not love his father, but he loved the stories he told him, of Pomeroy in particular. He had held the Mount for weeks on end against thousands of Edward the Fourth's troops. Literally thousands of soldiers had tried to usurp Henry and gain the Mount, to draw him out. They had laid siege to him and his band of men and he had held out for nearly six months. The odds were against him, but the Mount was special. It held a special power, a strong force that willed men on to defend it. This land, this small yet important granite outcrop of Britain had stood since long before man could even begin to understand its value. It withstood earthquakes, tsunamis, and wars. Lazarus intended to make sure it stood for many more years, with him as its ruler.

If the navy thought they could take it from him they would be forced to think again. They could not fight the infection. How can you kill something that cannot be killed? You can chop off the arm or the leg of a zombie and it will keep coming. Chop its head off and it will still bite you. No, the navy were misguided. They still thought they were in command. Lazarus was in charge of this piece of England.

He tried sleeping, but woke constantly. He fidgeted and tossed and turned until, unable to waste any more time, he got up. The storm had blown itself out and he opened the window from which Keisha had so gracefully 'fallen' last night. The sea was calm and the autumn sun was illuminating the Cornish coast, blinking off rooftops and shooing away the last dark rain clouds. Morning was rapidly approaching. The only sound Lazarus could hear was the lapping of the ocean on the rocks below.

He would wake the others and send a group onto the mainland. If they were to defend themselves, they would need all the ammunition and weapons they could find. If there was to be any kind of siege they would need plenty of food. The navy might try to force them off the Mount. Thankfully, with a fresh spring on the island, water was not an issue he had to deal with. With so many mouths to feed though, he wanted to build up stocks as much as possible. The vegetables and crops they grew were not enough to feed nearly thirty men forever.

There was another issue to act upon too. If the men knew the navy were just around the corner, waiting in their armoured ships to whisk them away, they might *want* to leave. It would be ridiculous, of course, but they needed telling what to do. If they were allowed to think for themselves, they would all go their own way. They would die out there for that old notion of king and country. What was the point in getting yourself killed over a king who was already dead and a country that was dying? It was better that they stay here and defend the Mount, defend Lazarus. They could build a new empire. They respected him. The men knew he was superior and could ensure their safety. If they left, would they be safe?

Lazarus dressed and decided he would go down and see first what, if anything, Ed had managed to find out overnight. It was imperative that he nipped this in the bud now. He had been foolish last night. He should have made Tim stay on the radio. Lazarus couldn't afford too many people finding out about this new development. Perhaps he could use this to his advantage. Tim was going on the scouting party and the mainland was a dangerous place. Accidents happened all the time. With millions of zombies wandering the land freely, who knew what might happen.

Lazarus put his long black coat on and opened the bedroom door. Walker was asleep in the chair outside, a sheathed sword by his side. The door clicked shut and Walker jumped to his feet.

"Lazarus. Morning, sir. You're up early today. Anything I can do for you?" Walker rubbed his face awake.

"Yes, go down and check on Norm will you. He's been helping himself to the entertainment lately. He thinks we don't know about it. Teach him what's what, will you?"

"Yes sir. Anything else?"

"Yes, I'm sending a scouting party over this morning. When you're finished with Norm, get it arranged, will you. I want them ready to go at 0700. Get Tim, Honok and Shane and bring them to the back door. I want to speak to them before they go."

They walked down the grand stairway together saying nothing. Walker continued on down to the cells whilst Lazarus went outside and made his way down the hill to the houses. Each one was quiet, but in a couple of hours, they would be a hive of activity. You had to earn your keep on the Mount and Lazarus made sure they all worked hard. There was plenty of hard labour to be done in repairing the buildings and preparing the land for sowing more seeds and grains. Some of the men would be put on watch, patrolling the castle and the grounds, ensuring there were no uninvited visitors, especially ones with sharp teeth and deadly infections.

Lazarus approached the stone house and opened the door. He didn't knock or wait for an invitation. This was his kingdom and he could walk straight into wherever he pleased, whenever he pleased.

Ed jumped up, shocked at the intrusion. Lazarus was pleased to see Ed looked tired. His usual grin was absent and he had dark bags under his eyes. He pulled off a headset and placed it on the desk in front of him by the radio set.

"Ed."

"Sir."

"Report?"

"Yes, I, er, did hear something. Here are the notes I made, mate, I mean *sir*."

Ed held out a couple of pieces of paper and Lazarus took them without letting his eyes leave Ed. "Tell me what you heard."

"Well, Tim told me about the British guy, McCulloch. He's definitely the bloke in charge. HMS Daring he's on. They're somewhere out there off the south coast, but he didn't give specifics. He was talking to the American Captain Samson. McCulloch said they were running low on provisions but had enough for about another week. He said they keep trying to contact command HQ but are getting no response. He thinks they're all dead. He said they're going to try to dock in a couple of days and make one last attempt to see if anyone is alive on the mainland. McCulloch said they've been sending out an automated message telling any survivors to head to some extraction points. Get this sir, they're heading for Penzance."

Lazarus's eyes bore down into Ed. In the small house his tall figure seemed even larger than he actually was and Ed felt nervous as the imposing Lazarus stood over him. "I wonder what they're actually going to do when they get here, Ed. The Daring is a destroyer so it's not designed for rescue missions, nor is it going to be able to dock at Penzance. The harbour isn't big enough to cope with it. No, I would think they're going to come in close and then send out a smaller boat to see what's going on. It's probably just a reconnaissance mission to check the lay of the land, so to speak.

"Ed, we must be cautious. This is a time of war you understand. If the navy is looking for survivors this long after the infection wiped out Britain, then they must be desperate. They need men, supplies, and ammunition. They're looking to salvage and steal, not help us. Ed, we are going to have to make sure they don't see us or find our location."

"I suppose so, sir," agreed Ed frowning. "I thought that they would help us though, wouldn't they? Tim told me all about it. He said he was looking forward to being rescued, that we'd be able to get off this bloody island. They might know of somewhere safe to go, somewhere..."

"Ed." Lazarus took a step closer and Ed thought he was going to strike him. "Ed, you're not stupid, but you don't need to think about this. You shouldn't be listening to Tim either. He's got a big mouth. I'll be making sure he doesn't go gossiping again. You know what happens when people start rumours, don't you?

"Why would we need to escape the Mount? This isn't a prison, it's a sanctuary. If there was somewhere else safe to go, the British navy would be there already wouldn't they? This just proves the point that there is nowhere to go. I imagine the people on that ship are demoralised and desperate – and that makes them dangerous. No Ed, they're not here to help, they're here for us. They want what we have: this place, this castle, the Mount. This is safe. Do you see the infected here? Do you not get a square meal every night? Do I not provide you with women?"

Ed nodded. He thought Lazarus might not be completely right, but there was no way he was going to disagree and end up like Ricardo. He made a mistake and ended up dead. Ed knew Tim was in for it. He had been sloppy and talked out of turn. Ed had no intention of being put in the same pot as Tim. "There was something else too, sir. The past five hours there's been no contact at all. I think they signed off for the night. Before they did, Samson said they were heading for provisions and would be in contact again with McCulloch. Samson said they had something of interest that McCulloch would want to see, something that might help in winning the war."

"Did he suggest what?"

"Not really, sir. He just said it was something the USS Wasp had picked up in Texas. He said they were carrying out tests and would know more soon."

"Interesting...Ed you need some rest. Go get some sleep. You can leave the radio for now. I don't think we're going to get much more out of it for a while."

Ed got up. "Thank you, sir." Ed walked past Lazarus who watched Ed leave. As he opened the door, Lazarus spoke. He forced his lips to smile, but his eyes were cold and hard.

"Ed, I don't need to tell you that this is confidential. Everything you've heard in here stays between you and me. Are we clear? Rumours and gossip serve none of us well."

"Absolutely. I won't breathe a word, you can trust me." Ed shut the door behind him and trudged across the yard back to his bed, desperate for some sleep and pleased to have left Lazarus alone.

Lazarus waited a moment and then left the house empty, traipsing through the cluster of stone houses back toward the castle. As he passed the pub, he saw Honok hauling a large black bag across the hillside. He was dragging it behind him with clear difficulty as it kept catching on the rocks. Lazarus watched for a moment wondering what he was doing. It was nearly seven and he should be preparing for the scouting party.

As Honok dragged the long black bag over a large rock, he felt a hand on his shoulder and whirled around, surprised.

"Lazarus! I mean, sir, sorry. I was not expecting..."

"Evidently," said Lazarus. "What are you doing, Honok? You should be up at the castle now. We've a job to do. Did Walker not tell you?"

Honok was a stumpy man and looked up at Lazarus who towered over him, his black coat reflecting the morning sunshine. Honok dropped the bag at his feet. "I just had to do this one job for Norm, sir. He said it was important."

"Did he now?" Lazarus bent down and unzipped one end of the bag. A woman's arm appeared, cold and limp. As Lazarus unzipped it further the woman's body appeared and he saw the bruises and cuts on her. She wore a ripped blue shirt and there were some jeans stuffed into the bottom of the bag near her feet. Lazarus recognised her as one of the women from the cells that Norm was supposed to be guarding. They had picked her up a week ago and she had been young, fit and healthy. Now she was the opposite of healthy. Norm was failing.

"Carry on, Honok, and then hurry up, will you. Don't worry about this. I'll speak to Norm."

Lazarus walked away as Honok picked the bag up. He dragged it a few more meters over the rough terrain and reached the cliff edge. Holding the two ends of the bag, he carefully tipped it over and the woman's body rolled out. Honok folded the bag up – they would need it again – and kicked the dead woman. Her body plummeted over the side of the cliff and landed on the sharp rocks below. Honok peered over and saw she had landed on one of the higher rocks. Its pinnacle had ripped her body in half. He watched her legs slowly disappear under the waves, but her torso and head remained stuck. She would have to wait until high tide before the rest of her became fish food.

Honok grunted and then began the walk up to the castle. He had tried to keep her hidden from Lazarus. It wasn't his fault. Norm was the one who would have to answer for her death. Honok's short legs made swift work of the hillside and he made his way through the castle toward the meeting point. He had been to the mainland a few times on missions. He enjoyed them. It meant freedom for a few hours. He was happy working here at the castle for Lazarus, but when he got the chance, he loved to go ashore. He had spent all his life working for someone else and he longed for the time he could be himself, away from watching eyes.

He heard noises coming from the dungeon below, but knew better than to investigate. If Norm was down there, he would be facing the music. Norm was an idiot. Honok didn't even know why Lazarus put up with him. He was too stupid to be of any use. That was probably why he was put on sentry duty for the prisoners. It was an easy job that even an imbecile could do.

Honok walked down a cold stone corridor. It was nothing like the rest of the castle. There were no decorations adorning these walls unless you counted damp and moss. The floor had a slimy sheen over it. Dampness pervaded the whole building once you got down low enough. At the end of the corridor were some small steps that wound downward to another room. Honok had walked this path many times.

He entered the room and felt his spirits lift immediately. There were the boxes and stacks of food and drink he had helped gather from previous trips. They kept cool and fresh down here, away from sunlight and prying hands. There were no windows down in this room and one entrance, a large oak door set into the stonework that could only be unlocked by Walker or Lazarus. A set of rails ran through the middle of the room and they headed straight for the door. The cart was there, empty and waiting for him. Honok unlocked it and quickly checked it over. It was fine, as he knew it would be. It would carry them easily, just as it had ferried people for years.

Honok heard footsteps and talking. Walker and Tim came down the steps and their noise echoed around the underground cavern.

"Honok, all good to go?" asked Walker.

Honok acknowledged him with a curt nod of the head. "Why is *he* coming?"

"Lazarus wants him to. There's no problem, is there?" said Walker.

"No sir."

"You're such a prick, Honok," said Tim as he ran his fingers over the cart. "So how does this work? I can't see an engine. There's no ropes either so it's not on a pulley system. Where does it go?"

"To the mainland," said Lazarus as he entered the room. There was a noticeable shift in the atmosphere when he appeared, as if the temperature in the cold room had suddenly dropped another few degrees.

"You push it. Think you can manage that?" said Honok to Tim.

Another member of Lazarus' trusted men, Shane, appeared. Shane often went with Honok on these trips. He was loyal to Lazarus and had been a bricklayer before the infection. He could be relied on to do the hard graft nobody else wanted to do, or was capable of.

"Right then, listen up," said Lazarus. "Shane, Honok, I want you out there today looking for the usual: tins or packets of any useful food, alcohol too if you can. I want you to get Tim to help you. Remember, he hasn't been out on a run before so watch each other's backs. I don't need to remind you that Walker will check you when you come back. Any bites, scratches or signs of infection will see you with a one-way ticket back there on your own, permanently.

"There's something else too. I need you to find guns. The more the better, quite frankly. I don't want to go into any details, but we need to be able to defend ourselves and we will be better prepared if we can fight fire with fire."

"One question," said Tim. "How do we get around out there? I mean the tunnel to the mainland doesn't take us straight into Penzance, does it?"

"No, you idiot," said Honok shaking his head. "Fucking hell, when do you think this tunnel was built? It's over a hundred years old, moron. It goes in a straight line to the nearest point on the coast. There's nothing there, but we have a vehicle parked up. *I* have the keys. We get over there, drive to the nearest town and start looking. For weapons we'll probably have to get into Penzance. I doubt we'll be back before the sun goes down. You think you can do this, *Timmy*?"

"Listen, Honok, you've got an attitude. You want to start something, then let's go. I'm not afraid of you."

As Tim glared at Honok, Walker put a hand on Tim's arm. "Tim, cool it. If we can't trust you to keep a cool head in here, what are you going to be like out there? Do you remember how it is? How we found you? Shut up and get on with it."

Honok unlatched the cart as Walker unlocked the doors and swung them back. The tunnel ahead was dark and cold. Tim could smell the water above, the salt mingling with the icy cold air and he stifled a sneeze. Honok began pushing the cart on the tracks and Tim took the other side.

"Don't forget," Lazarus said quietly to Shane. "Remember what I told you."

"Don't worry, sir, I'll see to it," said Shane as he lumbered after the cart.

Walker closed the doors and locked them again. "What was that?" he asked Lazarus as they left the underground cavern.

"Nothing. Just a little extra job I asked Shane to help me with. Did you see to Norm? Looks like he's been getting carried away again. I caught Honok this morning disposing of one of the girls."

"I saw to him, sir. He'll behave from now on. I'm afraid we're down to one. The older woman, Tanya, passed last night. I don't know exactly when, but I've asked Norm to tidy up the mess. It looks like she managed to off herself at last. There's blood all over the place."

"Fine, fine, whatever. Just deal with him. Walker, we might have trouble coming. Come upstairs with me, I want to speak to you about it. We'll have some breakfast and figure it out. And if the boys are lucky we might get some new recruits today. Going into Penzance is more dangerous, I'll admit, but it brings more rewards. Who knows what, or who, they might come across."

CHAPTER EIGHT

As Tom laughed, Heidi marvelled at the way Tom's blue eyes creased at the edges. They were sitting in the kitchen munching peanut butter on rye bread for breakfast, having awoken a few minutes earlier. The kitchen was at the rear of the house and elevated so they could afford to open the curtains without being seen from the road. The window looked out over nothing more than a field of crops and it almost felt like normality. It was going to be a clear autumn day. The window was open and the air was cool and crisp.

"So you've really never seen Star Wars?" Tom laughed again. "I can't believe it. We'll have to see if we can sort that out one day."

Heidi grinned back at him. Jessica had been true to her word and found some clothes for her. They were a little baggy, but at least she felt warmer now in the maroon tracksuit Jessica had given her. She noticed Tom had marks on his arms, red lines and scars that looked like they had healed without having been treated properly.

"How did you get those?" Heidi asked him.

"These? They're nothing really. It wasn't easy getting out of the city and we've had a few scrapes along the way. All of us have some scars."

"They look sore, do they hurt?"

"Not any more. I'm quite lucky actually. I managed to avoid the infection, God knows how."

Jessica came into the kitchen and helped herself to some breakfast. She had already dressed and looked wide awake, ready for the day, even though it was barely seven o' clock.

"They're his war wounds," she said ruffling Tom's hair. "I think he's proud of them."

Tom looked up at her and she winked at him. Heidi watched, unsure if this was a private joke or not. She pushed her chair back and got up.

"Here, Jess, you can take my seat, I'm done anyway. I'm going to take something in for Mum and Dad if that's okay?"

"Go for it," said Tom. As Jessica sat down, he watched Heidi leave, her wavy blonde hair striking his eyes as it contrasted with the red tracksuit she wore.

"Earth to Tom, hello? I said what's the plan today?" Jessica kicked his shin under the table.

"Oh, sorry, um, yeah I was talking to Harry, Jackson and Laurent last night. I assume you've looked out front this morning?"

"Yeah, they're still there. There are hundreds of the dead bastards. What are we going to do? Rosa's freaking out and I can't say I blame her. Christina's upstairs with Caterina now trying to calm her down. She thinks she's going to have the baby in this house. I mean she's not even due for another three months."

"I can understand why she's worried though. I think we have to leave. The ship is due in Penzance tomorrow. If we stay here, the dead could find a way in or at least block us in. We don't want to get trapped in this house. Harry reckons we should just go for it today. Find somewhere closer to Penzance to stay tonight so we're ready in the morning. Plus, what if they come early? We don't want to find our ship has sailed." Tom took another slice of bread.

"I agree with Harry," said Jackson. He looked old and tired. He was followed by Leonard who was still wearing the same pyjamas they had found him in. Jackson had tried to coax him into getting changed. They had plenty of spare clothes in the house, but Leonard refused. He liked his pyjamas, he had said, and Carol wouldn't recognise him if he changed now. How would she find him if he got changed into a stranger's clothes, he had argued. Jackson wore a blue and white chequered shirt and baggy jeans, the only things he found that came close to fitting him. Tom thought he looked a little like an old gold-era prospector.

Heidi had given her parents some food, but they were exhausted and still rousing themselves from a bad night's sleep. Heidi followed behind Jackson and Leonard and stood in the corner of the kitchen, desperate to hear more from Tom. Whatever was going on, she wanted to be a part of it. She felt like she had missed so much from being cooped up at home that now she wanted to know, and be a part of everything.

Jackson grabbed some bread and spread some peanut butter thinly across it. Then he took a bottle of water and poured some into a glass. He held them out for Leonard.

"Many thanks, Mr Jackson," said Leonard. He held the glass and bread and then looked around the room for a seat.

Tom stood up and let Leonard sit down, who proceeded to down the water, then nibble on the bread like a rabbit gnawing on a lettuce leaf.

"How is he?" asked Tom.

Jackson gave a non-committal shrug. "Hard to say. He's essentially fine, but I think he might be suffering from dementia. He refuses to change and he keeps saying he wants to go back and get Billy. I think it was a friend he was staying with. I managed to get out of him that he lived in a big old house with lots of other people like him. I think it was close by."

"Oh yeah, the old codger's place that's just around the corner from ours," said Heidi. "It was anyway. He must've come from there and ended up in our back garden. Bloody hell, he gave me a fright I can tell you. What was that old folk's home called...? 'Peaceful' something or other...I can't remember."

"Peaceful Valley Rest Home," said Leonard suddenly. "I should say they'll be wondering where I am soon. Is Carol coming to get me? I do so like her visits. I hope the bad people have gone by then. Oh, have we got any biscuits? Bourbons are my favourite." With that, Leonard resumed nibbling on his bread, picking out small grains and carefully putting them on the tablemat.

"Carol's his daughter," said Jackson.

"Is she..?" asked Tom in a hushed tone.

Jackson shook his head. "Look, Tom, what the hell are we doing? How are we going to feed another four mouths when we can barely feed ourselves? No offence, Heidi."

"None taken. I'm just glad you helped us out yesterday. If you hadn't, well...look we'll pull our weight. I want to help you. Mum and Dad will too. Honestly, after what I heard last night I'm not going to waste any more time sitting on my arse doing nothing. We've been doing that for too long."

"Thanks, Heidi," said Tom. He didn't notice Jessica roll her eyes. "Look, let's go into the lounge. Whatever we're doing we need to decide together. I want everyone in on this. Is everyone up yet?"

"Yeah, but I think it best to leave Cat upstairs with Christina. She's a bit delicate this morning. I'll talk to them when we're through," said Jackson. "I think Leonard is happy enough here too. Isn't that right, Leonard?"

"Mmm-mm," muttered Leonard through a mouthful of bread, crumbs spurting out of his mouth over the table. "Mr Jackson, I told you, please call me Lenny. My friends call me Lenny. Only Carol calls me Leonard."

"Okay Lenny," said Jackson. "We're just going into the other room. Stay here and help yourself to more if you want. We're going to find a way back to Billy."

They left the kitchen and went to the lounge where Daniel and Glenda were rolling up the blankets that had been their bed for the night. Rosa was sipping a glass of water and Harry came downstairs. Moira threw open the curtains and drew them back, tying them to the hooks on the wall. Bright sunlight came streaming into the room.

"Moira, what are you doing, they'll see us." exclaimed Rosa. "Quick, close them again!"

Moira shook her head. "There's no point. They know we're here, Rosa. Since last night, they haven't dispersed. In fact, if anything, they've grown in number. It's too late to hide behind the curtains now."

Heidi snorted a laugh and Jessica glared at her before turning her attention to Tom. "Maybe we should get started? I know the zombies outside aren't going anywhere, but that doesn't mean we like having them there, staring at us. Jesus, I can hear them. I don't like this."

"Listen," said Tom, "for the sake of anyone who isn't up to speed, here's the deal. We have one day to get to Penzance where, hopefully, a ship from the British navy will be docking with the intention of extracting any survivors; that's us. We have transport and yes it'll be crowded, but even with the extra numbers we can make it. I think we can squeeze into the van. The only difficulty really is getting past those things out there."

"Excuse me, Tom? Who says we're going anywhere?" asked Daniel. "We're grateful and all, but our lives are here. My wife and I have built up a strong business in Longrock and I'm not sure we should just abandon it to go on some wild goose chase. How do we know this ship you speak of will be there? Our home was our business and we have lived here for over thirty years. The insurance will cover the rebuild and..."

"The insurance?! Dad, look around you. Longrock is as fucked as the rest of the country!" Heidi pointed out of the window and Glenda stifled a sob.

"So many poor people," she whispered into her husband's shoulder.

"Heidi Cooper, do *not* use foul language like that to me and your mother." Daniel stared at his daughter disapprovingly as Jessica smiled.

"Without putting too fine a point on it, Daniel, your daughter is right," said Tom. "There's no point glossing over the truth of the situation we're in."

"You can't polish a turd," said Harry quietly to Jackson who hid his laughter behind a well-timed cough.

Tom continued. "Staying here is not an option. We can't wait this out. The dead out there are *not* going to stop and they're *not* going to leave, so *we* have to. Mr and Mrs Cooper, Heidi, if you want, you can come with us. I can't promise you the ship will be there, but there's damn all else to do other than sit around and wait to die."

"I'm coming with you," said Heidi. "Sorry, Mum, but I can't stay here any longer. Longrock was fu...really boring, even before this infection thing."

"Heidi, I don't know," began Glenda. "Daniel, what do you think?"

"With all due respect, I need you to debate whether you're coming with us or not on your own. Right now, we have little time left to work this out," said Tom. "Firstly, *we* are going to Penzance today. We cannot wait, so the sooner we get moving, the better. Once we get there, we have to find somewhere safe to stay the night, *and* figure out a way to the harbour."

"Secondly," said Jackson, "we have to get past those zombies out there. Do you think we could just batter our way through them, Harry? Get in the van, rev it up and plough our way through?"

Harry shook his head. "No, they're too thick and they're funnelled into the driveway. We wouldn't get more than a few meters before their number stopped us. With all those bodies in the way we'd be surrounded in minutes with no way forward or back."

"We could try to burn them," said Moira. "We've several lighters. We could try to chuck the lighter fluid over them from up here. I'm just not sure we have the time to wait for the fire to take enough of them out. The storm put them out last night, but it's a clear day today."

"Jesus Christ - burn them? Mow them down? Can you hear what you're saying?" said Daniel. "I don't know what you people have done to get this far, but these are God's creatures. I don't know what's going on anymore. Where is the respect for the deceased? Thou shalt not kill, remember?"

"Daniel, can you come here, please," said Moira.

He walked over to the window and she grabbed him, forcing his unshaven face up against the window. His breath began to fog up the glass.

"Look at them. Look at their faces. Look at the way they walk, the way their slack mouths hang open, the way they still try to fight their way in here even without arms and legs and beating *fucking* hearts. These are not God's creatures anymore. God has long since fucked us over."

Daniel struggled out of Moira's grip and rubbed his neck. "Say what you like, but I won't have it. Glenda agrees with me. I cannot permit atrocities on the scale you are talking about. This is some kind of joke, right? In his wisdom he chose to put man on this Earth and there is no greater power than that. We must..."

"Oh, enough of this bullshit," said Jackson. "I'm sick and tired of this religious bullshit and cod psychology. There is no higher power at work. This is nature giving us a reality check. The Plague, tsunamis, earthquakes, aids, bloody flu and E-bola outbreaks. This is just another in a long line of Mother Nature's attempts to cull the most destructive being on the planet: man. I mean come on, I just don't believe that this is God's work, nor is it man's. Some scientist created this infection in a bottle and – oops – let it out by accident? Not likely. No, something crawled out from under a rock or the jungle and got twisted, warped somehow.

It's like bird flu or swine flu or something. Something out there is carrying a disease that we have no cure for."

"It's alien," said Tom sighing. "Sorry, Jackson, but you're not quite right. This infection that kills decent people and turns them into walking dead cannibals isn't a message from God, nor is it manmade. It wasn't here on Earth either. It didn't crawl from the belly of some creature into the human food chain. No, it came from somewhere up there." Tom raised one finger and pointed upward. "Fuck knows how, or why, but it did. This thing is alien. That's why we have no cure for it."

The room fell silent.

Jackson began to laugh. "Tom, I respect you, but you sound like a raving lunatic. You're really talking about aliens? Are you saying we are being attacked by zombies from Mars?" Jackson slapped his palm against his head. "This is…this is just crazy"

"I tend to agree, Tom, why would you think this is alien? Are you lying to us trying to make us feel better 'cause if so, I don't get it," said Jessica.

"It's true," said Christina coming down the stairs. "Tom's not lying."

"You too?" said Jackson. He sat down and threw his hands up in the air. "Sheesh."

"You don't have to believe me or Tom," said Christina. "Quite frankly that's up to you, but this infection is alien."

"How so?" said Harry. "Where did you get this?"

"Ferrera," answered Tom. "We talked to him back at the airport before he...anyway, before he left us, shall I say. He filled me and Christina in on what this thing was."

"This Ferrera bloke, how did he know? Who was he?" said Moira. "Can we talk to him?"

Tom sniffed. "Nope, you can't talk to him, he didn't make it. He was a soldier, but he's dead now. He had no reason to lie to us. And what he said makes sense."

"Maybe," said Harry. "But if it's alien, and I'm prepared to concede it's possible, then why? Did something crash here? Was it an accident? Or was this thing sent here on purpose? If it was designed specifically for man, presumably with the intention of wiping us out, then you have to say it's doing a damn good job."

"That doesn't explain how it spread around the world so fast," said Jessica. "If some kind of alien disease started in London I can see how it would spread around the country, but that doesn't explain France or anywhere else."

"Oui, it's true, Paris was hit hard by the infection. I heard of other incidents around the country in Lyon, Marseille, all over, even stories of infected coming over the border from Germany. It was some kind of viral outbreak that they couldn't contain. This was not a disease from England. This is not like your beef with the foot and mouth, eh?" said Laurent smiling wryly. His attempt to inject a little humour to dissolve the tension only annoyed Jackson.

"Now hang on," interrupted Jackson, "I've tolerated this up to now, but I can't take much more of this nonsense." Jackson got up and began pacing the floor.

"Jackson, sit down, mate. There's no need to get angry," said Harry.

Jackson sat down on the sofa and folded his arms. He couldn't summon up the energy to argue anymore. He ground his teeth and wished he could rewind the clock. He wished he had not gone into work that fateful day and had stayed home with Mary. Instead of being here now, arguing with strangers, having spent the last few weeks killing zombies, he could be with her, his wife, in Heaven. He had no death wish, but sometimes he thought Mary had gotten the best deal of the two of them.

"We need to focus," said Tom. "Let's save the debating for another day. Every minute we spend here today is a minute wasted. I've got an idea of how to get out of here, but I need everyone on board."

"Okay, let's talk about the Martians another day. Let's hear the plan," said Moira still keeping a cautious eye on the driveway below.

"We need a diversion. Two or three of us can get out back into the field easily enough without being noticed. We track back around to the road and make a scene; shout, scream and get their attention. Not all, but a lot of the dead will go for it. You'll have to be quick on your feet though. Run down the main road and lead them out of town as far as you can. There's a petrol station a mile out of town. Make it there and hide. If you can slip inside without being seen the dead will keep running. Meantime, the rest of us will pile into the van and get out of here. We'll then get the dead to follow us, lead them back into town. We'll circle around and pick you up from the petrol station. Then it's off to Penzance."

"I think it's insane," said Harry, "but I think it might work. I can't see a better option. Anyone else?"

"Do what you like," said Daniel, "but me and my family will stay here, thank you."

"You don't have to come with us," said Harry, "but I wouldn't stay here if I was you. Once we leave, we can't shut the door behind us. Some of those things will get in and you won't be safe. From what I hear you can't go home."

"Dad, listen to them. Even if just for now, we need to stick together." Heidi looked from him to her mother. Glenda was quiet and downcast, her eyes wet.

"Fine. We'll go along with you, for now," Daniel replied.

"I'll go," said Laurent. "I'm a fast runner. I don't mind being the bait. I'm getting used to it anyway, eh, Tom?"

Tom nodded at Laurent who was smirking. "I'll come with you."

"No, Tom, you need to drive the van. I'll go," said Harry.

"Me too," said Rosa.

"What? Why? You don't need to!" exclaimed Jessica.

"Yes I do. It's going to take more than one or two of us to get noticed. The more the better. Besides, we're not easily all going to fit in the van, are we?" Rosa knew that Jess was the tough one, but she wanted to make a point and do something. This was her chance.

"Thanks, Rosa," said Tom.

"Us too," said Daniel. "Me and Glenda are coming with you and Laurent."

"Look, Daniel, you don't have to..."

"Yes I do. I need you to protect my daughter and the safest way is for her to ride with you. If me and Glenda can help you get away, then try and stop us."

Heidi looked horrified. "Dad, come on, I'll be fine, stay with me. There's enough room for..."

"Heidi, go with Tom and the others," said Glenda. "Your father's right. You heard Tom, we'll be fine, you're going to come back for us, so don't worry. Just look after yourself, honey." Glenda took her daughter and held her tight.

"Okay, Laurent's in charge," said Tom. "Out there you listen to him, follow him and do exactly what he says. He'll lead the way. Harry, Rosa, for God's sake, take care out there. Everyone else, gather up your shit. We're leaving in five minutes."

* * * *

Laurent jumped down into the back garden and began scaling the low fence into the field. It was full of un-harvested wheat, and weeds had already begun to take a hold, slowly strangling the crop. Harry followed behind him and Rosa swiftly after him. They were nervous, but kept their emotions in check. They had spent weeks on the run, learning how to hide and move out in the open, avoiding making any noises and movements that would get them noticed. Rosa glanced behind her as she entered the field and saw Daniel and Glenda right behind her. She thought they might chicken out, but to their credit, they were coming. They must love their daughter a lot, she thought as she fought her way thought a thick cluster of overgrown stalks that pulled at her feet.

Back in the house, they had gathered their belongings together and were filling up the van. Tom and Jackson sat in the front, with Christina, Caterina and Jessica in the back. The final two seats were reserved for Leonard and Moira.

Moira was keeping a look out upstairs and as soon as Laurent and the others had drawn away most of the dead, would run down and give Tom the signal to go. Leonard was in the toilet as he was worried about going outside again. Wandering outside was not normally allowed and the nurse, Wendy, had told him off on more than once occasion.

Moira heard the van start and saw some of the dead at the start of the driveway begin to turn away from the house. She couldn't see Laurent or any of the others though as the road was hidden by the last few houses on the edge of town. She smiled as more and more of the zombies were drawn away from the driveway. So Laurent must have made it. She waited a minute and eventually the driveway looked clear enough.

"Lenny, come on, time to go!" Moira raced to the bathroom and banged on the door. It swung open and she was surprised to find it empty.

"Lenny? Lenny, where are you?" Moira called out, but the house was quiet. She began to panic. Where could he be? Was he hiding? She raced upstairs and checked in all of the rooms, behind the doors, even under the beds, but he was not in the house. She called out again, but still got no answer. There was no time to wait. She couldn't leave the others out there. Moira ran down to the garage and jumped in the van. She clicked her seatbelt in and Tom started the engine.

"Where's Lenny?" asked Jackson.

"He's gone, I couldn't find him anywhere. He must've snuck out when I was looking out the window."

"What? Where the bloody hell did he go?" said Christina shocked. "Oh, my God, we can't leave him."

"There's only one place he could've gone and that's out the back after Laurent." Tom put the van into gear and took off the handbrake. "If he's lucky he kept up with them. We can't go looking for him now. We'll pick him up later when we get to the petrol station. Harry, do it. Everyone else, buckle up."

Harry pressed the automatic garage door opener and it swung upwards smoothly revealing the driveway. The others had done a good job of drawing the zombies away. There were only a few left and Tom put his foot down on the accelerator. The van charged out of the garage at speed and instantly ran over three dead boys who crunched under its wheels. Caterina cringed and kept her eyes shut as the van bumped its way down the driveway, knocking over bodies and running over any zombies in its path.

Blood splattered the front of the van and Tom flicked the wipers on to clear it so he could see. As an old woman bounced off the bonnet, her long black hair caught and pulled off one of the wipers, leaving bloodied strands of her scalp stuck on the window. The van jumped and skidded as more bodies slipped under its wheels and Tom carried on, relentless, having long since tuned himself out to the horrors of what they had to do to survive now.

The van bumped over the pavement at the end of the driveway and Tom braked quickly. They came to a juddering halt in the middle of the road. To their left, the road was clear. To the right, he saw the zombies, hundreds of them, loping and running down the street after Laurent, Harry, Rosa, Daniel and Glenda.

"Right, let's get their attention, shall we?" Tom hit the horn and kept his hand on it as he pulled the van away after them. He needed to get as many as possible to follow the van, giving time for the others to reach the petrol station and hide.

Leonard heard the horn blaring and stopped. He had gotten lost in the field of wheat and was worried. What would Billy do if he got lost and couldn't get home? He looked down at his pyjamas covered in dust and dirt. Carol would not like seeing him dressed like this and he began to think it hadn't been such a good idea to follow Mr and Mrs Cooper. They had seemed like such a nice couple. He ran forward, following the sound of the horn and hoped he would find his way out of the field before the bad people found him.

CHAPTER NINE

Jimmy prised the last nail from the door and put it in his pocket with the others. He removed the plank and carefully carried it through to the lounge, laying it down quietly behind the out of tune piano. He went back to the kitchen and put his hand on the doorknob. This was it, there was no going back. Once he opened that door, they would be exposed.

The door creaked open and Jimmy looked at the street before him. The house across the road had indeed burned down, but the flames hadn't reached any others nearby. The burnt out shell looked like a rotten decayed tooth in a row of otherwise perfect teeth. Jimmy pushed the door back so it was wide open. The air tasted good. The sun had barely risen so it was gloomy outside, but Jimmy felt happy. He wasn't nervous about going outside. His mother had been caught out, unprepared, but Jimmy knew what he was doing. He needed one of them, just one of the dead, and his father would see sense. Actions speak louder than words, as his father was fond of telling him before giving him a slap on the back of the head.

Jimmy walked down the pathway from the front door and began whistling. Anyone listening would've heard a badly out of tune rendition of Crowded House's 'World Where you Live.' It was the first song that popped into Jimmy's head. He waited, listened and then, sure enough, a solitary zombie appeared. It had been crouched between two cars a little down the road, apparently eating something as it still carried the bloody entrails of something between its dead hands. The zombie looked like it used to be a woman, but its body had decayed badly and its flesh was thin and scraggly.

Jimmy whistled again to make sure he had its attention and then ran back inside the house. Now he would go and wake his father up and show him *why* they had to leave. He glanced at the clock. His father was never awake before seven, he would still be sleeping. Probably sleeping it off, Jimmy thought.

"Dad! Dad, get up!" Jimmy bounded up the stairs two at a time. He opened his parent's bedroom door and David was on his feet. He was wearing just a pair of dirty boxer shorts and brandishing a knife.

"What? What's happened?" David's eyes were sleepy yet wild with surprise. He stared at Jimmy. "What the hell's going on, lad?"

Jimmy was surprised that his father was so alert for such an early time of the day. "Dad, we have to go, they're here. One of them broke the door down. Come quick!"

Jimmy rushed out of the bedroom and David followed him downstairs into the kitchen. Jimmy stood there proudly by the front door which was wide open. "See? I told you."

"What the..?" David couldn't understand how the door had been broken down. It looked fine and there were no zombies milling around the house.

Suddenly, the dead woman that Jimmy had whistled to appeared and dropped the meat it carried in the doorway. The zombie reached out for Jimmy and David lunged at the same time. He managed to grasp the dead woman as Jimmy ducked out of the way. He hadn't expected the zombie to actually get *into* their house.

"Dad?!" Jimmy recoiled in horror, pressing himself against the wooden table as his father rolled around on the floor with the dead woman. Jimmy could see blood coming from his father's arms where the woman had scratched him and torn at his flesh.

David managed to roll over and get on top of it. He sat astride the zombie with his knife plunged firmly into its head. As the woman finally stopped moving, David pulled the knife from her skull and he wiped it on his boxers. He turned to face his son, his face red and sweaty. He spat on the floor and Jimmy noticed his saliva was thick and red.

"Jimmy, what the fuck have you done? What the fuck have you done, you idiot?!"

Jimmy felt sick. Perhaps he should've tried talking to his father first. "Dad, I..."

Another zombie suddenly appeared in the doorway, a boy that Jimmy recognised from school. It literally jumped on David's back and sank its teeth into his shoulder, ripping out flesh and tissue. It bit him again, ravaging his neck, drinking in David's sweet warm blood. David tried to throw the boy off, but it was holding him firmly. Exhausted, David sunk to his knees.

"Jimmy," he rasped, "get out of here. Go!" David's eyes were locked on his son. His knuckles were white as he made fists and hit the zombie biting him. He tried to shake the monster off his back, but it was too strong.

"Dad, I can't, I..."

David felt himself weakening. He was acutely aware that he was losing a lot of blood and the pain was overwhelming. The dead boy on his back refused to give up and continued digging its teeth into him.

"Please, Jimmy, I love you, son."

Jimmy watched as his father dribbled blood from his mouth and sank to the floor. The zombie continued its relentless attack, gorging on the rare fresh meat it had suddenly found. Jimmy picked up the large screwdriver from the table with which he had unscrewed the nails earlier and approached the zombie. It was so intent on eating his father, who was now unconscious, that it was oblivious to Jimmy.

The screwdriver entered the zombie's head through one ear and the tip came out the other side. Jimmy held onto it as the zombie keeled over onto the floor. When he was sure the zombie was dead, Jimmy pulled the screwdriver out.

"Dad?" he whispered. It was too late though. David was already dead. Jimmy bent down and touched his father's wrist. There was no pulse. Should he run, like his father had said, or try to board the door up again? What about his father? He couldn't leave him like this. Jimmy stood up again, staring at his father, unable to believe he was really dead. As Jimmy stared at his father's bloody corpse, David's left leg twitched. Jimmmy flinched and stepped back. Surely his father wasn't going to come back? He wouldn't, would he?

Jimmy heard the roar of an engine outside and turned to the doorway. The noise was growing louder and he peered around the door carefully, but saw no more of the dead. Tentatively, he stepped outside clutching the screwdriver and saw a van coming down the street. It was being followed by hundreds of zombies. Jimmy recognised it as being the same van that he had seen last night and ran out into the road to flag it down.

* * * *

Harry shouted at Tom to stop, but there was no time to avoid the figure in the road. It had run right out in front of them yet Tom instinctively knew it wasn't one of the dead. The figure was waving its hands above its head and holding a weapon of some sort. Tom saw the boy's eyes and knew he was alive. He yanked the wheel down hard and the van careered over the pavement and crashed into a parked car. It missed Jimmy by an inch and he felt the air rush past him as the van whisked by his head.

Harry coughed and looked across at Tom who was conscious but had a bleeding nose. The van had no airbags and they had both smashed into the front of the vehicle. Luckily, they had been wearing their seatbelts.

"Is anyone hurt?" said Harry turning slowly in his seat. He felt like a ton of bricks had been thrown at him. There were murmurs and groans from the back seat, but nobody spoke. He looked in the mirror and saw the army of dead advancing.

"Tom, can you start it?"

Tom wiped his bleeding nose on his sleeve and turned the key. The van did not even turn over. He tried again and again, but the van stayed silent.

"It's dead," Tom said slapping the steering wheel in frustration.

A face appeared by his window and Tom pressed himself back in his seat. He felt down the side of the driver's seat and curled his fingers around a tyre iron. The face at the window stared at Tom in amazement before speaking.

"Please, you've got to help me, my dad..." said Jimmy. Seeing the blood on Tom's face, Jimmy's amazement turned to concern. "Are you all right? I didn't mean to..."

Tom unclipped his belt and opened the door. Jimmy stepped away and Tom got out, still holding the tyre iron.

"We've got to help *you*? Are you fucking kidding?" shouted Tom.

Harry got out of the van too and helped the others. They were dazed, but otherwise unhurt.

"Tom, we've got to go. Leave him be, he's just a boy," said Jackson. "Those things will be on us in a minute."

"Shit, Tom, what do we do now?" said Jessica looking down the street at the numerous zombies running and lurching toward them.

"We have to run for it. Come on."

Tom ran down the road and everyone followed, heading away from the walking corpses coming for them. Jimmy hesitated and looked back at his home. His father David was stood in the doorway, his near naked body covered in blood. Jimmy ran after the others leaving his dead father chasing after him.

Tom turned a corner and let the others catch up. Harry and Heidi reached him first.

"We're going to have to find somewhere to hide, try to give them the slip. When they've dispersed, we'll try to find a working vehicle and go get the others."

"I don't like the look of any of these houses, Tom," said Harry. "There's no cover, no safety. We don't know what's in them."

"We should go down there," said Heidi panting. "Godolphin Road leads to the main road out of town. There's a mini shopping complex there. You know, like a supermarket and some warehouses and stuff. Maybe that would be safer?"

Moira and Jessica caught up and heard the conversation.

"Let's keep moving. I'm not dying out here today," said Moira. She had managed to grab a rucksack and rifled through it quickly only to find it was full of books. Right now, a weapon would have proven far more useful than a well-read paperback.

Jackson and Christina appeared from around the corner with Caterina. Her normally pale face was almost purple. Christina had managed to grab a bag too and Tom guessed it would have Caterina's things in it, mostly medicines and vitamins.

"Heidi, lead on, quickly," said Tom.

As Heidi ran, they all followed. Jackson ran up to Tom.

"Where's Lenny? We can't leave him."

"I don't like it either, Jackson, but what choice do we have?"

"I'm going to look for him. We didn't leave Benzo behind, did we? I can't do it. When I've got him I'll meet you at the petrol station."

Tom opened his mouth to argue, but Jackson suddenly ran off to the left, down a small residential street, his oversized shirt flapping in the wind. Within seconds, he was gone.

"Damn it, Jackson," Tom said hurrying after Heidi. He glanced over his shoulder and saw the dead in the distance. Between him and the dead was the boy who had run out into the street. Tom saw he was crying and slowed down to let him catch up.

"What's your name?" said Tom as the boy approached him.

"Jimmy."

The boy was still clutching the screwdriver and looked terrified.

"Jimmy, stick with us, we're going to find somewhere safe, okay? Don't worry about before, it was an accident. Come on."

Tom saw the complex that Heidi had been talking about. She was running across a deserted car park headed to a series of low-rise buildings. He saw a supermarket, but the front windows had all been smashed in. It looked as if someone had rammed them with a truck of some sort. The shop was decimated and rubbish blew around the storefront. Next to the supermarket was the entrance to a mall. It was dark inside, but Tom could see that the shops had been looted and the entrance to the mall had been destroyed. Tom guessed that someone had driven a truck or large van into the mall, probably the same one that had ram-raided the supermarket. The large metal grill that should've been in place was on the ground. There was no way of shutting the doorway and the mall would be useless.

Heidi had obviously noticed the same thing and was running around it, down the side, past a burnt out coffee cart. She paused and waved for everyone to follow her. There was a garden centre next to the mall and a tall fence surrounded it. Tom could see a huge array of plants, trees, shrubs and flowers through the fencing, but wondered how Heidi was planning on getting in, if that was her plan. They would need a ladder twenty feet high to get over the fencing. Taking a look over his shoulder he saw the zombies giving chase. He hoped that Jackson had made himself scarce and quickly.

Tom and Jimmy ran past the coffee cart and down the side of the mall. They were sandwiched between the back wall of the shopping centre and the tall fence. Everybody stopped where Heidi had and Caterina and Christina were on their knees gasping for breath. Tom looked around and they were out of sight of the road. They had a few precious seconds out of sight of the dead before they were found. He ran up to Heidi.

"Any ideas?" he asked hopefully.

Heidi's face was flushed. "I thought maybe the shopping complex would be safe, but it's been trashed. I can't believe it!"

Tom looked around. The mall would offer little protection from the horde that was only sixty seconds away. Like the supermarket, there was nowhere to hide and nothing to barricade themselves in with. He looked at the garden centre. The building looked intact, but the fence around it looked insurmountable. Tom scanned around looking for inspiration.

"Hey you, let us in!" Harry shouted.

"What? Who's there?" said Tom.

"I see them too," said Jessica. "Look, behind those rose bushes, there's someone there."

"Hey, you, we're not infected. We need help!" shouted Harry again.

The rose bush rustled and then a man stepped out from behind it. He jogged up to the fence and looked at Harry. The man was dressed in overalls and apparently worked there. His face and hands were covered in dirt, but he seemed healthy otherwise. Despite all the dirt he was covered with, his white eyes sparkled brightly. He looked African and had a round cherub-like face and short dark hair.

"Who are you? Where did you come from? Are you with them?" asked the stranger in a deep and urgent tone.

"Please," said Tom approaching the fence, "please let us in. They're coming. We just need somewhere to shelter for a while. We're no trouble, I promise."

The man's brown eyes looked Tom up and down and then settled on Caterina. "She pregnant?"

"Yes, she is. Can you help us?" pleaded Christina as she helped Caterina to her feet.

"Over there, there's a gate in the fence." The man pointed to one corner and then raced over to open it.

Tom and Heidi ran to it and the man was there already unlocking it. He pushed the gate open and let them in. When the last of them was inside he shut it and locked it again.

"Better get inside then. No one knows I'm here and I'd prefer it to stay that way. Follow me and keep quiet."

The man led them down an aisle of tall shrubs and Tom saw that many of them were dying. Looking around at the other plants, many of them had dead leaves and the soil was dry. Evidently the occasional storm wasn't enough to keep them alive. Tom wondered if this man had any water and how he had managed to survive in here on his own.

They walked into the garden centre through another door that the man locked behind them. Inside it was cool and dark. It smelt like fertiliser and the air was bad. They were quiet, as he had asked, and followed the man past well-stocked rows of gardening equipment: forks and spades, lawnmowers, hedge trimmers, trellis, and even an array of outdoor furniture. The man led them into a back office, not locked, and then through into another room. It appeared to be the worker's restroom. There were two vending machines in the corner, a couple of sofas and a small kitchen area with a microwave, kettle and assorted dishes.

As they all settled down into the seats, Tom approached the man who stood by the door watching them all. "Thanks. I'm Tom."

"Macklin. But call me Mac."

"Thanks, Mac. Is there anyone else here or..?"

"Just me." Mac ran his grubby hands over his head. "Shit, I'm just...I thought I was the only one left around these parts. Where the hell did you lot come from?"

"That's a long story, Mac," said Tom. "I'll fill you in later, but right now, I've got to figure how we're going to get out of town. We've more people out there and they're relying on me. I can't leave them out there."

"More people?"

"Hey, Tom, are we good?" said Harry. He shook hands with Mac and introduced himself.

"Yeah, they can't get in, don't worry," said Mac. "I haven't had any trouble in here - not from those dead fuckers anyway."

"You asked if we were 'with them' when we were outside. Who were you talking about?" asked Tom. "Is there someone else in Longrock we should know about?"

"I suppose you've not been here long then? You don't sound like you come from here and I don't recognise any of you. Well, that blonde chick looks vaguely familiar actually. Anyway, I wasn't always on my own in this dump. I only moved to this town recently. Man, how much would I love to be kicking back with my friends in Jo'berg right now? Assuming they're not zombies of course.

"When it all kicked off, there was me, Sally and Keisha. We all worked here and it seemed the safest thing to do was stay put. There wasn't much choice, outside was...well, you know, how it is. We wouldn't have lasted two minutes. We managed to get a shit load of food and drink from the supermarket before it was cleared out completely. We just locked up and stayed put. I haven't been outside since.

"Over the past couple of weeks we saw these creeps come around. There was always two or three of them and they'd come and check out the mall, take stuff and leave. They drive an ambulance, but I'm pretty sure they're not ambulance-men. They didn't look like it to me. Sally reckoned we should join them. She thought they must have somewhere safe nearby. I told her not to go, but she wanted to leave and she convinced Keisha to go with her. I think they probably got cabin-fever being cooped up in here with me.

"A few days ago, Sally and Keisha left. I watched them approach the ambulance and a guy came out the back. He was a short, ugly looking bloke. They talked for a minute or two then they got in the back, drove off, and I haven't seen them since."

"These men driving the ambulance, you don't think they're on the level?" said Harry.

"I didn't like the look of them one bit. I hope the girls are all right, but..." Mac shrugged his shoulders. "What could I do, I couldn't force them to stay, could I."

"Mac, we were on our way out of here when we had a bit of an accident. We've got friends out there. I don't suppose you know where that ambulance went? Maybe we can find your friends? You helped us, we'll help you, right?" said Tom.

"I hope your friends are okay, but if they're outside...I heard them talking once, the ugly bloke and another one with a funny accent. Reckon he was Australian or something. They drove around the garden centre and must've figured it wasn't worth it because they stopped and had a look but left us alone. One of them said they had to get back to the boss, but if you're thinking of joining them, I'd think again. You'll never get there anyway. The ugly bloke said they had to get back to the Mount. I think that's where they are, on the Mount."

* * * *

Laurent kicked open the door and ran into the petrol station foyer. Rosa was right behind him. The station's glass doors were shut, but they found a back door which took them inside. It was quiet inside and they were exhausted from running. The plan had worked well so far. The pack of zombies trailing them had largely turned around, once Tom had brought the van onto the street. Some were still following them, but they had managed to keep well ahead of them.

"Hurry up," shouted Laurent.

Daniel and Glenda were not far behind, but were finding the run hard. Laurent could see that there was still about twenty or thirty dead behind them. Glenda pulled ahead and reached the station. Rosa grabbed her hand and Glenda gratefully took it, letting Rosa lead her into the station. She looked back through the large glass frontage and saw Daniel straining to reach the station.

Laurent watched on, worried that Daniel might have a heart attack as he stood in the doorway urging Daniel on. "Come on, Daniel, you're almost there. Hurry!"

Overgrown fields bordered either side of the road, and from the undergrowth, a dog suddenly bounded out. Laurent saw it was already dead. Its mangy body was covered in sores and much of its fur had rotted off. It chased after Daniel and nipped at his heels. Daniel stopped, no more than ten feet from the station, and kicked out at the dog.

"Get away, get out of here," he said, repeatedly kicking the dog in the head.

Suddenly, another dog appeared, then another and another. Laurent counted six in total, all very large, powerful dogs, and all very dead. There was a variety of breeds: Labradors, Alsatians and some he didn't recognise. They were in various stages of decay. Their teeth were still razor sharp though and their senses keen. Laurent watched, his stomach churning, as the pack of dogs circled Daniel and pounced on him. Laurent faintly heard Glenda scream and was aware of a struggle behind him as Rosa held Daniel's distraught wife back.

Daniel was dragged to the floor and the dogs tore into him, muscular jaws clamping around his arms, legs, and face. Laurent picked up the door he had kicked down and placed it in the doorway. It wouldn't hold much back, but it might help keep them out of sight of the dead. Daniel screamed and pleaded for help, but there was nothing they could do now. From inside the station, Laurent heard the sounds of Daniel's bones crunching as the dead dogs ate him alive.

Glenda fainted and Rosa dragged her behind the counter. "Laurent, we have to hide, help me," she said, kicking away the cluttered mess of bottles and newspapers on the floor.

Laurent stood watching Rosa, too shocked to move. "Did you see? Did you see Daniel, he..."

"Yes, I fucking saw!" said Rosa. "Now fucking help me or we'll be next!"

Laurent was instantly snapped out of his awe and picked up Glenda. They carried her behind the counter and crouched down.

"Well, that didn't go as planned," said Rosa. "Fuck." She sat on the floor and listened to the sounds from outside the station, of the dogs eating and the zombies approaching. "They know we're in here, surely. If they can't see us they can smell us, sense us. Fuck, Laurent, what are we going to do?" Rosa was trembling and he took her hand.

"I hope Tom hurries up with the van," said Laurent trying to give Rosa a reassuring smile. "I don't know how long it will take before they figure out a way in here. Tom will come soon. If he doesn't..." Laurent didn't want to say what he was already thinking.

"He'll come," said Rosa. "He *has* to, or we'll be as dead as Daniel out there."

PART FOUR: PATHOGEN

CHAPTER TEN

"I can't believe we've got an ambulance," said Tim. "Surely, there must be something better we could use, something bigger that could carry more things? What about a truck or a van? They can't be that hard to find."

"This is fine," said Shane. "Not too big, not too small. Easy to drive and manoeuvre. More importantly, it's easy to spot when you're out on the street and need an escape. You don't want to jump into the wrong truck and find yourself in a confined space with a hungry zombie."

Honok was driving whilst Shane and Tim had squeezed into the passenger seat. They were driving into Longrock along the coastal road, a path that Honok and Shane had travelled together many times recently. On their last trip, they had happened upon two girls at the shopping complex. They hadn't even had to coerce them into coming back to the Mount, they *wanted* to go. Honok still smiled when he thought about that now. Sometimes luck was on your side and things just fell into your lap.

"So where first?" asked Tim. He was chattering endlessly like a schoolboy on his first trip away from his parents. "Straight to Penzance or what? What do I do? Can I do any of the driving?"

"You can be quiet, Timmy," said Honok. "I'm driving. Shane is working. While you shoot your mouth off we're looking out for something that could be useful; supplies, weapons, maybe more recruits even. Of course, there might also be things out here we don't want to meet. Look, there's one now."

Tim saw a zombie on the side of the road. It was nothing more than road-kill now. Honok had driven over it so many times that the lower half of its body had been flattened. He had been careful to avoid the head though so it still struggled to get up off the road it was stuck to. Tim felt slightly queasy.

"Gross. I hope we don't run into any of those things today. Say, shouldn't we have weapons or something, in case we get attacked?"

Shane sighed. "They're in the back. Now shut up."

"But where are we going? If I'm going to help I need to know what the plan is."

Honok and Shane looked at each other. They were approaching Longrock and Honok slowed down. The road ahead was unusually busy. Just past the petrol station there were nearly thirty zombies.

"Holy shit," said Tim. "Look at them all."

Honok brought the ambulance to a standstill, but left the engine running.

"Something's brought them out," said Shane, scanning the fields. "They don't normally gather in numbers like this unless they've found a meal."

"A meal?" said Tim nervously.

"Hey, Tim, you're right, we need something to defend ourselves with. Why don't you go grab something from the back?" Shane shuffled in his seat to allow Tim out.

Tim jumped out excitedly and ran around to the back of the ambulance.

"One minute, okay?" Shane said to Honok as he slid over the seat and jumped out after Tim. "I just need to...take care of something." Honok nodded, and waited.

Tim pulled open the back door and cast his eyes over the assortment of weapons in the back: axes, swords and spades. He picked up a sword and was impressed at how heavy it felt in his hands.

"Let me see that," said Shane.

Tim passed him the sword. "Cool eh? That should do us nicely, I reckon."

Shane gripped the sword with both hands. "Tim, do you know what Lazarus told me before we left today?"

"What?" said Tim eagerly. He was looking forward to getting on with their mission, yet equally anxious about standing around in the open with the zombies so close.

"He said you were a liability and that I had to kill you."

Tim laughed nervously. He could see that Shane was serious. Shane raised the sword so that the tip was pointed straight at Tim's throat. "Shane, you wouldn't? What did I do?"

"You've a big mouth, Tim, but don't worry. I'm not going to kill you."

"Well, yeah, um, thanks. Look, I know I've a tendency to go on a bit, but..."

Shane wielded the sword above his head and brought it down on Tim's shoulder. He cleaved off Tim's right arm with one clean slice and blood spurted from the exposed joint. Tim screamed in agony and dropped to the ground.

"Do you ever shut up? Jesus Christ. Like I said, I'm not going to kill you. I'm going to let those things eat you." Shane laughed and put the sword back in the ambulance before closing the back doors. He went back to the front seat, leaving Tim writhing in agony on the road, blood pouring copiously from his severed limb.

"We all good?" asked Honok as Shane got back in. He had been watching them both through the side mirror. Whatever Tim had done to deserve it, Honok was not going to lose any sleep over it.

"All good," said Shane, closing the passenger door firmly. "Tim's going to help us by getting their attention." Shane pointed at the mass of zombies who were leaving the petrol station and heading toward the ambulance in the direction of Tim's screaming. "Then we can go check out that station and see what got their attention. Could be a little bonus to take back for Lazarus."

Honok drove forward and pulled over to the side of the road. "After Norm fucked up the entertainment last night, I hope it's a female bonus."

They sat quiet and still, watching the zombies lope past them to Tim. They took no notice of the ambulance and Shane was surprised when a pack of infected dogs trotted past. They looked like they had feasted recently. Their teeth were bared and blood dripped from their mouths. Shane was never less than bemused by the dead. He found it fascinating to see them now and often imagined how they used to be before they were infected.

Honok watched in the rear-view mirror as the dead leapt onto Tim who was rapidly submerged beneath a pile of rotting, biting zombies. His screams abruptly stopped as they ripped his body apart and Honok turned the engine over.

"Right, let's check it out and be quick. Tim won't keep them satisfied for long. If there's someone alive there, we'll grab them and head back to the Mount. If not, we'll carry on."

Honok drove the ambulance up to the petrol station. In the forecourt, amongst sticky pools of oil, lay a body. It was mangled and had been mostly eaten. They could not even recognise if it had been a man or a woman.

"Do you think that was it?" asked Shane.

"Let's check inside, there may be others," said Honok. He left the engine running and jumped out. The vague vapours of petrol and blood wafted up his nose and he fought the urge to sneeze. Before he got more than three feet, a man with long curly hair came running out of the station.

"Tom, thank God, you..." The man stopped and frowned when he saw the ambulance.

"Hey, are you all right, can we help?" said Shane nonchalantly.

Honok pinched his nose and buried a sneeze. "Are you alone?"

"No, I'm with two others. Sorry, I thought you were someone else," said Laurent. The two men facing him looked odd. One was tall and thin, and the other short and fat. They didn't dress like officials and had obviously stolen the ambulance. "Look, we're okay, our friend will be here soon. Any moment now, in fact. So..."

"Who else is with you?" said Shane approaching Laurent.

"Oh, just a couple of friends of mine, but we're okay, we don't need any help," said Laurent. "One of my friends fainted, but she's fine, really, thank you, but..." Laurent had a bad feeling about these two men. He would rather take his chances with the zombies than fall in with this odd couple. He was quite sure that the taller man had blood splatter on his shirt. In itself that was not unusual, fighting off zombies was a dirty job. But the blood on this man's shirt was still fresh, and Laurent knew that you did not get such bright red blood from a dead body.

"The way you came running out of there it sure seemed like you needed help," said Honok. "Shane, we should help this man and his friend who fainted. I'll help our friend here." Honok drew a knife from his belt and let it hang by his side. He made sure Laurent saw it, but kept his eyes locked on Laurent as Shane made his way into the station.

Laurent noticed that Shane had drawn a large knife out too and wished he had had the forethought to take something with him. "Look, we don't want any trouble. My name is Laurent. My friends in there..."

"I'm not really interested in your name. Listen, Laurent, this is a one-time offer. Those things that killed your friend here are going to be back very soon. Now, your two friends are coming for a ride with us. You can join them if you like, come back with us to where it's safe. Or you can stay here and take your chances. You can have, oh, five seconds to decide."

Laurent thought about running. He thought about trying to fight this odd, stumpy man standing before him, but Laurent was unarmed and the man had a knife. He had fought off the dead before, but none of them had been armed. He thought about staying and waiting for Tom, but he couldn't let them take Rosa and Glenda like this.

"Oui. I will come with you," said Laurent. "Please don't hurt my friends, they've been through a lot. We won't cause you any trouble."

"Just get in the back," said Honok showing Laurent to the back of the ambulance.

As Laurent was climbing in, he noticed the assortment of weapons on the floor of the vehicle.

"Don't even think about it," said Honok, kicking them away out of Laurent's reach.

Shane reappeared from the station with Rosa. He was carrying Glenda who was still unconscious.

"What's wrong with her?" said Honok. "Is she infected?"

"No, she just fainted," said Shane smiling. "That's her husband you're stepping in."

Honok looked down and realised he had walked through Daniel's remains. Disgusted, he wiped his shoes on his trouser legs. "Fucking shit," he said aiming a kick at what was left of Daniel's skull.

Rosa climbed up into the back of the van next to Laurent and Glenda was bundled in beside them. Shane scooped up the assortment of weapons and took them out to keep beside him in the front.

"Sorry, Laurent. He said if we didn't come with him, he was going to kill you," said Rosa.

"It's not your fault. I shouldn't have run out unprepared like that. I heard the engine and I assumed it was Tom."

Laurent and Rosa cradled Glenda as the back doors were shut on them. Honok and Shane got back in the ambulance and pulled out of the petrol station just as the dead were returning. Tim had been devoured, only blood stains on the road marking where he had been. Even his bones were nothing but food to the dead. The ones that were too strong to break they carried and gnawed on. The pack of dogs had Tim's pelvis and femurs between them and were fighting over them.

Honok pulled the ambulance onto the road and then suddenly stopped. Up in the road ahead was a man in pyjamas. He was walking toward them slowly, carefully following the white lines in the middle of the road.

"What the fuck is this?" said Honok winding down his window.

Shane put a hand on the door handle, ready to jump out.

Leonard stopped by the ambulance and looked up at Honok. "Have you come to pick me up and take me home? I'm afraid I got a bit lost. Have you seen my friends? Billy? Glenda?"

Honok turned to Shane. "Have we, Shane?"

So this man had been with the others, thought Shane. "He could be useful. I'll put him in the back with his friends." Shane jumped out and bundled Leonard into the back of the ambulance with ease. They decided it would be best to head back to the Mount now with their prize. Lazarus would be pleased. They would still have time to go out and find the guns he wanted later.

As the ambulance headed back down the road, away from Longrock, Jackson stood up. He had been crouched down in the corn field watching the whole scene. He had managed to avoid being seen by anyone, living or dead, and had been about to head over to the petrol station when the ambulance suddenly appeared. He watched one man slice off another's arm and leave him in agony to draw the zombies away. He watched them take Laurent, Rosa and Glenda away at knife point, and then Leonard. But to where?

Jackson watched as the vehicle rounded a bend on the road and vanished. He thought about running after them, but who knew how far they were headed, or where. How would he keep up with them and avoid the worryingly large group of zombies still out there. If only he could have stopped them. He felt so frustrated. He knew he was going to have to go back to the others and try to track the ambulance later.

Jackson recalled they had been going to an out of town shopping centre. He had found his way here through a back road and then overgrown deserted fields. He could retrace his steps and hopefully avoid the zombies. Most of them had been drawn away from him, following the ambulance to wherever it was headed. Jackson disappeared back into the abundant corn and began to head back to the others, hoping he would be able to find them quickly. That ambulance could be headed anywhere, and Jackson was worried they might lose them altogether.

As he crept through the field, one of the dogs that had killed Daniel suddenly dropped Tim's femur it was chewing on. It could smell something, living, just a faint trace on the breeze. There was something close and tantalising out there, something fresh and meaty that would be far tastier than a stripped bone. It ran off into the field to hunt it down. The rest of the pack quickly joined it in the hunt for fresh meat.

* * * *

Tom, Heidi, Mac and Jessica were strolling around the interior of the garden centre. With Mac's help, they wanted to look around to see if they could use anything inside to help them rescue the others and escape to Penzance. Christina had stayed behind in the restroom to look after Caterina. Jimmy was very quiet and pale and refused to talk. He settled on the sofa and curled himself up, so Christina volunteered to keep an eye on him too.

Moira and Harry decided to take a look around and keep watch on the outside. A lot of zombies followed them to the complex, but lost them when they'd gone into the garden centre. Harry found that Mac had dragged several of the plants and trees together outside so he and Moira could use them to monitor the car park without fear of being seen. The foliage provided good cover and they were there now, watching as the dead shuffled around the cars, in and out of the mall, unable to find their quarry. Moira kept Harry company and also used the time to check out what they managed to bring with them. Their supplies were next to nothing now, since they left most of them behind in the earlier panic.

Inside, Tom picked up a chainsaw and swung it about lazily. "This could be *very* useful."

Heidi nudged him. "Boys and their toys, eh?"

Tom laughed and put the chainsaw down. He felt a pang of guilt about laughing when his friends were out there. Heidi somehow made him feel more positive about things though. She was cute and looked at him in a way he wasn't used to, not like the others. She treated him less like a leader and more like an individual. Sometimes, he wondered if the others even knew him at all.

"It's not a *toy*, Heidi," said Jessica. "Tom's right actually, it could be useful. We need as many weapons as we can get."

"Unless you have an incredibly long extension cord, then it's useless I'm afraid," said Mac. "Even if you did, there's no power."

Tom picked up a set of long-handled shears. He drew them apart and snapped them back together, the sound echoing around the room. "These could be handy. Here," he said handing them to Heidi. He picked up a Bow Saw and handed it to Jessica. "How about this, Jess?"

"This is going to be messy," she said, looking up and down at the sharp blade.

Mac led them down another aisle and took a pair of telescopic ratchet loppers down from the shelf. "These bad boys are what you want. Ain't nothing going to get close to you if you got these."

"Mac, we sure appreciate your help," said Jessica.

"Don't worry about it. I'm glad of some company for a change. Plus if you're going after your friends, then you're going to need all the help you can get. You really think you're going to find them at that petrol station?"

"I hope so," said Tom. "They should be there, locked up tight, waiting for us. I don't want them out there too long. They weren't supposed to stay there and we didn't even give them anything to defend themselves with. I should've thought about it."

"I hope Mum and Dad are all right. I shouldn't have let them go." Heidi began to well up and bit her lip.

"We'll get them," said Tom putting an arm around her.

"In case you're forgetting, Heidi, Rosa's there too. Not to mention Laurent, Jackson...but it's all about you, isn't it. Shit, whatever. Thanks, Mac, I'll see you later, I'm going to see how Christina's getting on," said Jessica. She rolled her eyes at Heidi and then abruptly left.

"She okay?" said Mac watching Jessica leave.

"Yeah, she's just worried about Rosa," said Tom. He couldn't help but wonder if there was something more to it. It wasn't like her to get upset and she kept making barbed comments to Heidi. Tom couldn't understand why they weren't getting on. Heidi wasn't a threat to anyone and she had happily offered to help them. He still had feelings for Jessica, but he knew he was never going to be able to act on them. They were close, but he had grown accustomed to her treating him more like a brother as time went on. Tom realised he still had his arm around Heidi and withdrew it.

"So what's the idea, Tom?" said Heidi. She wanted to change the subject. She was upset about her parents, and Jessica's reaction was uncalled for. If she knew they were doing something positive, something that would get her back to her parents, she would feel better. Tom's arm had already made her feel better. He had gripped her shoulder and a warm fuzzy feeling had spread throughout her.

"Well, there's no point in all of us risking our necks. We'll decide who goes to get the others, and on the way, we're going to have to look for a vehicle. I don't fancy going to Penzance by foot. It'll take too long and it's far too dangerous." Tom picked up a strong metal spade and tucked it under his arm. "I'll take a group and head out now."

"You're still going to try for Penzance?" Mac shook his head bewildered. "Do you still think the navy is coming? Penzance is a shallow dock, so there's no way you can get a naval ship in there anyway."

"Really? Hmm, well we have to try," countered Tom. "What's the alternative? This is safe, but for how long? What were you planning on doing when the food ran out? We have to do *something,* Mac. If the navy says that's where they'll be, then that's where they'll be. I wish you would reconsider coming with us."

"Maybe, maybe. Look, get your folks, get a vehicle and then maybe. I guess I hadn't thought too far ahead." Mac scratched his head, trying to figure out what exactly he should do next.

Suddenly, a long scream echoed through the vast warehouse and they all jumped.

"What the hell was that?" asked Heidi.

"Shit, that sounded like Jessica." Tom kept a hold on the spade he carried and ran off in the direction of the screaming.

As Heidi and Mac followed, Tom thought that something must have found its way in. A lone zombie had somehow found its way through the fence and took a chunk out of someone. Please God, not now, not now, not now. He raced through into the restroom ahead of Heidi and Mac.

"What was that?" he shouted.

Christina and Caterina were on their feet, worried expressions on their faces.

"I don't know. It came from out there," said Christina, pointing through the door to the outside area.

Tom pushed past Heidi and rushed outside. He saw Harry, Moira and Jessica standing in a circle of rose bushes looking down at the ground. Tom was still holding the spade and when he saw what they were looking at, he raised it above his head, ready to strike.

"It's okay, Tom, it's dead," said Harry.

Moira had hold of Jessica. Tom could see he had been correct, that it had been her that had screamed. Her eyes were full of tears and she was shaking.

"It came out of nowhere!" said Harry. "Bastard thing just flew in over the fence there and nearly took Jess out. Bloody good job she had that saw on her."

Tom stepped closer to the thing on the ground. It was like no animal he had ever seen before. The saw had cleaved it in half and evidently, when it had landed, Harry had stomped on it to make sure it was dead. There were two elongated wings on either side of its body, although there were no feathers. They looked more like a bat's wings, all leathery and veiny. The body of the creature was fat and covered in thick black fur. There was a tail still flailing about connected to the dead body and it trailed to a pointed, glistening tip. A gloppy brown liquid was oozing out of the tip over the ground at Harry's feet.

Tom looked at the other end of the creature where its head had been. Despite Harry's heavy feet, Tom reckoned it had been a cat once. It had two heads and the whiskers, the small pink nose, and the pointed ears were all undoubtedly feline. One head looked fairly normal, but the other was covered in a rash of huge blisters that must have obscured its vision. If it had once been a cat, then it had mutated into something else, something hideous and deadly. He lowered his spade.

"Jesus Christ, what is that thing?" said Heidi rushing up behind Tom.

"It's dead, that's the main thing," Harry replied, stamping on its two heads once more. The tail finally stopped moving whilst the brown liquid continued seeping from it.

"Call me insane, but to me it looks like it was a cat once," said Moira.

Jessica threw the saw to the ground and rushed inside, barging past Tom without looking at him.

Harry knelt down to examine it more closely. He grabbed a twig from a nearby bush and poked the creature's carcass. "Look at this. Its legs have been pushed up into its body. I wonder if this was two cats. There are so many joints and bones...I think I can count at least six legs here. They're all shrivelled up though. Fuck knows how a cat grows wings."

"I told you," said Tom bending down beside Harry as he poked and prodded it, "this infection is alien. We don't know what it's capable of. So far, it seems to take humans and kill them, reanimating them into hungry walking dead ones. We don't know what else it can do. What if it's evolving somehow?"

"What do you mean?" asked Moira.

"Well, we figured this infection was maybe an accident, right, some sort of alien disease that can turn any living thing into a zombie? What if it's more than that? What if the disease is a living thing too, like a parasite? What if it's taking the creatures on this planet and using them for its own design?"

"Design?" Heidi stood behind Tom, careful not to get too close, but fascinated to see the strange thing that had flown in and nearly killed Jessica.

"I think Tom is suggesting this might not be an accident," said Harry. "Perhaps this alien infection has a purpose? Maybe we're being targeted."

Mac let out a long whistle. "This is all very interesting, but your friend's scream seems to have brought us some visitors."

The zombies in the car park were beginning to converge on the garden centre, alerted by the noise and activity.

"I'm going to see if Jessica's okay," said Tom. "We'd better get back inside." He didn't want the zombies to get too excited and was unsure of how strong the fences were that currently protected them.

"I'll stay a bit longer," said Harry. "I just want to make sure nothing else comes through or over that fence."

"I'll stay with you," declared Moira.

Tom took Heidi back inside and Mac followed them, picking up the discarded saw on his way.

Harry watched as a large zombie staggered out of the supermarket and headed toward the garden centre. Plastic bags whirled around its feet and then away into the middle of the car park, swept up in a mini-tornado. He watched them rise and fall, swooping through the air before the wind disappeared and they dropped casually to the ground. More and more zombies were headed their way. Beyond the rubbish and the leaves, the abandoned cars and the dead, a figure shambled toward them. There was something slightly different about this one. Whilst the zombies tottered around unsteadily, this one was walking directly toward them.

"Hey, Moira, look over there. That one's headed over here. See how it looks different to the rest?"

She looked to where Harry was pointing and saw the one he was talking about. She squinted and looked at the figure. It was a man, wearing baggy trousers and a checked shirt. Moira's eyes opened wide.

"Holy Shit, it's Jackson!"

CHAPTER ELEVEN

The sun was shining and Lazarus had to shield his eyes from the glare. It was almost white, tearing through the low clouds, ripping them apart without mercy. Lazarus turned away from the window. He had informed Walker of what they had heard about the navy and instructed him to make sure everyone on the island was busy. He also told him to watch Ed. Lazarus was fairly certain Ed could be trusted, but it didn't hurt to have him watched, just in case.

Lazarus made his way through the castle, admiring the pennants and flags on the walls. They were symbols of the olden days, when life was miserable and cold and hard. Civilisation had gotten fat and lazy and now the hard times were back. He intended to take all those fat and lazy people and make something of them, of himself. He had tried following in his father's footsteps a few years back, but could never live up to the old man's ideals. Where his father had taught Classics at University, Lazarus could only get a job teaching history at a private school. To anyone else it would have been an impressive job, but to his father it was a failure. Where his father had raised an intelligent son with a loving wife, before the cancer had taken her, Lazarus had failed to hold down any relationship and therefore failed to produce any offspring. His father had regularly berated him for his deficiencies. In his youth, Lazarus had felt the weight of a leather belt across his backside many times. When he was older, it was his father's harsh words that cut him.

A year ago his father had told him how his mother had considered an abortion early on. They were young and hadn't prepared to have a child so early. To look at him now, his father said, he wished they had gone through with it. He had named his child Lazarus with the hope that such a grandiose name might inspire him to achieve something in his life. As Lazarus soared, so should he.

Lazarus had studied and worked hard, but could never compete with his father's ideals. If he had been anointed King of

England his father would still find some excuse to castigate him. Six months ago, his father had been shouting at him across the dinner table, his face getting redder and redder until abruptly the shouting had stopped. Lazarus had watched as his father suddenly keeled backward clutching his chest, knocking the table over as his chair fell over. Lazarus had watched as his father suffered a massive heart attack there in his living room. With his father dying at his feet, Lazarus poured himself another glass of Shiraz and sat down on the piano stool. He played some Haydn and a little Bartok whilst he finished the bottle of wine. Eventually, only when he was sure his father was cold and dead, he called 999.

Lazarus stepped outside into the fresh air. Down on the slope he could see his men working. This thing with the navy had made him uneasy though. It might pay to check on his insurance plan, just in case. He made his way down, through the village, and went to the stone house where Walker was monitoring the radio. Lazarus poked his head around the door.

"Anything?" he asked.

Walker shook his head from side to side. "Just static. I'll let you know if I get anything."

Lazarus left him and followed a small path that went further down the hillside. There was a crude pathway carved into the hillside and Lazarus followed it round, out of sight of the village. He made sure nobody saw him. The path curved around the Mount and took him to its rocky base. Nobody ever came down here, there was no need to. He could see the grisly remains of one of the women on the rocks ahead, but ignored them and slipped into a cave. It looked out to sea and only Lazarus knew what secrets this dark hole contained. In the gloom, he felt along the wall as the water lapped at his feet. He felt the rope where he had left it and pulled himself along it. There she was. She was still tied up where he had left her: Pandora.

She was a sailing yacht in perfect condition that he had secured here at the start of the outbreak. Wherever you were, no matter how safe you felt, you should always have an escape plan, his study of past wars teaching him that lesson well. Nobody knew about the boat, not even Walker. Lazarus had no intention of letting anyone else know it was here either. He looked it over, smiling, pleased to see she was still in good order. The darkness of the cave hid her well. Unless someone took the steps down the cliff base this way and knew to go into the cave, they wouldn't even know there was a boat there.

Lazarus exited the cave and climbed back up the hillside to the village. He looked in on Walker once more, but to his surprise, found the radio unmanned. Why would Walker leave his post? He knew how important this was. Lazarus began to wonder if Walker could be trusted too, when Ed suddenly bumped into him.

"Sorry, sir, I got here as quick as I could." Ed sat down at the table and picked up the headphones.

"Where's Walker? Why are you back here so soon, Ed?" Lazarus tried not to let his rising anger show. His right hand clenched into a tight fist and he released it, trying to let his anger evaporate with it.

"Walker said Honok was back early. He just got word no more than two minutes ago so he asked me to take over. Sounds like they found some people. Awesome eh?"

"Thanks, Ed. Stick to it, okay? I want to know the second they're back on the air. When you hear something, anything at all, then come and fetch me."

Lazarus left and strode up the hillside toward the castle. It wasn't even noon, yet Honok had returned. He was intrigued as to what, or who, was so important that he would come back so soon. Lazarus made his way into the castle and downstairs. He approached Norm on the way, who was cleaning the cells and washing the steps with a bucket of cold water and bleach. He was sporting a black eye and a cut lip. When Lazarus passed by, Norm tensed and stood up straight.

"Get back to work," grunted Lazarus as he walked past Norm. The odious man was beginning to grate. If Honok found others, perhaps there would be more recruits. Lazarus was beginning to think he needed some fresh blood in the ranks. Autumn was setting in, but it was time for some spring cleaning.

As Lazarus descended the steps to the tunnel entrance, he heard raised voices, male *and* female. Lazarus smiled.

"Oui, now get your fucking hands off her!" shouted a male voice. Lazarus heard shrieks and cries followed by the sound of scuffling.

"Okay, okay, just stop hurting him," begged a young female voice.

Lazarus took the last step and was surprised to see the room so busy. Honok and Shane had hold of a man. In the cart sat another man, only much older and apparently dressed in pyjamas. Walker had a woman pressed up against the wall, a knife to her throat and in the middle of the room stood another older woman. Christopher had forced her to strip and he held a large blade to her neck.

"Now then, gentlemen, would someone like to tell me what is going on?" said Lazarus surveying the room. The room went quiet. The tunnel door was still open and a cold breeze came in. He was glad he still had his black coat wrapped around him.

Walker pushed the young girl down to the floor. "Sit!"

"We picked up some waifs and strays, sir," said Honok proudly. "They were messing about in Longrock. Any later and they would have been brunch for half the town. They should be grateful really."

"I trust you have checked they're *clean*," said Lazarus. "We wouldn't want anyone here with any sort of infection would we."

"They're clean," said Shane. "Christopher's helping us check them, but I'm sure they're fine."

"What the hell are you doing?" shouted Laurent, struggling to free himself from the vice-like grip of Honok and Shane. "You can't do this. Where are we?"

"Honok, who is this? Did you get any names or information yet?" Lazarus walked over to Walker and looked at the young girl sitting at his feet.

"Yes sir. This is Laurent, and these are his friends. That woman over there is Glenda. Her husband got nailed by the zombies. Over there with Walker is Rosa. That man cowering in the cart is Leonard."

Lazarus looked around. The naked woman, Glenda, was shivering. The other new faces were looking at him fiercely. He walked across to the girl on the floor and told her to get up.

Rosa stood and spat at him. Saliva dribbled down Lazarus' cheek as Walker slapped the newcomer and held her back. Lazarus was happy to see the hatred burning in Rosa's eyes.

"Christopher, take Glenda to Norm. I'll take this feisty one with me. Walker, I want you to take Mr Laurent to the cells and ask him a few questions. I suspect they have more friends out there and it would be useful to know where they are. They haven't survived on their good luck, so I want to know how. They must have supplies and weapons."

Christopher shoved Glenda down the wet stone steps into the cells. They were still wet from where Norm had washed away the bloodstains and she slipped, crashing headfirst onto the stone floor.

"Lock that up, Norm." Christopher turned and left hastily. He had seen Norm's face and knew better than to upset the boss.

Norm reached down and gave Glenda a hand up. She reached to her head and saw blood on her hands. She felt dazed, dizzy, and she stumbled into the cell with Norm where he shoved her onto a dirty mattress. She was aware of a door closing and heard keys jangling.

"And you are?" asked Norm, standing the other side of the locked door.

"Glenda Cooper. Where, where am I?" Glenda looked around for a rag, a piece of clothing, anything to cover herself up with. There was nothing at all. The cell was empty aside from the mattress she sat on and a bucket in the corner which smelt, literally, like shit.

"You're in the dungeon. What does it look like? Shit, how hard did you bang your head? And that wasn't my fault, you slipped," said Norm defensively.

As Glenda looked around, she saw Norm more clearly. He was an obese and dirty man. He was looking at her closely and she felt like she was under a microscope. She crossed her arms and sat back against the wall. "I don't understand. What's going on? Where are my clothes?"

"Look, you don't need to understand. It's probably better if you don't, actually. There's a lot of blokes on this island and it's a small place. Occasionally, they need to let off steam, you know...you're here to help them...relax. I'm here to look after you."

"But...my husband...my daughter's out there. Please, can't you let me go? I promise I won't tell anyone where you are or anything. I don't even remember how I got here." Glenda touched her head as the pain grew.

Norm chuckled. "Look, darling, just sit tight. You're going to get some visitors soon. I suggest you relax and get some sleep while you can, eh?"

He left her alone and Glenda wondered how she had ended up here. They had been running toward the petrol station and Daniel had been killed. God, how she wanted Daniel with her now. And Heidi was out there alone now, without her mother or father. Glenda felt sick.

She lay on the mattress and began to sob. Daniel was a stubborn man, an old-fashioned man, but he always put his family first. She loved him so very much. What would Heidi say when she found out her father was dead, eaten by zombies.

Glenda lay there for a while, occasionally slipping off to sleep, only to awaken with a fright, her vivid nightmares shocking her mind. There was a tiny window high in the wall, too high for her to see out. There was sunlight coming through it and she could see the edge of a blue sky. She remembered her home, back in Austria before she had moved here. There, it had always been sunny and bright. In the mountains it seemed like the sky was perpetually blue. Oh, if only she were there now. Glenda fell asleep again and dreamt of the mountains, the fresh, clear river water and the green grass.

Her dream was cut short with the sound of the keys jangling again. She looked up. Seeing the light was dimmer, she assumed a few hours must have passed at least. She turned over and saw Norm opening the door. A man walked in and stared at her as Norm shut the door and left. Although she was already pressed up against the wall, she tried to move further back, away from this man. He was sweaty and covered in dirt. It looked like he had been doing some physically demanding work and his face was streaked with grime. He wiped his hands on his tartan shirt and then whisked it off over his head.

"Couldn't find anything younger, eh, Norm?" the man shouted.

"Who are you?" said Glenda.

The man just smiled and unzipped his trousers. Glenda stifled a scream as she realised what was about to happen. She finally realised why Norm had told her to get some rest and why she was being kept prisoner down here. As the man came closer, she shut her eyes. She could smell his foul breath on her face. Please protect Heidi for me, please protect my daughter, she thought as his hands grabbed her.

* * * *

Rosa spat once more at Lazarus. "Fuck you, we won't tell you anything." Rosa thought about Jessica, wishing she was back with her now. Who were these monsters?

He wiped the spit from his cheek and merely smiled. "I'm not going to waste time asking you questions, my dear. I can think of something *far* more fun to do with you."

"Let her go, you animal," ordered Laurent. "Let us all go! We're no good to you. I'm not going to tell you anything, or where our friends are."

"Walker, bring the girl over here by the cart please. Rosa, wasn't it? Honok, Shane, bring Mr Laurent over here."

Lazarus went over to a corner of the room and came back with a club. It was made of steel and the end of it was rusty. Lazarus leant over the cart where Leonard was sitting. He was hunched over, his hands shaking and his eyes shut tight.

"Who was this again, Honok?"

"Leonard, sir. I think his mind's gone, stupid old fucker."

"How...disappointing. Leonard open your eyes, please. I want to talk to you," said Lazarus.

Leonard slowly opened them and looked up at the scary strange man staring back at him. They had hurt Glenda and he was scared. Laurent and Rosa were there too, but they looked frightened of this man.

"I want to go home. I want to see Billy," said Leonard. "Carol will be wondering where I am if I don't go back soon."

"Let me help you, said Lazarus offering Leonard a hand. He helped Leonard out of the cart and then pushed it away as the old man stood in the centre of the room. He was clearly bewildered.

"It's okay, Lenny, ignore him, don't talk to him," said Laurent.

"Shut up," said Shane, punching Laurent hard in the face, breaking his nose.

Honok grinned and held him up as Laurent reeled. Laurent refused to cry out, defiantly looking at Lazarus as blood poured from his nose.

Leonard wet himself and Lazarus could literally smell the man's fear as it spread through his pyjamas and puddled on the stone floor.

"Laurent, Rosa, *Lenny*, let me tell you something. This is *my* place. What you want is irrelevant to me. Anyone on this island is either with me, or against me. Now I am quite sure that you are not going to work for me, which means you are my enemies, my prisoners. Mr Laurent, you have information which I want, so Walker is going to ask you some questions. How painful the answers are is up to you. In the meantime, I shall take your friend Rosa someplace else. She looks tired if you ask me. I think we should find a nice comfortable bed for her, don't you agree?"

"Who are you?" said Laurent. "You're no better than those things out there."

"We men are wretched things. I do not expect you to understand. But I do expect you to do as I say. My name is Lazarus. Welcome to the Mount." Lazarus smiled.

Laurent and Rosa screamed as Lazarus took the club and raised it in the air, smashing it against the side of Leonard's head, instantly splitting his fragile skull. Leonard roared as Lazarus brought the club down again. He smashed Leonard's hands and arms, shattering the bones with each blow as the old man tried to get out of the way. Lazarus continued to rain blows upon Leonard's old body as Honok and Shane dragged Laurent away.

Blood and bone flecked Lazarus' face as he bludgeoned Leonard to death. When the old man stopped moving, Lazarus threw the club aside. Leonard was hardly recognisable anymore. His body had been smashed and battered, and he lay in a crumpled bloody heap.

Walker laughed as Rosa struggled, unable to escape the man's strong hold. He watched as Shane and Honok took Laurent away up the stairs and deeper into the castle. The man was fighting, but Walker would get what he needed to know out of him. Today was going to be a good day.

Lazarus exhaled and ran bloody fingers through his thick black hair. He pointed at Walker. "Take that girl to my room and tie her up. Then clear this shit up. Tell Honok not to waste anymore of my time bringing me old rubbish like this. He would've been nothing but a drain on our resources. When they have Laurent locked up, I want him and Shane back out there right away."

Lazarus turned and went upstairs as Walker pushed Rosa ahead of him. She was bawling her eyes out, praying her death would be quicker and less painful than Lenny's had.

* * * *

Lazarus rolled his head and stretched his neck. He grabbed a towel and ran it across his back, the rough texture of the dry towel absorbing the sweat from his muscular body. He reached down to the floor, discarding the towel and began to dress. "Now where was I? Oh yes, your friends."

Rosa was naked, tied to his bed. Her ankles and wrists began to bleed from the tight binding and she turned her face away from him. She had lost track of time since he had brought her up here and tied her up. It must have been an hour or two, she thought. They had gone through a long underground tunnel to this place, and every passing minute was another minute closer to death and further away from Jess. Lazarus had spent a considerable amount of time in fucking her. He hadn't said anything to her, just grunted and ground away on top of her, ignoring her pleas for him to stop. Eventually, she had given up and blocked him out. She tried to think about Jessica, Tom, home; anything but here and the pain she was feeling.

"You might as well tell me, Rosa, your French friend has probably spilled his guts to Walker already," Lazarus chortled. "If not, then no matter. You'll tell me, won't you?"

She didn't answer him. Rosa was thinking about Jessica and the last time she'd seen her. It had been in the house in Longrock on the morning before they'd split up. She had gone with Laurent because she wanted to prove a point. She wanted to prove to Jessica that she wasn't a pushover or a flake, and that she could handle herself. Now look where she was; tied up and raped, her life at the mercy of a madman.

"Still not talking to me? Shame." Lazarus walked around the bed to face her. He held her head with one large bony hand so she could not turn away. "Fine, have it your way. I'm going to send you downstairs to your friend. Gwen or whatever her name was. Do you know what my men are going to do to you?"

Rosa stared back at him, refusing to speak. She was scared of what was going to happen to her, but was more scared what would happen if she told him where Jess and the others were.

Lazarus let go of her and pulled a shirt on over his head. He put on his boots, his long black coat, and picked up a small sword from the drawers beneath a window. He bent over Rosa and she braced herself, waiting for the cool steel blade to slice through her skin. Instead, Lazarus cut her ties and freed her. He grabbed her arms and she felt the sword pressing against her back.

"We're going on a little walk, my dear. If you try anything, I will cut off your tits and let you bleed to death."

Lazarus frogmarched her out of his bedroom and down the stairway. He kept a strong hold of her all the way down to the cells where he passed Christopher coming out. "Christopher, wait there please."

Lazarus threw her down the steps into the cell and barked at Norm to lock her up in the spare cell. Once he had seen Norm close the door on her, he went back upstairs to find Christopher obediently waiting for him.

"Christopher. I want you to go and tell everyone there is to be a meeting tonight at six. Until then, everyone can relax, stop work and have a break. Tell the men we have new entertainment for them and they don't need to wait for my permission. Tell them to come right away, in fact. Think of it as a little present from me."

"Yes, sir, right away." He didn't think twice about what the meeting was about. He had finished with the older woman, but now that the young one was available, he intended to go back for her. She was slim and pretty. "The boys are going to have a lot of fun, thanks sir." Christopher gleefully left the castle to inform his colleagues and friends of the good news.

Lazarus made his way down the hillside to the village and entered one of the houses as Christopher spread the word.

"Ed, anything?"

"Perfect timing, sir, they've just started talking again. I was about to fetch you."

Ed held out the headphones and Lazarus sat down at the radio.

"Ed, we've some visitors. Go and see if Walker needs a hand will you?"

Ed left to go find Walker whilst Lazarus reached for the volume button and turned the dial clockwise. Through the static, he began to hear the voices, one British, one American.

"...luck with it McCulloch. Seriously, I hope you find some people. I'm starting to feel like we're the last ones alive on Earth," said the American voice.

"Thanks, Samson, I'll let you know how we get on, of course. We're not going to take any risks, but we can't call it off now. We've been sending the message out and we're just hoping someone heard it. We'll know by 0730 tomorrow one way or another. Penzance is our last hope."

Lazarus recognised the second voice as being British and guessed it was that of McCulloch, the British naval Admiral.

"I've been in discussion with Blaine on the USS Gerald Ford, and he's in agreement with me. He thinks we should get together too. We've been unsuccessful in reaching anyone on the mainland and we're better prepared for this thing with you than without you. Are you still in agreement?" said Samson.

"Absolutely. I can't wait to meet you face to face, Samson. I've told some of my men and they're keen to get going. We can put our heads together and come up with a plan. I'm sure of it. Things are pretty hairy down here. We've seen some strange shit."

"You mean worse than the zombies?" asked Samson.

Admiral McCulloch coughed before answering. Lazarus wondered if he were hurt, or just being very British and polite.

"In the ocean. Marine life around here isn't usually very exciting, but...some of my men reported seeing things in the last couple of days. There are things floating on the surface of the sea. They look like harmless lumps of seaweed, but if you look closer, they're alive. A couple of my men got hurt. It sounds crazy, but these long tentacles reached up out of the water and stung them."

"McCulloch, I hope you put them in quarantine."

"Oh, yes, of course. They've been sedated, but they're not doing well. We even saw dolphins yesterday, but..."

"Go on."

There was static and Lazarus wondered if he had lost the frequency for a moment before the British voice resumed.

"The dolphins tried attacking the ship. They rammed themselves into us. God knows what they thought they were trying to achieve. It was hard to see clearly, but they didn't look well. I'm thinking that this infection thing isn't contained to humans. The dolphins were covered with blisters and cuts. They looked terrible. After a while, they must have figured out they couldn't get at us and gave up. We fired a few warning shots, not that they took much notice of them."

"Well, the dolphins are much friendlier over in the Caribbean," said Samson. "The USS Gerald Ford is sitting tight there. They're going to wait for you and me to join them. I told you there's something we wanted to share with you yesterday and I mean that, McCulloch."

"Tell me, Samson, what have you found. You said you picked it up near Texas right?"

"Yeah, you're not going to believe it when you see it. What we've got here is nothing short of a miracle. It's one of them. It's a goddamn alien."

Lazarus took off the headphones. So the Americans had captured an alien? Was that how this infection had started? He was amazed. He hadn't been naïve enough to believe man was alone in the cosmos, but an alien here on Earth, alive? He put the headphones back on just in time to hear the two ship's captains saying their goodbyes. No wonder there hadn't been a cure for the disease and no wonder it had spread so quickly.

Lazarus got up. He needed to go see Walker. If this infection could spread to animal life, then it wasn't just zombies they were dealing with. They were going to need a large arsenal and Rosa's friends could help them. Lazarus left the stone house, slamming the door behind him.

CHAPTER TWELVE

"We need another distraction," said Harry. "He'll never get past all those things to the fence. Quick, go tell the others."

Moira sprinted into the garden centre whilst Harry kept a watch on Jackson. Jackson wouldn't exactly know their whereabouts of course, and Harry could see the confusion on his face. Jackson was looking at the shopping mall, the supermarket, trying to figure out where to go. He also couldn't keep still as the zombies had noticed him and were gathering around him, getting closer all the time.

Tom and Jessica came sprinting back with Heidi and stopped behind Harry.

"It's him? What's he doing here?" said Tom.

"I don't know, but we need to do something fast or he won't be here for long," said Harry.

"Over there. We have to go the front of the centre and shout and scream, get the zombies to follow us. Harry, Jess, you come with me. Moira, stay here and hide. When the coast is clear, open the fence door, get out there and wave for Jackson to follow you. We'll keep them away from you as long as we can."

Tom didn't wait for an answer and rushed through the bushes into the open, heading for the opposite corner. There were a hundred zombies in the car park and he began hollering and whooping. Harry and Jess followed suit and began jumping up and down, trying to make as much noise as possible. Slowly, the zombies headed in the direction of all the noise. Tom and Harry kept a safe distance from the fence so no prying fingers or hands could reach them. Jessica stood behind them with half an eye on the sky. She hadn't forgotten the strange creature that had nearly decapitated her only five minutes earlier.

When the majority of zombies had moved away, Moira slipped the door open quietly and jogged down the side of the building. She waved her arms over her head and Jackson spotted her. He ran toward her, a line of zombies following his path. They looked like they had formed a bizarre conga line. Only ten feet away from salvation and a dead shopper emerged from the supermarket between Moira and Jackson.

Jackson stopped in his tracks and Moira did not hesitate. She swung the bow saw at the zombie and lopped its head off. Jackson raced past the falling body and Moira led him back through the door into the garden centre. She locked the door behind her and dragged a bush over it. Some of the zombies had seen where they had gone through the fence and the whole centre was now surrounded.

Exhausted, Jackson sank to his knees. He was panting, out of breath, and Tom and Harry helped him to his feet. Together, they carried him inside.

"Get him some water!" shouted Tom when they reached the restroom.

They laid him down on the sofa and Mac brought a bottle of water out to him. Jackson took a sip and looked around the room. All eyes were staring at him expectantly.

"What the hell, Jackson? We thought you were going to wait at the petrol station for us?" said Harry. "What happened?"

"Oh, my God, Rosa, is she..?" Jessica brought a hand to her mouth.

"She's alive," said Jackson, draining the water from the plastic bottle.

"My parents? Where are they?!" Heidi clutched Tom's arm.

"Okay, hang on, everyone. Give him some room." Tom ushered everyone away. They waited for Jackson to respond. Heidi was holding her breath and gripping Tom's arm.

"It went wrong. Jesus, it's all fucked up." Jackson face was bright red and he let out a sigh. "Heidi, I'm sorry but your dad..."

"Oh, my God." Heidi gripped Tom's arm tighter. "Mum?"

"She got away."

Heidi threw herself at Tom and he held her there. He could feel his chest getting wet through his shirt from her tears.

"What happened, Jackson?" Christina sat down beside him and he inched away from her.

"It was so fast that I hardly know. I went after Lenny. I traced my way back to the house, and to the fields out the back of the house. By the time I got there, I couldn't see Lenny, but I saw the petrol station. Laurent and Rosa got inside with Glenda, but

Daniel...he was too slow...the zombies, they..." Jackson didn't want to tell Heidi what he had really seen, how he had seen those dogs rip him apart.

Christina touched Jackson's arm and he flinched.

"Don't touch me. Sorry, but just don't, okay? Look, the others got into the petrol station, but then someone else turned up. They were in an ambulance of all things."

Tom looked at Mac who nodded. Jackson went on.

"There were three of them to start with, but they killed one of their own. They just maimed him and fed him to the zombies. Then they got to the station and before I could do anything, they got Laurent, Rosa and Glenda. They were armed with knives and swords and they just bundled them into the back. They took Lenny too."

"Those motherfuckers, I knew it. I knew they were bad news." Mac began pacing up and down. "Well, I guess I know where Sally and Keisha are. Fuck, we have to go get them."

"Steady on," said Tom. Heidi had stopped crying and Tom gingerly pushed her away. Caterina took her to one side and consoled her.

Jessica watched. Maybe Heidi's tears were real this time. Her father *had* just been eaten alive. Jackson was right, this was fucked up. "He's right, Tom. Rosa's there, so we have to go get them. What did these men look like, Jackson? Do you know where they were going?"

Jackson shrugged. "I'd recognise them again, but I don't know where they were going. One was a short fat man, the other average looking. Big butch man though. Thick hands and arms. If we're going looking for a fight, I think we'll get one."

"Oh, God I can't believe this. We were so close." Christina put her head in her hands. The thought of reaching that naval ship tomorrow had been her focus for so long now that it had kept her going. She had planned to get Caterina on that boat no matter what. Now Laurent and Rosa had been kidnapped? That boat wasn't going to be back. They had to be on it tomorrow, they just *had* to.

"Excuse me," said Jimmy clearing his throat. "I don't mean to interrupt, but there are nine of us in this room. Just to play devil's advocate, but it sounds to me like you're proposing going to rescue your friends? What if you don't? These men took four people, two of whom you hardly even know. One of them is an old man, right?"

Christina looked at Jimmy. She had comforted the boy, got no more than two words out of him the whole time, and now here he was giving a speech about how they should leave their friends behind? "Jimmy, shut the fuck up before someone shuts you up," she said calmly.

"I'm not leaving my mum!" cried Heidi.

"Are you for real?" said Jessica. "Who the fucking hell are you anyway? It's your fault we're in this mess, you little shit! We should be leaving *you* behind."

"We're not leaving *anyone* behind," said Tom. He picked up the garden shears and rested them against a shoulder. "Jimmy, you're way out of line. I don't know what rock you crawled out of but you'd better start growing up fast. We can always throw you outside if you'd prefer. Heidi, Jess, we'll go back for them." Tom sighed. He had to get some control of things before people started going their own way. If Jimmy kept talking that way, he was liable to get lynched. Tom watched a red-faced Jimmy slink into the background. "Jackson, what about Laurent and Lenny, did they seem okay?"

"Yeah, I suppose so."

"How about you? Are you okay?"

Jackson looked at Tom and didn't answer.

"Jackson, tell Tom you're okay," said Christina.

There was no response.

"No, no, no," whispered Christina, a horrified look dawning across her face.

"When the ambulance left, I knew I wouldn't be able to follow it," said Jackson softly. "The only option I really had was to get back and find you to tell you what had happened. I thought I was well hidden in the cornfield, but turns out, I wasn't hidden so well. There were so many of them, so many of the dead."

"Oh fuck, no. Did you get bitten?" said Harry.

"Sort of. I got quite far through the fields before I realised something was following me. I thought I was going to make it back, but I knew I wouldn't. I came to the edge of the field and then I saw them. It was a pack of dogs and they were all dead. I guess they could smell me. I didn't have anything on me so I had to run for it. Unfortunately, dead dogs can run quite fast."

Jackson leaned over and rolled up his trouser leg. There were two sets of bite marks on his shins where they had bitten him. The skin around the bites was already bruising and Tom saw the tell-tale sign of the infection already, a line of white blisters spreading up his leg. Jackson rolled the trousers down.

Christina leant over and gave Jackson a hug. "I'm sorry, Jackson, I'm so sorry," she whispered in his ear.

"Well, better me than one of you lot," said Jackson stoically. "I've had a good inning and I do miss my Mary. I know she's waiting for me."

Tom smashed the shears down on the table and stormed out swearing. Harry followed him.

"I'm sorry, Jackson," said Caterina. "Thank you for trying. Thank you for everything." She came over and planted a kiss on his cheek.

Jackson brushed Caterina away, keen not to let her get any closer. "You'd best all keep your distance from me." He shook himself and shuddered. "Well, sod this, I'm not dead yet. Now who are you, young man?" He began talking to Mac.

Heidi sank down into one of the sofas and held a cushion to her chest. She had stopped crying, but was sniffing and dabbing at her eyes. She couldn't believe her father was dead. Her mother was alone out there. Daniel had been a rock for her and Heidi was worried that without him, her mother might crumble. Where was she now?

Jessica saw Heidi holding back the tears and thought it might be time to mend some bridges. She sat down beside her. "Hey, I'm sorry about your dad."

"Thanks. He was…" Heidi choked up as so many memories of her childhood raced through her mind. She had to try and think about that later. Her mother was still alive. "I'm worried about my mum."

"I told Rosa not to go, but she's pig-headed sometimes. If she's with Laurent, she'll be okay. Glenda too. Laurent's a good man. He'll look out for them."

"So you and Rosa are…together?" asked Heidi innocently.

"Yeah, no problem with that, is there?" Jessica had enough to worry about without having to worry about homophobia too.

"Of course not, I'm not my dad. I just wasn't sure. I thought maybe you and Tom..."

"No, we're good friends, but that's it," said Jessica.

"I can't get him out of my head," said Heidi. She knew Jessica and Tom were close, that they had been through this since the beginning. She still wasn't sure quite how their relationship worked, and wanted to try getting some understanding of how she might fit in. "I know this isn't exactly the time, but I can't help it. There's something about him. Shit, if he can get my mum back, I will have his babies." Heidi wiped her eyes and tried to smile at her own lame joke, hoping Jessica might open up. "I've never met anyone like him. You know him well. Did you know him before all of this? You think I should say something to him?"

Jessica gritted her teeth. She had been wrong to think that Heidi would fit into their group. She was too immature and Jessica was fed up. She was worried about whether Rosa was alive or dead, yet all Heidi could talk about was boys? "I think you need to grow up. He isn't interested, okay? I've met plenty of pretty girls like you before, all tits and blonde hair, and I'll meet plenty more when you're gone. Just leave Tom alone. He's got bigger issues to deal with right now than your hormones."

Jessica left Heidi looking on bemused as she grabbed a drink and walked out of the restroom. She hadn't meant to snap, but there was something about Heidi that pushed her buttons.

Jessica heard voices and tracked them down. She made her way past the garden furniture display into the gift area and found Tom and Harry in deep discussion. "Mind if I join you, it's getting crowded in there." Jessica was feeling pissed off and didn't want to be in the same room as Heidi anymore.

"Sure. How's Jackson doing?" asked Harry.

"Surprisingly chirpy, considering," she answered. "He's chatting away with Mac."

"How's Heidi coping?" asked Tom.

Jessica shrugged. "Fine." She wasn't about to tell Tom what Heidi had said. He had other things to be thinking about right now, like how they were going to get Rosa back.

"We were just saying that we need to do something sooner rather than later," said Harry. "Mac doesn't have a very high impression of these guys and from what Jackson tells us, I agree. If Laurent and Rosa were taken at knifepoint, then we have to assume the worst. Mac says they would've been taken to the Mount."

"What's that?" queried Jessica.

"A big fucking problem," said Tom crossing his arms. "It's about two miles away. We didn't see it on the way here because we came from inland. This place is out to sea, about two or three hundred yards off the coast I think. It is *literally* a mount. There's a castle on top of it and it's difficult to access. You can get across the beach when the tide is out, but otherwise, you'd need a boat. It's built on granite mostly, and the terrain is tough. It gets battered by any storm before the mainland and it's had its share of bloodshed over the years."

"So why would they be there? Sounds horrible." Jessica popped open the can of lemonade she had grabbed from the restroom.

"Sounds perfect to me," said Harry. "It's pretty inaccessible which means it's easy to defend. If anyone or anything got to the island, you still have to work your way up a steep rocky hill to get to the castle. If they've kept it clear of infection, then it's a pretty good place to be right now. Whoever's in charge over there is onto a good thing and they know it. I'm guessing they use the ambulance to run errands, you know, come to the mainland now and again and see what they can pick up? They probably didn't figure they were going to pick up Laurent and Rosa today; that was just a fluke."

"So how do we get them back? We can't just knock on the door, can we? What would they want with Rosa? Lenny's just an old man, what use could they have for him?" Jessica absent-mindedly picked up a trowel.

"Best not to think about it," said Tom. "Look, we're going to have to do something. We handled Brad and we can handle this. If we can get to them and back without being seen that would be best. We don't know how many people are on the Mount and the less that know we're here the better. I'm thinking we run a small scouting party up there, two or three of us at the most. Find a way in, get our friends and get out of there quickly."

"You just said it was inaccessible," Jessica argued. "We don't have a boat and by the time you've got across the causeway and up the hill, they'll have had plenty of time to see you coming."

"True." Tom's eyes were vacant. Jessica could see him mulling something over. "Ask yourself, where did that ambulance come from? You're not telling me they keep it on the Mount and drive it back and forth over the beach. I bet there's a tunnel."

* * * *

Tom, Harry and Jessica explained to the others what they planned. It was simple. Whilst Christina, Heidi, Jessica and Mac distracted the zombies outside again, Tom and Harry would sneak out and make their way back to the crashed van. Their supplies were still in it, hopefully, and that meant guns. They had surmised that if the men from the ambulance only had knives, then they didn't have any serious weapons or guns. Tom and Harry would then look for the ambulance and the tunnel to the Mount. All being well, they would be back with the others and they could head to Penzance as planned for the rendezvous with the ship tomorrow morning.

"I should come with you as far as the van," said Moira. "You can't carry all the guns and bags with you, so whatever you don't need I'll bring back here."

"I'm coming with you too," said Jackson coughing.

"No way, you need to rest," said Tom.

Jackson stood up and grabbed the long-handled shears. "If you think you can stop me, Tom Goode, you just try it. I'm not sitting around here waiting to die while my friends are out there in trouble. I need to do something and I'm coming with you."

"You sure?" said Harry.

"Don't worry, I don't bite," said Jackson, "yet."

Tom laughed and they all joined in. Jackson had a black sense of humour sometimes. Tom could not believe his friend was dying. As Jackson pointed out though, he wasn't dead yet.

"Right, let's do this," said Tom.

"I'm worried," said Caterina as half the group left the restroom.

"Me too, honey, but have faith. We've gotten this far and Tom and Harry know what they're doing," countered Christina. "Besides, you need to worry about nothing but yourself, okay? We've talked about this."

"I know, but what about Jackson. Will we see him again?"

"Probably not, Cat. When he said goodbye just now he knew it was the last time. He's a brave man. He wouldn't want some big fancy goodbye. He'll help get Rosa back, and the others too. We just have to wait now."

* * * *

Tom and Harry watched as Moira began jogging back to the garden centre, laden down with bags of ammo. They had ditched the food and water. There was too much to carry, and with the arrival of the navy tomorrow, they would have plenty of food and water soon enough. Tom and Harry took two guns apiece and enough ammo for both.

"Think she'll be okay?" asked Tom.

"She'll be fine," said Harry. "I've been out there with her a lot and she can handle herself."

"What about us?" asked Jackson. He was carrying a pair of shears and a saw. He didn't want to be carrying the guns so that, if the infection took hold and he couldn't carry on, they wouldn't be lost.

"Lead on, Jackson. You said the ambulance went down the coast, yeah?" Tom slung an automatic over his shoulder. They had kept it from the encounter with Ferrera at the airport and Tom was glad they had.

"This way."

Jackson trotted off down the street. They had gotten away from the garden centre with only a few of the zombies following them. The majority had been drawn to the fence where Heidi and the others were shouting and screaming. Tom nipped down alleys and small streets until they had managed to lose the zombies. It felt odd being out in the open. There was no sign of any dead out here on the road, but Tom still kept one hand on the trigger. Jackson had been caught unawares and if he and Harry were caught too, then the group would be in serious trouble.

They jogged down the road together in the mid afternoon sun, the ocean on their right with empty fields and broken houses on their left. After a while, the road began to turn inland slightly, but they always kept the ocean in their sights. They passed a caravan park and more houses, but there was no sign of anything alive. The salty sea air breezed past them and Tom remembered how much his mother had loved going to the seaside. She had always loved the smell of the ocean. It was a shame they could not enjoy it now, and Tom was desperately hoping they would find the ambulance soon.

A honking flock of geese suddenly flew low above them, traversing the coastline. Harry watched them fly away in a V formation, as they kept jogging. "What do you think that thing was earlier, Tom? That monstrosity that attacked Jess?"

"I don't think even God knows what that was. I just hope we don't run into any more of them. It's not just zombies we have to watch out for anymore. And not just bad guys either. Now we have these...monsters? Things that can fly and crawl and who knows what."

"Look at that," said Jackson. He stopped and pointed to something on the side of the road. It appeared at first to be a dead rabbit. A rat was sniffing around it, deciding whether to make a meal of it or not. The rat was thin and breathing heavily. It looked as if it had not eaten in days and was weak. Jackson jumped back, astonished, when tendrils burst from the rabbit's stomach and snared the rat. They wrapped around the rat's body and it squealed, unable to escape. Its feet lost contact with the ground as the tendrils hoisted the rat into the air and curled around the rat, squeezing it tighter and tighter. Blood seeped from the rat's eyes and mouth as the tendrils began to crush its bones until with a loud crack, it squashed the rat completely. It exploded like a jar of jam in a microwave, shards of blood flying in all directions and sticky red rat blood spurting out over the road.

Tom raised his gun and pointed at the rabbit creature that had made a meal of the rat. The tendrils were growing, now a foot long, and seemed to be swaying in the air as if searching for something. They went stiff and then bent low, pointing at the ground, pointing toward Harry. Tom pulled the trigger and blasted the dead creature. The rabbit's body exploded just as the rat had done moments earlier.

"Let's hurry this up, shall we?" Tom slung the gun back in his belt and left the bloody entrails of the rabbit and the rat on the road.

"That ship had better come tomorrow," said Harry as he jogged after Jackson and Tom toward the Mount.

CHAPTER THIRTEEN

Jackson was the first to spot it. "Look, over there, I see it. The ambulance!"

The road they were on had turned back toward the coast and they had religiously followed it until they saw the Mount. They had not seen any more zombies since leaving Longrock. There seemed to be another small town the closer they got to the Mount, with little houses, shops, cafes and a school. Their progress slowed as they proceeded more cautiously, unwilling to rush for fear of stumbling across a zombie, a flying undead cat, or worse. They passed a slip road that was signposted as leading down to the beach for vehicular access to the Mount at low tide. The ambulance wasn't there, so they continued on, looking for its hiding place.

When they did come across it, it was easy to spot as the ambulance wasn't hidden particularly well. There was a seafront café and the ambulance was parked in the vacant lot next door, right out in the open. Harry and Jackson waited behind the café whilst Tom approached it. It was unguarded. Tom tried the doors, but they were locked. He peered inside, but nobody was around. He signalled for Harry and Jackson to come over.

"What do you think, Harry?"

Harry was looking across to the Mount. It was silhouetted against an orangey-blue sky streaked with flat clouds. The tide was in as the causeway between it and the mainland was covered in water. The Mount itself looked deserted. There was no sign of movement either on the hillside or the castle atop it. He still couldn't be sure that a dozen eyes weren't watching them now and he felt nervous.

As Harry looked at the Mount, he felt a shiver run down his spine. It was not the castle in particular that perturbed him, but the Mount itself. It was as if the island was looking at him, the dark watchtower of the castle standing tall and dark against a colourful sky, waiting for them to come. Harry felt that with every step closer to the Mount, they were closer to death. The plague of zombies receded from his mind and he almost felt like bowing down and weeping before the Mount's miserable majesty. He hadn't felt so dejected since he lost his son.

"I think we need a change of plan," Harry said leaning against the ambulance. "We all go in there and we don't know what will happen. We don't know what's in there or how many of them there are. We also need to find *how* to get over there. The tide's up so we need to find this tunnel."

"It can't be far," said Jackson wandering over to the cliff edge. "Look, there are some steps over here leading down to the shore. It makes sense they'd leave the ambulance close by. They wouldn't risk parking it miles away from the tunnel entrance and having to go through the town to get it. They probably reasoned that nobody was going to come along and steal it either."

Tom joined Jackson and looked at the steps. "Let's check it out."

"Okay, okay, but hang on." Harry joined them at the top the steps. "Say the tunnel entrance is down there, then what? We shoot whoever comes out? Force them to take us over to the Mount at gunpoint?"

"Works for me," said Jackson.

"And what if they refuse? What if they're being watched? What if someone's watching us right now? What if they come out armed to the teeth and we all get gunned down? We can't do this without a solid plan. If we fuck this up, then our friends are dead."

"What do you have in mind, Harry?" asked Tom curiously.

"How do we get around the zombies when we need to? Other than blowing their brains out, we create a diversion. That's *exactly* what we need here. As soon as they come out of that tunnel, they're going to lock it up again. One of us needs to get their attention so the others can slip in unnoticed. Our strongest weapon is the element of surprise."

"So who does the shooting and who does the sneaking?" queried Jackson.

Tom looked over at the Mount. It was a foreboding place. The castle looked impregnable, the rocky ground and hill impassable. A rescue mission was going to be difficult. But staying put was equally fraught with danger.

"Harry, you and Jackson should go. Let's get down to the beach and find the tunnel. You two find somewhere to hide. I'll wait up on these steps and when they come out, I'll start shooting. That should give you the time you need to get in the tunnel."

"What will you do, Tom?"

"I'll lead them away from you. See if I can lead them a merry dance around here and away from you, buy you some time."

"Just take care," said Jackson. "Don't forget there are still zombies around here and I saw one of them kill one of their own in cold blood. They're not going to hesitate to execute you if they catch up with you."

"Then I'll have to make sure they don't catch me," said Tom resolutely. "I'll give you 'til nightfall. If you're not back up here by the ambulance in a couple of hours' time I'll know something's gone wrong. I'll head back to Longrock and get help. I'm not leaving you out there alone. Right, come on, let's do this."

Tom stood halfway up the steps while Harry and a wheezing Jackson carried on down to the beach below. They found exactly what they wanted at the bottom. There was a small hut on the beach, nestled against the cliffs, its doors opening outward onto the golden sand. In the doors were two small cracked windows and Harry peered through them. Inside the hut were more doors that seemingly led straight to the rock face. Harry noticed on the hut floor two lines where something had been dragged from whatever lay behind those doors. He looked around for somewhere to hide. The beach was empty and stretched out for miles, curling around the bay until it reached Penzance in the faint distance. Harry motioned for Jackson to join him and they hid behind a large rock, just ten feet away from the hut. Then they waited.

Tom scoured the horizon for any sign of the navy. He looked for boats, small or large, masts, sails, tugs, but there was nothing. To the west, he could make out the faint skyline of Penzance. Where are you, he thought. Are you really coming? Could there really be a ship out there with dozens, maybe hundreds of people on? Or was he wasting his time, leading himself and everyone else into a dead end? He looked across at the Mount. Whoever was tucked away on that small island had taken up a good position. It was naturally fortified and if they had provisions they could last months, years possibly. The zombies would struggle to find that place. If the worst happened, Tom fully intended to make sure that with his last breath, he would lead every zombie in the vicinity to that castle.

They had waited no more than twenty minutes when Harry heard noises coming from inside the hut. There was a screeching, scraping sound as the inner doors were opened. Bangs and chains rattled until finally the outer doors swung open. Jackson pressed himself against the cold rocks, willing himself not to cough. His lungs burned and his blood ran cold. He could feel the infection spreading throughout his body and knew he didn't have long left. He was not beaten yet, and there was no way he was going to let this thing stop him from helping Harry onto the island.

Harry watched as two men stepped outside. One was a short stout man, the other tall and well built. Neither spoke. The small one began closing the hut doors whilst the tall one began ascending the steps up the rock face.

"Ready?" whispered Harry.

Jackson just nodded in reply. He dare not open his mouth in case he gave away their position.

Suddenly a burst of gunfire interrupted the peace and Harry saw the beach ripped up, sand flying into the air as bullets whistled into it. The smaller man ran for the cover of the rocks, waiting at the bottom of the steps for the gunfire to stop. Harry watched as the tall man fell over the side of a railing and plummeted down onto the beach. He landed with a thud on the sand. He had been hit by a bullet and was screaming in pain. He had fallen about fifteen feet and had probably broken several bones too.

"Honok, help me, for fuck's sake! Honok!" the tall man screamed.

"Shut up, Shane," came the reply.

Harry took a step away from the hiding place and saw the stout man, Honok, slowly ascending the steps.

"Hey, you up there, what's your problem? We're unarmed! Let's talk, eh?" Honok advanced slowly up the stairs toward Tom holding the carving knife low by his side.

"How about I just take this vehicle of yours?" shouted Tom.

Harry heard Tom mutter an expletive and then he dropped the gun. Tom said something about being out of ammo, but Harry knew he had plenty on him. It was a ruse. Tom was drawing the small man out. Harry took a small step onto the beach and looked up.

Tom was backing up the steps and Honok had given up hiding.

"You've made a big mistake, my friend," said Honok climbing the steps. "You'd better run 'cause when I catch up with you, I'm gonna cut you up and feed you to the zombies piece by piece."

Harry watched as Tom climbed the steps with Honok following. The plan was working. When Tom and Honok had disappeared over the crest of the rock face, Harry and Jackson went to the hut doors. Honok had not had time to lock them and the doors opened freely.

"Hey, what are you doing?" said Shane. The pain had numbed him and he was lying on his side, exactly where he had landed. His blood was soaking into the salty sand right in front of his eyes.

"What are we doing? We're getting our friends back. The ones you kidnapped. I don't know who you people are, but…" Jackson stopped and coughed. The pain in his chest got worse and he covered his mouth as he doubled over, the violent coughing shaking his body. When he stopped, he saw droplets of blood on his hands. His leg was burning as the infection spread higher.

Harry walked over to Shane. "How many of you are there over there?"

"You're going over to the Mount?" Shane winced as he tried to move. He recomposed himself, knowing it was futile. He was going to die out here on this beach. "You've got no chance. Lazarus will kill you. There are thirty of us and we will defend ourselves to the death."

Harry thought for a moment. This man was not lying and sneaking past thirty armed men to find the others was sounding suicidal. An idea formed in his head.

"Jackson, help me carry him, will you? He's coming with us." Harry grabbed Shane's arms.

"You think this Lazarus will bargain for this piece of shit? Come off it, Harry, he's nearly dead. Don't waste your energy," said Jackson as he tried to calm himself down. His head was swimming and spots darted in front of his eyes.

Harry began dragging Shane toward the hut doors. "I'm not bargaining with anyone. I've met enough scum in my life to know when the time for reasoning is over. No, help me pick him up and I'll explain on the way over there. Let's get into that tunnel before anyone else comes along."

Jackson trusted Harry and so he picked up Shane's legs. They ignored his cries of pain, dragging him across the sand to the hut. Once inside, they saw the cart and put Shane inside. Harry and Jackson began the descent into the tunnel, pushing the cart with them, as Shane fell into unconsciousness.

"I hope you know what you're doing, Harry," said Jackson clutching his sides. The infection had spread rapidly from his leg to his chest. It wouldn't be long before it took the rest of him too.

* * * *

Laurent put his hands over his ears. He tried to drown out the whoops and hollering, but it was impossible. He tried to block out the crying, the sobbing, the screaming, the tormented wailing, but it was hopeless. He pushed himself further into the corner of his cell and screwed his eyes shut. He had tried to stop them. He had ordered them to stop, asked them, pleaded with them, and begged. He offered his life if they left her alone, but his desperate pleas fell on deaf ears.

At first, they had forced him to watch. One of them, an Australian, had stood over Laurent with a blade to his throat, forcing him to watch Rosa being raped. She was in the cell next to Laurent and had cried throughout the whole ordeal. When the second man came in, Laurent had been made to watch again. The second man was their jailer; an obese man whom Laurent had learned was called Norm. He had not taken long with Rosa, but it had been horrendous to watch. After he had finished, another six men came down into the cells. Laurent had tried to talk to them, but the Australian told him to shut up and had beaten him. Laurent had crawled away, bloodied and bruised, unable to block out the sounds of the men forcing themselves upon Rosa.

Laurent took his hands down as the sounds diminished. He heard doors slamming and keys clanking together. There was a faint whimpering and he turned around to face Rosa's cell. A thin reedy man was walking out, zipping up his trousers, whilst Norm locked the door after him. Norm walked away whistling and went up the steps, leaving the prisoners securely locked away.

Laurent crawled over the stone floor. He had two broken ribs from the kicking Ed had given him and a variety of bruises forming on his face. Despite the pain he felt, he wanted to get closer to Rosa. He knew the pain he felt was nothing to what Rosa was going through. She had barely left her teenage years behind and shouldn't be subjected to this. Laurent had not contemplated murder before, but he would gladly kill everyone on this island if he got the chance.

"Rosa," he whispered, "Rosa?"

She lay on the floor of her cell, breathing, but not moving. The mattress was propped up against the wall and she lay on her front with her face turned away from him. He wasn't sure if she was still conscious.

"You have to be strong, Rosa. I tried to stop them but I couldn't, I...I know you miss Jess, but they'll come for us. Tom, Harry, they'll come."

Rosa didn't answer. Laurent wondered if she had heard him, then she slowly turned over. When he saw her face, he gasped in horror. They had not only sexually abused her, but viciously beaten her too. Laurent didn't know precisely how many men had visited her cell. Her eyes were swollen, her lips were cut and she had deep lacerations across her cheeks. There was bruising on her neck too where they had held her. Laurent could see outlines of large hands, pudgy fingers that had left dark purple marks on her pale skin.

She opened her mouth to speak, but no words came out. She was too weak. Her cracked lips moved, but only blood and semen spilled out.

Laurent felt tears welling up and forced them down. He had to be strong for her. "Rosa, I'm so sorry. I promise we'll get out of this. I promise you."

He lay there on the stone floor watching Rosa. She drifted into unconsciousness and Laurent was pleased. He hoped she would not feel her pain there. He hoped she would dream about Jess, about something good. There had to be something good left in this world. Laurent refused to accept this was it, that this was how they would die. He couldn't accept that he had made it so far, past hordes of zombies and deadly creatures, only to die at the hands of a psycho.

After Lazarus killed Lenny, Laurent had been taken down to the cell where Walker had questioned him. He wanted to know where they had come from, where they were hiding, what weapons they had, how many of them there were. The questions did not stop. Laurent refused to answer honestly. He had told Walker it had been just them, just himself, Lenny, Rosa and Glenda. They both knew he was lying. Honok told Walker how they had found them, how Laurent had run out of the petrol station shouting about someone called Tom. Walker slapped him around a bit, but nothing he couldn't take. Walker told him he would be back later, when Laurent had time to think about things. Walker told him that if he didn't answer him honestly next time, that whatever happened to Rosa in the next two hours was nothing compared to what he could expect. That's when Walker left and the men had come for Rosa.

He didn't know where Glenda was. The cell on the other side of Rosa was empty. She had been there initially, but had been taken away once Rosa had been brought down. He asked, but had been told it was none of his business. He hoped that wherever she was, she was in a better state than Rosa.

* * * *

Harry banged on the door three times. The sound carried down the tunnel, reverberating off the damp stone walls, echoing loudly around them.

"This better work," muttered Jackson.

They stood there for three minutes and then Harry banged again. As he did so, the doors swung open and two men stood there facing him. Harry saw the puzzled look on their faces as two strangers stood before them, with an unconscious Shane in the cart.

"Oh, thank God, thank God," said Harry as he pushed the cart inside. "We weren't sure if it was true or not. Thank God you're here." Harry and Jackson drew the cart to a stop and the doors shut behind them. Looking around the room, Harry noticed it was cool and dark, full of boxes and weapons. There was a set of stairs leading up in the corner.

"Hold it, mate, who are you? What's happened to Shane here?" asked Ed. He held a rusty axe in his hands and was peering in at Shane who was all but dead.

"I'm Harry, this is Jackson. Your men were attacked. Some nutter with a gun went crazy out there. We've been on the road and heard the gunfire. Shane helped us, but he got hit. I'm not sure how badly, but he looks in pretty poor shape...the other one, the small fella, he got away and went after the gunman. Shane told us to bring him down here. He said you could help."

Jackson said nothing. He felt dizzy. The room was spinning but he couldn't collapse now or it would give away the fact he was infected. If this plan didn't work, it would be more than him winding up dead.

Ed looked from Harry to Shane. The other man stepped in front of Ed.

"I'm Walker. Put your weapons down now." He spoke slowly and clearly. It was unlikely Honok would've let two strangers down here, but Shane? Possibly. He watched as Harry and Jackson put their weapons down on the floor. They had been carrying guns and ammo. Lazarus would be pleased. "What happened to Honok? The other man – you said he went after the gunman?"

"Yeah," said Harry. "We tried to help your man Shane here, but…" Harry hoped that Shane didn't regain consciousness or they would be exposed and killed in seconds. He had seen enough to know that it was unlikely Shane would recover.

Walker looked at the two men. They appeared to be okay, but they had not had uninvited guests at the Mount before. The meeting was due soon and he couldn't let them wander the Mount unaccompanied. He decided it best to let Lazarus decide what to do with them. "Ed, pick up the guns."

As Ed scooped up the two guns from the floor, Jackson coughed, unable to contain it anymore. Ed handed one of the cold guns to Walker who pointed it at Harry.

"Hey, there's no need for that," said Harry. "We thought we were helping. We just need a bed for the night. I'm sorry about your friend. He told us…"

"How do we know *you* didn't shoot him?" said Walker suspiciously. "How do we know Honok isn't dead already? For all I know, you killed him, shot Shane, and came up with this plan to get over here. Thought you could get in the easy way instead of having to shoot your way in, eh?"

"Mr Walker, look, please, if we were that stupid, why would we have just given you our guns?" Harry lowered his hands. "We didn't even know if there would be anyone here. Like I said, we've been on the road for weeks and we happened to hear the gunshots."

"It's okay, Walker, put the gun down," said Lazarus.

They hadn't realised he had heard the banging on the doors too and had come down to investigate. He had been stood on the steps, listening to the conversation. As he entered the room, Walker handed him one of the guns and Lazarus smiled.

"Harry? Jackson? Pleased to have you on board. We can give you a bed for the night, after that you're free to leave. I think you'll find we have a good thing going here. We have food, water, shelter. In fact, we're having a town meeting right now to discuss a few things. Come and join us. I suspect poor Shane won't be joining us."

Harry looked at the man standing before him holding the automatic. A long black coat hung off his broad shoulders and he had bright penetrating eyes. Harry felt like the man was peering into his soul. "Okay, thank you, Mister..?"

Lazarus held out a hand for Harry to shake. "Welcome to the Mount. I'm Lazarus."

CHAPTER FOURTEEN

Ed led the way out of the castle with Harry and Jackson following. They headed down the hillside toward the settlement where the meeting was to be held. Walker and Lazarus followed them at a distance.

"You believe them?" said Walker.

"I'm not sure," said Lazarus. "They could be telling the truth. Then again...keep an eye on them, Walker. The old chap, Jackson, doesn't look too good. We need to see if it's just old age or anything worse. We need to keep the Mount clean of infection. After the meeting, take them back to the castle and check them over."

Lazarus scurried to catch up with them and fell in step beside Harry. "So, Harry, how did you get these guns?"

"Military checkpoint," answered Harry. "We were coming down into Southampton last week when we came across it. There was no one around so we took them. It seemed too good an opportunity to waste."

"So the both of you have been together all this time?" Lazarus continued his probing. "Just you? Nobody else? How did you manage to survive for so long out there? From my reports, I understand there are very few survivors on the mainland. The zombies are everywhere."

Harry cleared his throat. "We haven't seen anyone else alive for weeks until today. I worked with Jackson at a paper mill outside Reading. It got too heavy so we split, thought we might stand a better chance near the coast. You know, find somewhere less populated?"

"Then why head to Southampton?" asked Lazarus.

Harry paused. He hadn't had time to think of their back-story thoroughly and was making it up as he went along. If he got caught out now, he knew what Lazarus would do to them both.

"My daughter," said Jackson suddenly. "She moved to Southampton five years back. I was hoping we could find her, but...well, I guess she's gone now."

"I see, I see," said Lazarus. "Well, I'm sorry to hear that, Mr Jackson."

They walked on in silence until they neared the houses. Harry counted the buildings as they approached. Eight stone houses and a larger one slightly separated from the others by a well. It looked like the houses were in a circular formation and Harry wondered if they were heading to the large house for the meeting. He was worried that Lazarus hadn't bought their story. Their rescue could be over before it had even begun.

"Is that where the meeting is?" said Harry pointing to the large building.

"Oh no," Lazarus said. "That's the old pub. We have a well-stocked bar and there's large freezer at the back of the pub. We run it from an old oil generator to keep the food fresh. That way, we can serve decent meals instead of living out of tins all the time. I'll bet you haven't had a solid meal in weeks. I'll take you there tomorrow. For now, we've business to attend to. Just follow Ed."

Ed led them between two houses and Harry immediately tensed up. He heard Jackson draw in a sharp breath. Standing around the circle of houses were the island's inhabitants. He estimated at least twenty men and counted only one old woman. They were standing in an oval shape and the sun was casting tall shadows across the rough ground. In the middle of them all was a set of stocks. Harry hadn't seen anything like them before, only in history books, but he knew what they were for. He also recognised Glenda who had been locked into them. Her feet were in shackles and her hands bound together.

Walker and Ed made Harry and Jackson stand beside them as Lazarus strode into the centre of the village green. The grass had long since died and the ground was now muddy, littered with exposed sharp protrusions of flint and rock. There was a low murmur as Lazarus stood next to the stocks. Glenda was naked and appeared to be semi-conscious. Lazarus raised his hands and then, as he lowered them, the men hushed.

"I hope you have all had a productive day today, men. It has been an interesting one. I trust you enjoyed the entertainment I laid on?"

There were cheers and laughter. Jackson wanted to grab the gun off Walker and shoot every last one of these pigs down in cold blood. Harry could see the look in Jackson's eyes and shot him a stern glance. They couldn't expose themselves now, not without at least finding out if Rosa and Laurent were still alive.

Lazarus waited for the noise to subside before continuing. "Some of you may be aware that we have lost some of our own today. Tim and Shane won't be joining us this evening. They were brave men who went down fighting, laying down their own lives to protect us; to protect the Mount. Tim was killed by outsiders, Shane gunned down in cold blood too. When you dine tonight, I ask you all to raise your glasses to these men and offer a prayer for their souls.

"Another of our own, Honok, is still out there. We do not know yet what has happened to him, or if he'll be coming back. These are dangerous times, gentlemen. Probably the most dangerous we have experienced since setting up base here. We are facing many dangers and we must be prepared to face our enemy."

"Who are these bastards?!" shouted a voice.

"Let's get out there and find them!" shouted another.

As more and more voices joined in, Lazarus asked the men to quieten down. "We shall have our revenge, but we do not need to go looking for these people. Whoever they are, they will come to us. We have captured some of the aggressors. We must defend the Mount when they come, and surely they will. This woman here is one of them. Honok and Shane managed to bravely capture four of them. Two of them are locked up right now and will be questioned further. I believe you have all already met one of them, a lovely young thing called Rosa."

Harry bristled at her name. From the chorus of laughter and wolf-whistles that accompanied her name, he surmised that she was in trouble. If this vile band of nefarious men had her locked up in a cell there was no telling what they would do to her, or had done to her. Harry wanted to get to her as quickly as possible.

Lazarus cupped Glenda's face and picked up a sword from the ground. Harry and Jackson could tell she had been beaten badly and was having trouble focussing.

"This is one of them. This is an outlaw, one of the people who mercilessly killed Tim. What should we do with her?"

"Throw her over the side!" shouted a voice from the crowd.

"Kill her. Kill 'em all!" shouted Christopher.

Harry and Jackson were shocked as the chorus of voices clamouring for her death rose. Lazarus let it reach a crescendo before drawing the sword across Glenda's throat. As her blood spurted out, the voices grew into a raucous cheering. Ed and Walker were enjoying the show and didn't notice as Harry put his hand on Jackson's arm.

"Steady," he whispered. "Steady, Jackson." Harry could see the steel in Jackson's eyes. If they revealed their true intentions now they would have an angry lynch mob on their backs and they would be as dead as Glenda within minutes.

Glenda still stood with her arms locked in the wooden stocks, but her life was nearly spent. Her knees wobbled and urine dribbled down her legs. Her last thoughts were of the mountains back home. She forgot the zombies and the castle, the agonising death of her husband and the rape. She pictured the snow-capped mountains and the lush green fields as her blood spewed out of her neck.

Lazarus took the sword, drew it back, and with one clean slice, lopped off Glenda's head. Her body sagged and quivered as her head rolled away across the ground. Her eyes blinked twice and then froze open, a deathly glaze covering them.

Jackson looked to the ground. He wished he could block out the cheers, the horrible applause and the hurrahs that were ringing in his ears. He wished this were over with so he could find Rosa, Laurent, and Lenny, and take them back to safety. Somehow, he doubted that was going to happen. The infection coursing through his veins was growing stronger. He would not live to see daybreak tomorrow.

The gleeful hollering of the men subsided once more as Lazarus raised the sword into the air, Glenda's fresh blood trickling down it onto his arm.

"Go now, men. Go eat, drink, and rest. I suspect we will need to fight before the next day dawns. May this pathetic woman's death serve as a message to all our enemies. Blood will be spilled on this land, for you will not take our home lightly. All sentry duties will be doubled. I want extra manpower around the island, all posts guarded twenty four hours a day from now on. We will take no prisoners, men. There will be no shirking from the battle ahead. No man or woman born, coward or brave, can shun his destiny. This is our time. Nobody is going to take the Mount from me, from us. This is *our* land!"

To unified acclaim, Lazarus left the circle as the men dispersed. He thrust the sword into Glenda's decapitated head as he strode back over to Harry and Jackson.

"Ed, clear that up, then get back to the radio. I've got something to attend to. Walker, make sure the men get organised after eating. I want sentries all over the place. I do not want any nasty surprises in the night. Get Norm to see if he can get any more information from our guests in the cells. Now take these two men back up to the castle. Inspect them thoroughly for any bites or sign of infection. If they're contaminated, kill them." Lazarus marched away out of sight around the back of the pub.

As Walker prodded Harry and Jackson along back up the path to the castle, Harry began to wonder if they hadn't bitten off more than they could chew. These men were enthralled by Lazarus, hanging on his every word. Harry had no doubt that they would rather die than give up their home on the Mount. He had lost his gun and was going to have to find an opportune moment to strike. He really hoped he would get one soon. He didn't like to think of Tom fetching the others to this place, and if Jackson was inspected, then he knew what would happen. There would indeed be much blood spilled.

* * * *

Ed sank into the chair and picked up the headphones. He hated having to get his hands dirty, but accepted it was part of living on the island. It was one thing offing a zombie. It was already dead, but Glenda had been a living, breathing human being. Her body was still warm when Ed tossed it over the cliff edge into the ocean. He had refused to touch her head, using a spade to scoop it up and put it in a bag. He had thrown her head into the ocean too and watched it bob away before returning to the radio.

The old woman of the group, Malini, had brought him a meal and a couple of beers. She was a good cook and ran the pub, such as it was. She kept the place clean, cooked everyone's food and kept quiet. She was nearly sixty and overweight. Her fat bulged out the side of her food-stained sari. She was of little use other than for cooking their meals, and it was the only reason she hadn't been tossed into the cells with the others.

The radio crackled and hissed, but there was nothing. He sat listening, waiting for the voices to come back. He wondered how his family were back home. He had been closest to his elder brother Evan. They used to go surfing together until Evan had got married. Then two kids had appeared on the scene and Evan became the family man. Ed had more time for partying and women and got into a few scrapes with the law. His father bailed him out of trouble several times, but eventually it got too much and he wound his way over to England via Bali. Ed had no trouble falling in with Lazarus. Since the whole zombie thing, the world had gone crazy. Lazarus was crazy, but he kept them together. He kept everything going. Ed reclined and let his mind meander back to Australia.

The radio beeped loudly in Ed's ear and the static abruptly gave way to conversation.

"McCulloch here on HMS Daring of the British Royal Naval Force, respond please, Samson."

After a moment, Ed heard the response come through.

"McCulloch, Samson here, USS Abraham Lincoln. It's good to hear your voice - I thought we'd lost you."

"How's it going, Samson? We've been trying to reach you for hours."

"Not good, McCulloch. Things are...difficult here. How are you?"

"We're okay. We're set for the extradition tomorrow at 0730 hours. We're keeping a safe distance for now. All quiet out here in The Channel. Unfortunately, we lost two men just a few hours ago. Remember I told you about the dolphins and the attack on us? The two men who got hurt died. We're going to have a ceremony for them shortly. There's no family to take their bodies back to, so we're going to take care of it ourselves. What's your problem, Samson, what's happened?"

"Where do I start? Jesus, the shit has really hit the fan. This morning, we lost contact with the USS Wasp. No coms at all. The ship's still on our radar, but there are no noises coming from them. We don't know if it's mechanical or a technical malfunction of some sort, but we're preparing for the worst. I still have communication with Blaine, of course, on the USS Gerald Ford. He's sitting tight near the Windies waiting for us. He's running a full crew and they're itching to get cracking, but he says he'd rather wait for our backup.

"McCulloch, Blaine said he picked up a signal from the Pentagon. God knows how. I guess these new Supercarriers have better equipment than we do. We haven't had a goddamn upgrade in fifteen years. It was a recorded message. It said the US was overrun and the President and his immediate security personnel and council were being evacuated to a secure location. We have no way of knowing if they made it or not. It went on to say that many world leaders are missing, feared dead. Apparently, your PM was in Belgium, but the European Council headquarters in Brussels was swamped by those zombies. Military jets destroyed the building. There were no survivors."

Ed scribbled it all down, not daring to miss a word for fear Lazarus would find out. He heard McCulloch sigh before the American continued.

"UN estimates currently put the reanimated at something like five hundred million worldwide. Can you fucking believe that? Five hundred million! Knowing the UN that was probably a conservative estimate too. Those idiots couldn't count to three on a fucking abacus. The message ended by saying that all military personnel were to await word directly from the President imminently."

"What did he say?" asked McCulloch.

"Nothing. We haven't heard from him. We haven't heard a word from anyone. The Pentagon's recorded message was dated over two weeks ago. Who knows what's happened in the time since they sent that out."

"Jesus," said McCulloch. "We really are on our own, aren't we?"

"Not exactly, buddy."

"What do you mean?"

Samson went on. "You remember I told you we had something? We captured one of them, one of the mother-fucking alien bitches who started this thing. Picked it up near Oklahoma. Long story. Anyway, it's still alive and we're talking to it."

"Alive? What's it like? What...what did it say?"

"Not much yet, but we're working on it. Trust me, the US Army knows how to get information out of people. We'll get it. So far, it's offered very little information. It's capable of speaking English, which is handy. It was very placid, very calm – until it realised it was on a ship out in the middle of the ocean. After that, it went psycho. We've got it contained, for now, but it was not a happy bunny. It said it was in danger, because the ocean was deadly. I asked if it would prefer to be on land with six million zombies and it said yes. Told you it was psycho. It said the things from the ocean and the skies were a thousand times worse than what was on land. It said there would be dozens and dozens of them, scores, hundreds, rising from the depths. Then it clammed up."

"Samson, you called it a bitch. Are you saying it's female? Is it humanoid?"

Samson laughed. "Yeah, it's humanoid, and it's definitely a female. Of the Queen Bitch variety."

"Anything else you can tell me? What was in the ocean that it was so scared of?" asked McCulloch.

"Listen up," said Samson.

Ed furiously wrote down the conversation until they were done. He was unaware that he had been listening, and writing, for hours. It was only when they had finished and he re-read the transcript that what they had said sunk in. Ed felt a chill run across him and almost released his bowels right there and then. He let the feeling of nausea pass and then stood up clutching the papers. Ed went outside into the dark night and made straight for the castle. Lazarus had to know about this immediately.

* * * *

"You're good to go," said Walker. Harry put his shirt back on. They were in one of the rooms at the castle. Walker had taken them both into one of the bedrooms. Jackson was finding it hard to focus on his surroundings, having to concentrate on his breathing.

Harry noticed the amazing variety and multitude of weapons still adorning the walls: battle axes, war hammers, crossbows, swords, bayonets, spears, daggers, maces and more. It was a treasure trove of antiquated weapons, suited to the bloodthirsty and the violent. Harry would quite happily have taken any of them at that point in time, but annoyingly, Walker was holding a gun and any attempt to grab one of the weapons so tantalisingly close would end in failure.

"Look, I need some fresh air, can I go outside for a moment?" asked Harry.

"No, wait over there." Walker prodded Harry with the gun and made him go sit on the bed. "You. Jackson. Take off your shirt."

"Now hang on," said Harry. "He's an old man, he just..."

"It's okay, Harry," said Jackson dejectedly. "Mr Walker, there's no need." He rolled up his trouser leg and exposed the bitten skin underneath, showcasing the boils and blisters that covered his shin.

"Holy shit, you've been bitten," said Walker. He stepped back and cocked the gun.

"Wait, hang on," said Harry. "We can sort this out."

"You knew about this, didn't you," said Walker.

"No, no, I didn't. Look, we can sort this out, Walker."

"Shut up and sit down. If I hear another word out of you I'm going to kill the both of you."

Walker kept the gun pointed at them and walked over to the door. He opened it halfway and called out. "Hey, Norm, get up here."

Moments later, Norm appeared in the doorway.

"Go get Lazarus, right now. Tell him it's an emergency."

Norm saw the gun that Walker was holding and frowned. "But I'm busy interrogating the guests. I'm supposed to..."

"Go get him, now!" yelled Walker.

Norm disappeared and Walker rested in the doorway, his strong back on the wooden frame. "I don't know what the hell is going on here, but you two can answer to Lazarus."

Norm came crashing downstairs and Lazarus was right behind him.

"Well?" said Lazarus looking at Walker.

"Harry's clean, but the old man, Jackson, is infected."

Lazarus pushed the door open and looked at them. Harry and Jackson both sat on the bed, their hands clasped. Harry stared defiantly back at Lazarus, but Jackson's head hung down. It was too much effort to keep holding it up. The play was over and they had lost.

"I thought we weren't going to have a problem, gentlemen?" said Lazarus unsheathing a sword from its scabbard on the wall. "I thought we might understand each other. We still haven't heard from Honok and it's getting late. I suppose we won't be seeing him again eh? Not that you would know anything about it, of course. Just like you didn't know you were infected?"

"I kept it to myself," said Jackson. He looked up at Lazarus.

Harry noticed that Jackson's eyes were sunken, even paler now than they had looked just ten minutes ago. It was as if the infection was finally catching up with him. Now the pretence was over, Jackson's willpower had ebbed away. His body was flushed with the infection and his brain was telling him to give up. His wife, Mary, was calling to him. Oh, how he longed to see her again.

"I got bitten a few hours ago, but I didn't tell Harry. I wanted to make sure he was safe. Look after him for me, please."

Lazarus ran his tongue across his bottom teeth. Could he trust them? Could he trust Harry? They *had* brought Shane back. Admittedly, Shane had died not long afterwards, but they had tried. They had willingly given up their guns too. It seemed the only real problem was with Jackson.

Harry watched as Jackson stood up. He wanted to reach out to his friend. He wanted to tell him it would be okay, but he knew it wouldn't be. He wished he could take away Jackson's infection, take him back home to his wife before all this had begun. He knew how much Jackson missed Mary.

Jackson cleared his throat and did his top button up. He stiffened his back and wet his fingers, then flattened down his hair. His knees were trembling and it was all he could do to not faint on the spot. His brain was fuzzy, his vision more so. Sweat dripped down the nape of his neck, soaking into the oversized flannel shirt he wore. He could literally feel the blisters on his skin popping. Despite the pain, he looked at Lazarus. "So what's it to be?"

"Come here, Harry." Lazarus held out the sword and passed it to Harry. "Do it."

Harry took the sword in his shaking hands. The handle was carved and embedded with three small emeralds. He looked up at Lazarus. Harry had faced down some tough criminals in his career: violent thugs, career criminals and the mentally insane. Yet never before had he felt such fear in the presence of a man.

"I can't, he's...he's my friend. I already had to put my son down. Don't make me do this…"

"Harry, in case you are hard of hearing, let me repeat myself. We are at war. The men on this island are soldiers. This island has seen a lot of blood spilled over the decades and it will see much more. If you are not with us, you are against us. Mr Walker and I are going to stand outside this room with the guns. When you are done, you can come out. If you come out alone, you are free to stay here with us. If you do not...well you saw what I do to my enemies at the meeting earlier."

Lazarus turned and left the room. Walker grinned at Harry and then followed him.

The door shut and Harry listened for the sound of footsteps, hoping they were bluffing, but there were none. Lazarus and Walker were waiting, as they said they would, right outside the room. Harry turned around to face Jackson. He still held the sword but lowered it to the floor. "Jackson I won't do it. There must be another way," he said.

Jackson could hear the desperation in Harry's voice. "I'm sorry about your son, Harry, but at least you got to say goodbye." Suddenly, Jackson fell to the floor and heaved. He spilled his guts on the floorboards. His vomit was mostly blood. He stayed there on his knees, unable to drag his body up again. "Tell everyone I said goodbye. I knew this was a one-way trip. Thank Tom for me. If it wasn't for him we wouldn't have gotten half as far as we have. Tell..."

Harry watched sorrowfully as Jackson dry-retched three times, unable to bring anything else up from his empty stomach except bile and drops of dark, red blood.

"Do it quickly," breathed Jackson. "Save Rosa. Save Laurent and Lenny. Do it quickly, Harry. Please."

Harry felt the quiver of his throat and the spasms in his stomach as he fought the urge to let forth his own wretched vomit. He raised the sword and let it hover in the air just above Jackson's bowed head. The three emeralds glimmered in the moonlight that shone through the window. Harry took in a deep breath. He raised the sword up high and tears formed in his eyes. "God bless you. Goodbye, Jackson."

CHAPTER FIFTEEN

Mac and Jessica were behind the rose bushes, watching the gathering zombies from their secluded vantage point, when they heard the throb of an engine approaching. Alerted by the unusual noise, they looked for its source. They could not see the road though as the garden centre fence had been surrounded entirely by zombies. With no other action in Longrock, the dead had finally all found their way here.

"Who is that?" said Mac.

Jessica strained to see, but could only hear the rumble of the engine. "I don't know, but I hope it's Tom back with the others. Come on, we need to clear a path for him."

Moira and Jimmy were on the other side of the centre. They heard the engine too just as Jessica came running up to them.

"We think it's probably Tom. We need to clear a way through for him to get to the gate."

"Probably? What if it's not?" said Jimmy. "What if it's someone else? We shouldn't take chances, we need to be careful. You heard what Mac said about those guys. They took his two friends and never came back."

"Shut up and help Jimmy," said Moira. She had been sitting with him most of the day, monitoring the outside, making sure the dead did not get through the fence. It was certainly wobbling with so many pressed up against it, but it was holding firm. Jimmy tried to talk to her, but she closed him down. She could tell he was weak. She pressed him about how he got out of his home earlier, but he wouldn't say. He steadfastly refused to be drawn on his background or what he intended to do. He told her he wanted to stay with them, get to the boat and that was it. Moira had her suspicions that Jimmy played foul in finding them, but she had no proof. The more time she spent with him, the more repulsive she found him.

They ran back to Mac and picked up the assorted tools they had gathered there: shears, cutters, hammers and spades.

Jessica picked up a bow-saw. "Jimmy, you go alert the others, then get back here. Everyone else follow me."

As Jimmy gratefully ran back inside, Jessica, Moira and Mac jogged over to a corner of the fence. The zombies were squashed against it, their hands and arms squeezing through the small gaps trying to get inside. Grotesque faces looked at the trio, teeth gnashing as they pressed harder against the fence.

"Let's make some noise," said Jessica, thrusting the bow-saw at an outstretched arm. The guillotined limb fell to the ground and Mac and Moira joined in. Mac jammed the ratchet loppers through the gaps in the fence, splintering skulls and bursting eyeballs. Moira took a claw-hammer to anything protruding into the garden centre. As they worked, they shouted and screamed, attracting more and more of the dead. Blood seeped under the fence and pooled at their feet. Occasionally, Mac would manage to jam the loppers through a zombie's head and it would drop to the ground, finally at rest. Another immediately replaced it, however, and they kept up their war-cry, inflicting as much damage on the walking dead as they could.

"It's working, guys, keep going!" shouted Heidi. She had raced out when Jimmy had told them Tom might be back with the others. Jimmy stayed inside, deciding he was better off inside in case of any problems out there surrounded by the dead.

Armed with a pair of long-handled shears, Heidi stood in the centre of the gardening section, watching as the zombies slowly swept around the fence toward the commotion on the far side. The engine noise suddenly increased and Heidi watched as an ambulance careered and slewed through the dead, their bodies exploding on impact. As blood and tissue rained down on the ambulance, it continued down the side of the fence, finally skidding to a halt just in front of the gate.

The driver's door opened and Heidi saw a dumpy man get out. She stood by the gate holding the shears aloft. "Who are you?" she asked, aware they didn't have much time before some of the zombies realised what was happening.

"Never mind that, just open the damn gate!" shouted Tom as he got out the other side, pointing a pistol at Honok.

A wave of relief washed over Heidi as she saw Tom, and she opened the gate. Tom pushed Honok through roughly and he fell to the ground. Heidi locked the gate quickly behind them, slamming the bolts into place before the dead could reach inside.

"Oh, Tom, I'm so pleased you're back!" Heidi said throwing her arms around him.

"Me too," said Tom before releasing Heidi. "This is Honok and he's got a lot of explaining to do. Get inside."

Tom waved the gun at the small man and they began walking inside. Mac, Moira and Jessica threw down their tools and rushed over to Tom, leaving the dead piled up at the fence.

"Where's everyone else? What happened?" said Mac.

Tom looked at him. Mac was covered in gore, fresh blood dripping from his overalls. "Here, take this and get everyone inside," he said giving Mac the gun.

As they trooped in, Tom took Jessica to one side. He paused by the door, out of sight of the zombies, watching as the others went in.

"Where's Rosa?" Jessica asked nervously. She almost dare not ask. All she knew was that Rosa wasn't here and that meant bad news.

"It's not good, I'm afraid. We got to the Mount and found this dude. He was with another man, but I shot him. Harry and Jackson have gone over to the Mount trying to find her. I don't really know what's happened. I waited for them to come back, but...Rosa is quite probably in a lot of trouble. Honok is not a pleasant chap and the things he's told me...look, I'll fill you in with the rest inside, but whatever Honok says, take it with a pinch of salt. He'll try to stir us up. He's a piece of work, but I'll sort him out. Just trust me, Jess, we'll get her back, I promise."

Jessica felt shell-shocked. She wanted to cry, scream, dance up and down on the spot, but most of all, she wanted Rosa back. Tom led her back inside where he found the others already interrogating Honok.

"Where are they? What did you do with my friends?" Mac was holding the gun to Honok's head, furious and frustrated at the lack of response.

Honok was sat on the sofa and smiling. He could tell Mac was mad, but he wouldn't shoot him. He wanted answers first. Honok had the power in this little game and he would drag it out as long as it took. "Your friends? I'm not sure...there are so many people on the Mount, I lose track. What were their names again?" he asked innocently.

"Sally and Keisha - the two girls you picked up outside here a few days ago. You *know* who I'm talking about, motherfucker."

The room was quiet, waiting for Honok to answer. The group stood watching as Mac kept the gun pointed at Honok's head.

"Oh *those* two," Honok said exaggerating his words, as if he had only just remembered them. "Yeah, we fucked the white one and then killed her. I'm not sure about the nigger. I suspect she joined her friend in a watery grave. Next question?"

Tom grabbed the gun off Mac before he could pull the trigger. Mac was outraged and landed a punch squarely on Honok's ugly squat face. Honok wiped the blood from his lip and laughed.

"What? Jealous? Hoping they'd come back for a little *nigger-love*, is that it?" said Honok sniggering.

Mac was well built and had spent his working days doing hard physical work. He raised his clenched fist again and punched Honok again. As he prepared to strike again, Tom held him back.

"Leave it, Mac, we'll deal with him. We need to get some straight answers first. You can beat the living crap out of him later."

Fuming, Mac stormed out of the room, slamming the door behind him.

"I'll go," said Christina, following Mac.

"Right, Honok, let's try this again," said Tom pointing the gun at Honok once more. "I need to talk to my friends, so you're going to be quiet for a minute. Understood? When I'm through, I'm going to ask you some questions and you're going to answer. Right?"

Honok snorted. "If you're going to kill me, you may as well get it over with now. I'm not going to tell you anything, so go ahead, pull the trigger."

Tom stared at Honok and then passed the gun to Moira. "Hold this, will you please, Moira?"

"With pleasure." Moira sat on the worktop with the gun aimed squarely at Honok's eyes.

She had not fired one before, but if it came to it, Tom knew she would not hesitate. He wiped the sweat from his brow and walked out of the restroom. Ten seconds later he came back in carrying a small pair of pliers. As he walked over to the sofa, the smile faded from Honok's face. Tom crouched down before him so he could look directly into Honok's eyes. He smelt bad and Tom wanted to throw him to the dead, but he couldn't. First, he needed information.

"No one is going to be pulling any triggers for some time, Honok." Tom waved the pliers in front of Honok's concerned face. "I imagine these could be used for a variety of purposes, wouldn't you say? I mean they're so dexterous, so easy to use. I could probably pull out all your teeth before I even get to snapping off your fingers and toes. Not to mention any other *small* appendages on your body."

Honok said nothing.

"Right, I'm glad we understand each other at last. Heidi, there's plenty of rope out there, can you get some and bring it back here. Tie Mr Honok up nice and tight please. I don't want him running off anywhere."

"Sure, Tom," said Heidi. She touched his arm as she left.

"Tom, what the hell is going on?" said Jessica. "I feel like my heart is going to explode I'm so bloody worried. What happened?"

Tom nodded. "Sit down. I want everyone to know so just hold on a second."

Jessica found a seat next to Caterina whilst Jimmy cowered in the corner, unsure what to make of this new stranger. Moira stayed where she was with the gun in her hands. Heidi reappeared with a bundle of rope and proceeded to tie Honok up with a grimace on her face. She bound his arms and legs tightly as Tom asked.

"He smells like dog shit," she said as she bound his hands and feet.

Christina entered the room with Mac behind her.

"I'm cool, don't worry. I'm not going to kill him, yet. I want some answers too," said Mac, leaning against the wall. He crossed his arms and stared at Honok.

"Okay," began Tom, "here's what I can tell you. Harry and Jackson are on the Mount. We made it back to the van, managed to get hold of a few guns each from the back, and got out of Longrock. That was the easy part. I think all the zombies in the vicinity are here. Once we left the town, they thinned out and we hardly saw any. We saw some freaky shit on the way, but that's another story. Once we found the ambulance, we waited. There was a tunnel over to the island so Harry and Jackson waited for a chance to get in.

"Honok and another man came out, so I started shooting. I shot the other one and led Honok away from the tunnel so Harry and Jackson could get in. They're over there now. I pretended I was out of ammo and this sucker fell for it. We waited a while for Harry and Jackson in the ambulance, but they didn't show. I *persuaded* Honok to drive us back here and so here we are."

"So when are Harry and Jackson coming back?" asked Christina.

"And the others and Rosa, what about her?" Jessica felt as though she was going to throw up, so she stood up, just in case she had to run to the bathroom.

"Laurent? Lenny? Glenda? Any news? Do we know where they are?" asked Caterina. "Shit, Tom, doesn't sound like it went well."

"We have to go get them. I promised Harry I would get them if he failed to show. We have a few guns left. He and Jackson are over on the Mount with everyone else."

"Not quite everyone," said Honok. "Your friend, the old man in the pyjamas? You won't be seeing him again. I'm pretty sure one of your lot got eaten by the zombies out there too. I saw what was left of a man at the petrol station. I think I've still got a piece of him on the bottom of my boot actually." Honok started wiping his feet on the floor.

"Who was it?" asked Heidi. "What did he look like?"

"He didn't *look* like anything, girly, he was dead. There wasn't much left of him, quite frankly."

"Tell us who you ran into at the petrol station," said Tom. "Who did you pick up there and take back to the Mount?"

Honok sighed. "Okay, there were two women, one old and one young. There was the old man in pyjamas and one other man. I forget their names. Who cares anyway? The man spoke with an accent. I think he might be French or something."

"And that was it?"

"Yep. The older woman was passed out. The younger girl, the one with the blonde hair, boy, she's a looker. She's going to have a *lot* of fun with my friends." Honok laughed despite the pain from his lip that had split when Mac punched him.

"Oh God," said Heidi. She started crying and ran out of the room, swiftly followed by Christina.

"Jesus Christ, you're just an animal. What do you mean 'fun'? Rosa wouldn't be interested in the likes of you," spat Jessica.

"Really? She told me she was looking for a man, a *big* man to satisfy her. She told me…"

Tom grabbed the gun off Moira and smashed it across Honok's already bleeding nose. He heard the bone crack and Honok bent over, shouting in pain, cupping his bloody nose in his hands.

"You're going about this all wrong, Honok. Lies we don't need, facts we do." Tom pulled Honok's tied hands away from his face. "You say anything like that again, if I hear any more racist comments, anything at all that I do not like, you'll have more than a bloody nose."

Tom handed the gun back to Moira. "You'd better hold onto this. I don't think I can trust myself."

"So should we go now?" asked Mac. "Let's tool up and go get our friends back. This piece of shit isn't going to help us."

"We can't go now," answered Tom, watching Jessica fight back tears. He had not seen her cry once since they had met. She was so strong he was surprised to see her looking so fragile. "It's nearly dark out and getting there past all those zombies outside is not going to be easy. Getting across to the Mount isn't easy either. They know about us and will likely be on their guard."

"You won't be able to use the tunnel," said Honok holding his broken nose. "Lazarus will have it well guarded. You go down there and it'll be like shooting fish in a barrel. You'll have to take your chances across the causeway."

"What's that?" asked Caterina.

"He means across the beach basically," said Mac. "At low tide you can cut across the sand to get out to the Mount."

"So when's low tide?" Caterina looked at the clock on the wall as if it had the answers.

"Dawn," replied Mac. "Tom's right, it's too late to go now. Damn it." Mac hit the desk in frustration as he realised they were going to have to wait another night.

"Tom, we can't wait, we have to go now, you heard him," said Jessica. "Think what they might be doing to Rosa, Laurent, or Glenda."

"Jess, we can't, think about it. I hate it as much as you, but we can spend tonight getting ready. This place is full of things we can use. We'll go at first light. Hopefully, we can still make that ship tomorrow."

"Hopefully? Oh God, it keeps getting better doesn't it," said Caterina.

"I have to agree with Tom. Whatever happens, whether we make it to the rendezvous or not, we *have* to get to the Mount. I'm not leaving without everyone else, but we can't go tonight," said Moira. "We should go at dawn."

"Honok, how many men are there on the island?" asked Tom.

"A thousand."

"A thousand? Is that so? Honok, I've just about had enough of your shit." Tom brandished the pliers and Honok shrunk back into the sofa.

"Okay, okay, thirty. Give or take, there's about thirty of us."

"And this Lazarus, who is he?" Tom knew it was better to know your enemy, and be prepared for who the fight would be against.

Honok smiled. "He's our leader. He is in charge of everything. He will kill you. He will kill all of you."

"Let's just shoot this fucker and be done with it," said Moira hopping down off the table.

"Not yet," countered Tom. "Honok here is going to tell us much more. He is going to actually answer my questions. I want to know about this Lazarus. I want to know who is on that island and what they're like, what their skills and their weaknesses are. I want to know the layout of the castle. I want to know where they keep their prisoners, as I suspect that is where we'll find Rosa and Laurent and the others. I want to know the best way onto the Mount from the causeway, where our best opportunity is to get in unnoticed. Honok is going to be very helpful."

"Am I, fuck. I'm not helping you. Fuck you, *Tommy*." Honok wiped his blood smeared face and looked around the room. All eyes were staring back at him.

Tom sighed. "Fine, we'll do it your way. Moira, Mac, can you help gather up the weapons. Anything sharp and pointy will be fine. Caterina, I don't want you exerting yourself, so maybe you can see if Heidi and Christina are okay. Jimmy, you need to go with Mac and make sure the fence is secure. We need to be able to get out to the ambulance first thing tomorrow. Jess, can you gather as many blankets or rugs as you can. We'll be spending the night here and we need as good a rest as we can get."

As everyone started shuffling out of the room, beginning their tasks, Jessica paused. "What are you going to do, Tom?"

Tom reached down to Honok and pulled on the ropes Heidi had tied around him earlier. He drew them tight so Honok's hands and feet couldn't move. Honok protested, but Tom ignored him. "I'm going to have a chat with Honok." He placed the pliers in the palm of his hand and looked at Jessica. "Close the door on your way out, Jess."

She smiled and did so as she left, leaving it open just a crack so she would be able to hear Honok's screams.

CHAPTER SIXTEEN

Harry swirled his whisky around in the glass and then swallowed it down, enjoying the burn in his throat.

"It's good stuff, Harry. Sixteen years old. Just how I like 'em," laughed Lazarus.

Harry gave a half-hearted smile, but was in no mood for company, especially that of a deranged, murderous psychopath.

"Come now, Harry, I'm sorry about your friend, but you have to know, once the infection has gotten hold of you there's no way back. I'm afraid it was for the best. You wouldn't have wanted your friend to turn into one of those things, would you? He wasn't the first and he won't be the last. One death is a tragedy, one million is a statistic."

"No, er, of course not. It's just hard to accept, you know." Every muscle in Harry's body told him to get out. Glenda and Jackson were dead and here he was sitting in the man's home, drinking whisky with their murderer. He had been forced to put a blade in Jackson's head and he would never forget it. Harry looked across at the sword leaning against the wall. It still glistened with Jackson's blood and he felt guilt surge through his body. He should've done more. Could he have done more? He hadn't even found Rosa, Laurent or Lenny yet. He had seemingly gained Lazarus' trust, but he was no nearer to helping his friends. He was going to have to go along with Lazarus for now.

"Is he going to stand there all night?" asked Harry.

Walker was standing behind Lazarus, watching Harry intently. Lazarus had insisted that Harry join him for a drink before retiring for the night. He was inquisitive about the newcomer, but still wanted Walker around for reassurance.

"Walker, go outside, will you? We'll be fine here."

"What about the preparations for tomorrow, sir?"

"We're ready, Walker. Everyone is on guard. All we have to do now is sit and wait. They'll come to us."

Lazarus watched as Walker left the room and stationed himself outside the door. He was loyal, like a pet dog. If he threw him a bone, Walker would get down on all fours and bring it back in his mouth if Lazarus told him to.

"Harry, you must stay with us. We need men, good strong men, and I think you'll fit in here. There's food, shelter...and if you've survived out there on the road like you say, then I know you can handle yourself. Hell, I saw how you handled your old buddy Jackson. What do you say?"

Harry thought about throwing his whisky glass into Lazarus' face. He wondered if that would buy him enough time to grab the emerald-encrusted sword three feet away and thrust it into Lazarus' heart. He glanced at the pistol resting in Lazarus' lap and knew it would not. If Harry died now, then who knew what fate would befall Rosa, Laurent and Lenny.

"I'm not sure. I mean I'm not exactly used to this kind of hospitality, you know. Since it all began, we've lived on the run, hiding anywhere we could. It seems strange to be able to sit here and relax and not worry about looking over my shoulder."

Lazarus reached for the whisky and poured himself and Harry another shot. "I understand, truly I do. I used to be alone like you. Always looking over my shoulder, wondering where life was taking me, what the point of it all was. *Then* the infection broke out. This place, Harry, this island, this rock, it's everything to me. I have made it strong again, the fortress it used to be. It's safe here. The men on this island will defend it to the last."

"What are the men like? I haven't really met many of them yet and it'd be good to know who I'd be living with."

"Walker you've met, Norm too, briefly. They used to be on the inside, just petty stuff, but enough for me to know they needed a leader. They were rudderless until I came along and gave them something to fight for. The men are an assortment of characters as you'll see. It's true some have done time for some serious crimes. But they are fighters and they are loyal to me. Most of them are lawbreakers, hard men: Honok, Shane, Christopher to mention a few. But I don't care what a man did before he found himself on the Mount. A man's past is his own. What matters now is the future. Where's yours, Harry? Are you always going to be on the run, living from one day to the next? What's the point in that?"

Harry remembered how difficult it had been these last few weeks, going from door to door, scavenging for food, and existing on meagre rations. Then he remembered the ship due tomorrow and what he was here for. If Lazarus wanted to make the Mount his home, then he was welcome to it. Harry's future involved getting off this island and away from all the death, not staying and looking for it.

"You're right, of course. I hadn't really had a chance to stop and think about everything." Harry could see how men fell under Lazarus' spell. He was a good talker, easy with his words. He was physically imposing too with his jet black hair and dark eyes.

"You should, Harry. Stop here with us and think about it. You don't need me to tell you that there is no going back. The human race is changed forever. When you look back now at the things we did, the stupid things men wasted their time on. Take this glass, for example. Have you heard of planned obsoletion, Harry?" Lazarus emptied the glass of its contents and threw it against the wall where it shattered.

"We create things and we destroy them. We build things to amuse ourselves, to keep busy, to find something else to spend money on. Why? We could've forged great things, but we kept churning out drivel, useless things that wouldn't last, things designed to break. We actually created things on purpose and invested our energy and efforts into something that was *designed* to fail. Just so we could do it all over again, spend more money and keep the merry–go-round turning. What a short-sighted, egotistical race we had become.

"Harry, this life ahead of us is different. There'll be no more flat-screen televisions, no more holidays in the Bahamas, no more new and improved washing powder, no pizzas, no laptops with even bigger memories or designer clothing with even bigger price labels. We shall exist as we were meant to, living off the land, forging alliances and killing our enemies with our bare hands. We have been given a chance, Harry, another chance at *life*.

"There is a tale of a man who was resurrected by Jesus after being dead for four days. Do you think he went back to work after that? Do you think he would've gone back to the office or the sweatshop and carried on as before? No, when you get a second chance, you take it with both hands. That is what I am doing, Harry."

Lazarus plucked another glass from a nearby bureau and poured himself another drink. He sat down again, resting the pistol back in his lap, one hand resting on it whilst the other held his drink.

"You're a very unique man, Lazarus," said Harry.

"Thank you. I would hate to be just another sheep."

"How did you know this was the place to come? I mean, I came across it by chance, but I'm assuming you didn't?"

"I was well schooled, Harry. I have my father to thank for that, at least. That, and my name. My father drummed a lot into me as a child. He was a professor, quite knowledgeable about every topic you chose to question him on. Apart from football – sport was banned in my house, denounced as puerile by my father. He was an intelligent man that's for sure. I swear there wasn't a book he didn't read. He taught me about the Mount. Many times he told me about the island's history and the battles fought over this place. Its strength is its position. I knew it would be the best place to go to when the zombies started appearing.

"There are thousands out there even just within a few miles. No doubt the cities are overrun, but once the food supply dwindles, the zombies will search further for food. They are in houses, fields, gardens, everywhere. Henry Pomeroy survived a siege here in the fifteenth century - admittedly not against an army of the undead - but if he can do it with lesser resources, then so can I. Nobody is taking the Mount. I won't break and I won't bend."

Harry was relieved when a knock on the door interrupted Lazarus' speech. He was trying to find a way to excuse himself so he could look around the island and find the others. There was only so much madness he could listen to in one evening.

Walker strode in with another man who was grasping a huge bundle of papers. "Ed wants to see you, sir. I told him you were busy, but…"

"You have to read this, sir, it's the navy, they've…" Ed stopped short when he saw Harry.

"It's alright, Ed. Walker, would you find a bed for Harry. I think he'll be staying the night. When you've shown him where he can stay, he's free to do whatever he wishes. Perhaps take him to the entertainment?"

Harry picked up the emerald-encrusted sword as he left, following Walker out of the room and wondering what was so important that Lazarus had to know straight away. The other man had mentioned the navy. Did they know the ship was coming tomorrow? Or was there something else?

Walker led Harry out of the castle into the cool dusk. Harry was already familiarising himself with the layout of the grounds. He knew the path they were on led to the other houses and pub. They passed the stocks and Harry glanced at them. There was no trace of Glenda now, just a smattering of dried blood on the ground.

Harry found himself standing outside one of the stone houses and Walker took him inside. It smelt like a toilet, but there were two beds in the corner.

"This was Shane and Tim's quarters," said Walker. "You can sleep here tonight."

"Thanks." Harry put the sword down on one of the beds adorned with thick grey blankets.

"You won't need that here. You should put it back," said Walker. "We don't need weapons on the Mount, unless you're on active guard duty. It's safe here. There is no infection, as you know." Walker grinned maliciously at Harry.

"Oh right, of course. I'll take it back tomorrow. I'm just so used to sleeping with a weapon by my side. If I can just keep it for now?"

"Well, take care, wouldn't want you having an accident in the middle of the night and falling on your own sword." Walker went to the door and stood in the doorway, letting the cold air sweep into the dark house. "Lazarus said you could enjoy the entertainment if you like. We've had our fill today so you'll probably get her to yourself tonight. If you feel like it, make your way back up to the castle and then down the stairs. First on the left are the cells. Norm will let you in."

Walker abruptly left, leaving Harry alone. The house was basic, but would serve as a bed for the night. Harry explored quickly once he was alone. There was a bathroom, a small kitchen, and another bedroom at the rear of the building. There was nothing of use and he sank down onto the bed next to his sword.

Entertainment? Walker had said he would get her to himself. Who were these barbarians? He knew Tom would come back for them, but it was getting dark. Harry doubted that Tom would be foolish enough to try staging a rescue at night. What with the zombies and strange creatures out there, they would be lucky to get out of Longrock. Harry knew he was going to have to do some exploring on his own. Lazarus seemed to trust him enough, at least for now. He picked up the sword, but it was heavy and he might need it tomorrow. If he went walking around with it now, Walker would take it off him for sure. He found some rusty cutlery in the kitchen and stashed a small knife in his belt, tucking his shirt over it so it was out of sight. He left the sword lying at his bedside, still coated in Jackson's blood.

Harry left the house and looked around. In the windows of the houses he saw a few candles burning and figures walking around inside. There was laughter coming from the pub, but he had no inclination to join them. He wanted to take a look around the island whilst he was free. Nobody else was outside. They were all inside in the warmth. Harry intended to retrace his steps up to the castle and check it out, but before then he needed to know if there was anything or anyone else on the island. Was it really safe, truly free from infection?

Harry walked around, occasionally tripping on an outcrop of granite, ignoring the cold air that accompanied him. He tried not to think about Jackson. Did Lazarus bury his dead? They wouldn't leave Jackson to rot in that room, surely? No, he suspected that Lazarus had little time for things that were 'useless.' Jackson would probably be buried or burned along with Shane.

Harry walked slowly and carefully, making sure he took everything in. Shortly, he came across a set of steps leading down the face of a cliff and carefully followed them down. They seemed to lead straight into the ocean, which made no sense at all. He kept following them. He hadn't made it to DI in the Met' without following his instincts occasionally. At the base of the cliff was a cave. Harry saw a rope nailed to the inner wall of the cave and took hold of it. The cave swallowed him into its darkness and then Harry saw it: a boat.

It was difficult to see clearly in the fading light, but there was a small mast and it looked seaworthy. It was moored up and appeared to be deserted. Harry left it alone and began ascending the steps carved into the cliff once more. He assumed that Lazarus had the boat there just in case. As much as he liked to think the Mount was defended by his men, it was not a complete fortress. Nowhere was impregnable.

On his way back to the castle, Harry saw nobody outside. Approaching the castle entrance, he saw two sentries up on the turret and two more by the castle's main doors. No doubt there were more around, keeping watch over the whole island. He remembered the instructions given to him by Walker and found the passageway leading down to the cells. As he descended the stairway, he wondered what he was going to find in there. He hoped Rosa wasn't in there. The cells were cold and damp. No good could come of her being locked away down in a dungeon with these people. Part of him hoped that she was in there. Searching the rest of the castle would be very difficult without being spotted.

"Did Lazarus send you?" asked Norm, getting up as Harry entered the cells.

"Yeah, he said I could come by."

"Knock yourself out. She'll be co-operative. If that other one gives you any trouble, just shout and I'll shut him up." Norm raised a fist. His meaning was clear.

Harry could see two figures in the cells, lying in the shadows, not making any sound. He took a few steps closer, past the first empty cell, and saw a woman lying on the floor. It was unmistakeably Rosa. Harry felt for the knife in his back pocket – he could slit Norm's throat in seconds. The obese man would not be able to outrun him, but he might raise the alarm. Getting back to the tunnel armed with only a knife was a suicidal idea.

"Hey, Norm, I forgot to say, Walker said you should call it quits for the night. He put me on guard duty, said I should make myself useful if I'm going to be joining you. He said you could have a night off."

Norm looked at Harry suspiciously. "Really? He didn't mention anything to me. Maybe I should go check."

"I wouldn't if I were you. He didn't look too happy when I mentioned I was coming here. Did you piss him off or something?" Harry took a gamble that Walker's name would carry credence and weight to his argument.

Norm grumbled something under his breath and rubbed his jaw. "Fine. This lot are more hassle than they're worth anyway. Good luck to you." He fished a set of keys out of his pocket and tossed them to Harry. Then he turned away and trudged upstairs.

When Norm was safely gone, Harry hurried to unlock Rosa's cell. He raced in and knelt down beside her, gently shaking her. "Rosa? Rosa, it's Harry."

She stirred and groaned. Harry took his jacket off and covered her with it. She was naked and it didn't take a genius to work out what had happened to her. There was a soiled mattress in one corner of the cell and a bucket in the other. The whole place stank of sex and excrement.

"Harry?" Rosa opened her left eye. Her right eye was swollen shut and she didn't have the energy to force it open. Her lip was split and her once blonde hair was now a dirty grey, tousled and greasy. She offered him a faint smile and he sat down beside her, cradling her head on his legs.

"Oh, Rosa, I'm so sorry we didn't get here sooner. How are you holding up?"

She shrugged and closed her one good eye. She didn't even have the energy to speak.

"Harry? Is that you?" came a voice from the other cell.

"Laurent? Thank God, I found you. Yes, it's me, Harry. Laurent, what the hell happened to you. Where's Lenny?"

"I promised I'd look after him, but I couldn't. I let him down. I let everyone down."

Harry heard a shuffling, scraping sound and then Laurent's face appeared at the cell bars. He too had been beaten and not just with fists and boots. Laurent's head looked like it had been used as a football. There were deep lacerations across his face and neck and his right ear was hanging on by a thread. Harry felt anger rising in his gut.

"There were too many of them, Harry. They threw us down here in the cells. That man, Norm, beat me. Rosa too. Kept trying to ask us where we'd come from and who we were with. We didn't say a thing, I swear. Rosa was so strong. I don't know how she did it. Glenda was here too, but they took her away. Do you know what happened to her?"

"She's dead, Laurent. They killed her."

"Good God. Poor Heidi. First her father, then her mother. These people are sick, Harry. They're evil. That Lazarus...he abused her and then he threw her down here with me. He sent his men in here to her. They raped her. They forced me to watch, but...I lost count, Harry, I lost count of how many men came and raped her and beat her and..."

Laurent began crying. He shrank back into the dark of his own cell so that Harry could not see his tears. He had managed to be strong all day, not showing emotion or weakness, trying to help Rosa. Now Harry was here, he felt like someone else could finally take charge and carry some of the burden. He tried to look after her, but he failed. He wept for her and his broken promises.

"I'm going to get you out, Laurent, all of you," said Harry after a while. "You, Rosa and Lenny. Where is he? Are they keeping him somewhere else?"

Laurent snorted, holding back a laugh and then immediately regretted it. Any movement just caused him pain. "No, he's dead too."

"What? How?"

"Lazarus killed him. I assume you've met? Charming man. He killed Lenny in cold blood. Made us stand there and watch. He took a club and battered him to death right there in front of us."

Harry rubbed his temples. Glenda and Lenny had died at the hands of this man. He should go up there now and run him through, to hell with the consequences. Harry looked down at Rosa. She needed him, now more than ever before. He couldn't leave her like this.

"Where's everyone else? What happened after we left the house?" Laurent's voice was fragile.

Rosa came to, but lay quiet and still, unable to speak, unwilling to move. Any slight movement only brought her pain.

"We ran into some trouble," said Harry. "Everyone else is set up back in Longrock in an out of town shopping centre. They're safe for now."

"Jess?" whispered Rosa.

"She's fine." Harry stroked her hair softly, holding her head in his lap.

"So you came on your own?" Laurent thought about sitting up, but realised he didn't have the strength. As he pushed himself up his head swam and he lay back down.

"No, Tom and Jackson came with me. Tom's gone back to the others. He knows to get help if we don't come back right away. He was going to wait a couple of hours and then go get help."

"And Jackson? Did he go back with Tom?"

Harry had hoped he wouldn't have to tell them now, not while they were so weak. He wasn't prepared to lie to his friends though. "No, he was with me. He...back in Longrock he got bitten. He came here with me, helped me get in."

"He's infected and they let him in? They let him stay? Are they helping him?" Laurent crawled forward again to the edge of the cell and his blue eyes stared at Harry who dropped his head. Laurent knew then that Jackson was dead.

"Once they found out he was infected...he's gone now. He's with his wife at last. I think he's happy now. He's at peace."

Laurent wanted to scream and roar, but all he could manage was a single tear. He felt so utterly lost that tears were useless. Laurent felt numb. "It's not fair. Poor Jackson."

Harry looked down at Rosa. She had fallen unconscious again. She really needed medical attention, but she wasn't going to get any in here. All Harry could do was try to comfort her. Her breathing was shallow, but her wounds were superficial. Physically, she would be able to recover, but mentally? Harry wouldn't have inflicted the torture and abuse she had suffered upon his worst enemies, except for maybe Lazarus.

"So why not get us out now?" said Laurent suddenly. "Where's Tom? Where's everyone else?" He was angry and the adrenalin gave him enough energy to sit himself upright, to push through the pain. "We could get back out the tunnel and nobody would even know. There are only three of us. We could still make it to Penzance and the ship tomorrow. What are we waiting for, Harry? Let's go!"

Harry shook his head. "It wouldn't work. Lazarus has doubled all the guards. They're everywhere: the tunnel, the castle, all over the island. The grounds are relatively clear, but there's nowhere to go. We need the tunnel to get out of here, or daylight at the very least to make it across the causeway. It would be impossible to sneak past them all."

"Fuck sneaking past them, I'll kill them!" said Laurent, his eyes blazing. "You've got a sword and you saw for yourself there are plenty more up there: swords, knives, axes, all sorts. What are you scared of, Harry? You don't know what we have gone through here. Rosa is...I mean look at her! We have to get her out of here. We can't wait any longer."

"They have *guns*, Laurent. I can't imagine what it's been like for you and Rosa, but we have to be patient. We have to wait for Tom. He'll bring the others. He's got guns now too. He'll get us out as soon as he can."

"What if Tom doesn't come?" said Laurent dejected. "What if he doesn't come, Harry?"

Harry looked down at Rosa, at her battered face and body, and held her, trying to warm her. "He'll come. He has to."

CHAPTER SEVENTEEN

Tom picked at the scab on his elbow, scratching and scratching until it came off and pus oozed from the wound. He dug a fingernail in and embraced the sweet pain it brought him. He dug his fingernail in deeper until he drew blood. It trickled down his finger and he watched as a single drop landed on the ground by his feet. The blood began to bubble as if it were being heated by an underground furnace. It spread out becoming a pool, a river, an ocean. Tom found himself swimming in an ocean of boiling blood, struggling to keep his head above the rising levels. As he flailed around in the viscous liquid something began sucking him down, tugging on his ankles. He tried to reach for something to hold onto, but there was nothing, no land, nothing solid to get hold of. He splashed around as his ankles were suddenly sucked down and he took a deep breath. As he sank beneath the blood, a zombie swam up to him, its teeth gnashing as it approached. The zombie was an old work colleague, Brad and his jaws opened to bite down on Tom's arms. Tom desperately tried to push the zombie away, but beneath the tide of red he couldn't. He opened his mouth to scream as Brad's sharp teeth bit down on his arm and blood poured into his throat.

With a start, Tom sat upright, his eyes wide open. He was sweating profusely, and looking around at his sleeping friends, realised he had the nightmare again. He glanced at the clock on the wall – five thirty. If it was the right time, it would soon be time to get up anyway if they were to make the low tide. He found it difficult getting back to sleep after the nightmares so he decided to get up.

He tiptoed out of the restroom, carefully trying not to wake any of the others. They would need their rest for later and still had time for a few more minutes precious sleep. Honok was still tied up, asleep or unconscious on the sofa, and Tom went into the garden centre, out past the large doors to the sanctity of the outdoor area. He could hear the zombies still at the fence, unable to get in. Ignoring them, he found a seat amongst some potted plants and sat down, looking up at the sky.

He hoped that Harry had succeeded in finding Rosa, Glenda, Laurent and Lenny. He knew that Jackson would be dead by now and wished him well, wherever he was. They were as well prepared as they were going to be for the day ahead. Tom hoped that the Mount wouldn't prove to be as difficult as he suspected. Who knew how long the navy would stick around? If they missed the rendezvous with it, he had no idea what they would do. His plans only extended that far.

He thought back to yesterday and the path from Longrock to the Mount. The road was fairly simple. It was almost a straight line and only a couple of miles. The difficulty was what was *on* the road. Jessica had told him about the flying creature that had attacked her and he was worried there may be more. He hadn't told her, or anyone else, about the tentacled dead rabbit they had seen. On his way back to the garden centre with Honok they had seen something else, something neither of them wished to talk about or see again.

As they had driven through Longrock, they had passed a two-headed dog. It had ignored them as it was busy with a meal. A large man, dressed in a flamboyant yellow shirt and naked from the waist down, half eaten, was in the dog's jaws, both of them. The dog, a bull mastiff, had no back legs yet clearly two heads. On its back were two small wings, covered in dirty brown fur. It was trying to fly up into the air, but it could not get more than a foot above the ground. It skittered about unevenly on the road, like a fawn on an icy lake, but it could not fly, it was too heavy. The jaws of the dog were clamped around the man's waist and refusing to let go, so every time it tried to fly it just stayed where it was. Tom watched from the ambulance as they passed it by. He'd asked Honok if he'd seen anything like that before, but it was clear from Honok's face he had not.

Tom had seen no reason to worry the others about it. This alien infection was creating not just zombies but monsters, abhorrent disgusting creatures that were putting two fingers up to nature. Tom began to think zombies weren't so bad. They weren't very intelligent, they could be distracted fairly easily and they could be put down with a clean head shot. These other things though, these bizarre beasts were becoming more and more frequent. Where they from the same infection? Was the virus or disease that reanimated humans, somehow affecting animals differently? Or was there more than one infection? What if there was a different strain? And what would it do to a human?

Tom's thought were interrupted by a booming thunderous noise from overhead. He looked up, expecting to see a dark cloud and a flash of white lightning amongst the inevitable downpour. He expected the stars would be obliterated by the oncoming storm clouds, but he saw a clear sky, twinkling stars and a bright crescent moon. The low rumble was almost unmistakeably thunder yet the source of it was hidden. Where were the clouds? He strained to see through the fence, past the overhanging branches and leaves of the small trees, but the early dawn refused to reveal its mysteries.

He crept quietly to the back of the centre to where it was clearer. He stood on an empty wooden pallet that rested against the garden centre wall and there above the fence, away from the zombies, he finally saw the source of the noise. Three mammoth creatures were flying above him, coming from the south. He could not identify what they were or used to be. They were not of this Earth. Their wings looked as big as houses and their bodies were long and cylindrical. Their dark black feathers matched the deep blue morning sky and he was grateful he could not see their features. He watched in silence as the monstrous titans of the sky continued on their path north, slowly flapping their giant wings, to what purpose he knew not. He was just pleased they were heading away. He felt an ominous sensation sprinkle over him and his stomach turned over. What was happening to the world? How could he possibly hope to find a future in this place of the dead and the diseased and the damned?

A ceramic plant pot behind him suddenly toppled over and smashed on the ground. He whirled around, whipping a knife out from his belt. A figure emerged from the bushes.

"Shit, sorry, Tom, I didn't mean to make you jump," said Heidi.

He put the knife back in his belt loop and jumped down off the pallet.

"Don't worry, you just caught me off guard. I thought I was alone."

"Mac started snoring. I couldn't sleep and I noticed you were gone. Is everything all right? What was that noise I just heard? Is there a thunderstorm coming?"

"You could say that."

Heidi looked up at the sky. "Doesn't look like it."

The dawn sky was enough light for Tom to see Heidi's attractive face. Her blonde hair and slim figure perfectly suited her bright outlook. A smile crept upon his face until he remembered Jess and Rosa, and all the problems lying ahead of them.

"You're an odd one, Tom," Heidi said. "One minute sitting in an office, probably hiding behind a pile of paperwork right, the next, leading a group of people past zombies to safety. What gives?"

Heidi leant back against the wall, grateful that there were no zombies in this area. With her and Tom out here, she didn't know how long that might be, but it was nice for a change for it to be just the two of them.

"The days of sitting at a computer, trawling through emails and filling in spreadsheets are long gone. To be honest, I'd only just finished college. I was kind of thinking my future was going to be boring, but things didn't quite work out how I'd expected. Mind you, I would swap it all to go back. There's so much death in the world now. I've lost my family, friends...for what? I'm sorry, Heidi, I know you only just lost your dad."

"Yeah...thanks...well, my mum's out there somewhere, so I'm not giving up yet."

They stood in silence for a while looking up at the fading stars.

"We should get going," said Tom. "We need to get everyone up and going. Mac reckons low tide is about six."

"Tom, when was the last time you relaxed, let someone else take charge?"

"A long time ago. Don't get me wrong, everyone chips in, in their own way. But I don't know, I guess they look to me for some reason."

"Harry, Christina, even Jess, they're all strong people. They're capable you know. You have to let them take the lead sometimes."

Heidi put her hand on Tom's arm and he smiled. She took a step closer to him and looked into his eyes. She brushed her hand over his cropped hair and he closed his eyes.

He felt so drained. It was nice to get some attention. Heidi's hands were soothing, caressing his head and rubbing his ear lobes. He felt her take a step closer and her breath was on his face.

Tom grabbed her closer and kissed her. He felt Heidi's warm tongue explore his mouth and he pulled her closer. He could feel her slender body pressed against his and she was pulling him into her. Tom slid his hands down her body to her waist where he untucked her shirt. His warm hands slipped around her soft skin and she moaned as they kissed. His hands moved up until he found her breasts and she ran her hands up and down his back as he caressed her.

Tom's head swam as he passionately kissed Heidi. She nuzzled his neck and her warm breath made him shiver. Suddenly, he pulled away. He longed to continue kissing and holding her and hold her, but he had to focus. Why had he let himself get so distracted so easily? Was he so weak that he caved in at the first girl showing an interest in him? Or did he really want her? "Heidi, we can't do this. We should…"

"Tom, forget 'should' for once, and do what you want. Do what you *need* to do." Heidi tucked her shirt back in and reached for his face, cupping his chin in her hand. "I like you, Tom."

"Hope I'm not interrupting," said Jessica walking around the corner of the garden centre. Heidi looked flushed and even Tom looked a bit embarrassed. As Tom stepped back, Jessica wondered if she had caught them in the middle of something more than conversation.

"No, what is it, Jess?" asked Tom. "We were just…talking."

"Well, everyone is stirring and keen to get going. You haven't forgotten what we're doing, have you? You ready? I hope you're not losing sight of what you're doing here, everyone is relying on you."

"I'm ready, and of course, I haven't forgotten." Tom marched off into the garden centre, annoyed that Jessica had questioned him, after all he had done.

"Why don't you cut him some slack?" Heidi folded her arms in front of her chest and hoped Jessica wouldn't see her flushed face.

Jessica literally looked Heidi up and down. She said nothing, but turned and followed Tom back inside.

* * * *

Back inside the garden centre, Heidi found things were well underway. They had stripped the shop of anything useful last night and bagged it up ready to carry. Caterina and Jimmy had bags of food and water to take. Mac and Jess were picking up the last of the tools and Tom was reminding everyone of their duties.

As they prepared to leave, there was a shrieking noise coming from the bathroom, followed by two loud bangs.

"That's Christina!" said Caterina.

Mac and Tom raced to the bathroom to find Christina coming out.

"What happened?" asked Tom.

"A bloody rat, that's what," she said.

"You've seen worse than a rat, surely?" asked Mac.

Christina looked at him. "You go look for yourself, young man."

Tom followed Mac into the bathroom and he saw what Christina was talking about. It looked like a rat had dragged itself out of the toilet. It was hanging half over the seat, its squashed bloodied face almost touching the floor. There was a broken cistern lid next to it. Tom guessed Christina had used it to kill the rat. What was most disturbing was that the rat had crawled *out* of the toilet. He peered into the bowl with Mac.

"I ain't never seen no rat like that before," said Mac holding his nose.

The back end of the rat trailed off into tentacles of varying length and thickness.

"It looks like its momma fucked a squid and this is the result," said Mac. "Look at that mess."

The rat was clearly dead, but the tentacles in the toilet were still moving around.

"Come on, let's get out of here," said Tom.

Back in the worker's restroom, they found Caterina sobbing. Tom tried to stifle his annoyance. She was hormonal, it wasn't her fault, he kept telling himself.

"Please, Christina, it's not safe, you have to stay with me," she was saying. "You just saw for yourself, there are weird things out there. Dead rats attacking us and that thing that attacked Jess yesterday. Now you're going out there with Tom and leaving me alone with him?" Caterina shot daggers at Jimmy who merely shrugged.

"Cat, now you listen to me. I will *always* be there for you, but I have to do this. I've took a back seat too long. Rosa, Laurent, Glenda, Harry and Lenny are in trouble and I have to help them. I'm a fighter and I'm not going to let some greedy pig split us all up. This Lazarus bloke has got it coming in spades. If you weren't pregnant, you'd be coming too. But someone has to stay and look after you. Jimmy's the youngest, he can drive and he can take care of you while I'm gone. It won't be for long."

Christina put an arm around Caterina and they walked off continuing their conversation.

"What was it, Tom? What freaked Christina out?" asked Heidi.

"You don't want to know," said Mac. He picked up a sledgehammer.

"Right, listen up everyone," said Tom. "This alien infection thing is getting worse. Whatever is happening to us is happening to the animals and birds too, only worse. When they die, they don't come back like they were. It's like they're being transformed into something else...some sort of hybrid created by mixing their own DNA and the aliens. Hell I don't know, all I'm saying is watch out. It's not just zombies we have to be careful about anymore.

"Moira is going to drive the ambulance with me and Caterina up front. Everyone else, jump in the back. We're going to turn the siren on so we get their attention. I want every blood-sucking freak show in the area to follow us to the Mount. When we get there, I'll turn the siren off and everyone follow me. Caterina and Jimmy are going to stay behind in the ambulance. When we've got Rosa and everyone else, we'll get back to the ambulance and straight around the coast to Penzance. Fingers crossed we find that ship. Anyone got a problem?"

Jimmy raised a pensive hand. "Um, Tom, what if you don't come back?"

"Then get Caterina to Penzance and to that ship. She is your priority now, okay? Your number one concern is for her and that baby. Think you can manage that?"

Jimmy nodded meekly.

"If anyone is not up for this, then now is the time to say. It's going to be messy out there. I need everyone armed and up for it. You aren't just killing zombies anymore, there's a good chance you're going to have to kill a person too, a real, living person. Just remember, it's them or us. If you hesitate, you will die. And so will our friends."

"Let's go, Tom," said Mac clutching the sledgehammer. "Kill the bad guys, rescue the good guys, and hurry the fuck up to Penzance to meet the navy. It's a cinch."

As Tom watched everyone file out heading to the ambulance, Jessica hung back.

"What about him?" she said pointing to Honok. He was still on the sofa where they had bound him. His hands and feet were still bound, although he was missing several fingers which Tom had thrown outside to the dead. His broken nose was crooked and he had a ball of wire wool stuffed in his mouth. He had watched everyone leave and was looking at Tom imploringly. "Should we take him with us?"

"Get everyone in the van. I'll see to him. Be there in a minute."

Jessica left, leaving Tom alone with Honok. Tom sat down beside Honok and removed the gag.

"What to do with you, Honok. That is a good question. What do you think I should do? What would you do if the table were turned? Would you let me go?"

"I...I would kill you." Honok looked a beaten man and for a moment Tom felt sorry for him.

"I know you would. Now that we're alone, tell me again what happened to Lenny?"

"You know what happened. Lazarus killed him."

"And Sally and Keisha, Mac's friends? What about them?"

"I already told you. Look, I'm sorry, we had some fun with them and...it just happened you know. It just happened!"

Tom moved closer to Honok. He was so close he could smell every stinking pore on Honok's contemptuous, nauseating body.

"Did you touch them, the girls? Did you touch Rosa?" said Tom quietly.

"Come on, man, what do you expect? We hadn't seen a woman in ages."

"Thanks," said Tom getting up off the sofa and picking up a large metal spade. "I just needed reminding."

Honok's mouth fell open and he began to bargain for his life. "No, please, I can help you, no, I...I..."

Tom launched the spade at Honok and the sharp tip went straight through his skull. It embedded itself into Honok's head and Tom had to tug on it to get it out. Half of Honok's face fell asunder. As blood flowed from Honok's decapitated skull, Tom lunged at him again and the spade took off the rest of Honok's face. His dead body fell sideways onto the sofa and Tom threw the spade down.

"Sorry, Honok, *it just happened.*" Tom spat on Honok's defiled corpse and walked out of the room to join the others waiting outside, picking up a new, clean spade on the way.

CHAPTER EIGHTEEN

As the ambulance sped away from the garden centre, Tom had to tell Moira to slow down.

"We want them to follow us, remember? At a safe distance, but make sure they do." He flicked on the siren and next to him Caterina put her hands over her ears.

Tom directed Moira out of Longrock, toward the Mount, continually checking the mirror to make sure the zombies were following. The mass of hundreds of dead bodies ran, jogged, walked, and slithered after them, drawn by the noise, the movement and the smell of living flesh. As they approached the slipway down to the beach, Moira slammed on the brakes.

"What the hell is that?" she said pointing up into the sky.

Tom recognised the two-headed dog he had seen yesterday. The yellow shirt was caught in one of its jaws and it was swooping down toward them, straight for the front windscreen. Tom wanted to laugh, it was such an absurd sight.

"Shit," said Tom. "Cat, move over, let me get to the window."

She let Tom clamber over her and he wound down the passenger window.

"What the hell, Tom? Close that or you'll get us all killed!" cried Caterina. "Moira, step on it!"

Moira watched calmly as Tom pulled a pistol out and took aim. He fired at the advancing dog which was now about fifteen feet away. The bullet struck the dog, but it did not slow the creature down. The bullet passed through its bloated body, sending blood raining down on the ground and the ambulance. It flew on, seeing the three people in the vehicle. Its jaws dribbled as it sensed the juicy flesh it was about to eat. It was close enough now for Moira to see the whites of its eyes and its razor sharp teeth.

"This country has gone to the dogs," said Tom. He fired again and succeeded in hitting the dog in one of its heads, the bullet entering straight through one eye. The dog jerked to the right and missed the ambulance by inches, slamming into the tarmac beside him. Tom jumped out of the ambulance quickly before the dog could regain its senses. The dog was confused. One of its heads hung limply while the other snapped and tried to gather itself for attack. Tom fired twice more into the dog's moving head, finally killing it. He jumped back in and Caterina recoiled from him. He was covered in gristle, tissue, and bits of brain from the dead dog. He had been standing no more than three feet away when he had killed it and hadn't even realised it had sprayed him with bits of its own rotting flesh when he shot it.

"Tom, what's going on? I don't understand. Flying dogs? Rats that can swim? What's going on?"

"Cat, it's not safe anywhere. We can't bottle ourselves up in a house or a shopping centre or *anywhere* anymore. This infection has spread to everything. Remember back in London, the rat that bit Freddy, that cat at the river? It's getting worse. Eventually, something will get us. We can't hide forever. We have to make that navy ship. *You* have to make it to that ship. If we don't come back from The Mount, you need to get to Penzance, okay? *Make Jimmy take you.*" He handed Caterina the pistol and she took it with a quiet thanks, stuffing it under her jumper.

Moira pulled the ambulance down onto the slip road and they headed down to the beach. She saw that Mac was right. The tide was out and the sand led all the way from the coast to the island. Looking at the Mount, she remembered where she had seen it before, some documentary on the History channel from years ago. A battle had been fought there years ago, one she struggled to remember now. All she could recall was the castle. It stood on the hilltop and she had to force herself to look away, at the road. She knew another battle was brewing, and she also knew this one was not going to be on any documentary programme. This was real.

Moira felt uneasy. The Mount had an imposing presence and the closer she got the worse she felt. Oh to be curled up at home with a good book now.

She pulled the ambulance up, turned the engine off, and jumped out. Tom flicked the irritating siren off and Caterina slid over as he jumped out too. Everyone was filing out the back and Tom told Jimmy to go sit up front with Caterina. He made it clear that if anyone else came back over the causeway he was to take Cat to Penzance.

"You and Cat need to sit down low in there and keep quiet. The zombies will file right past you. Once they see us on the beach, they'll follow us."

Jimmy went and sat behind the wheel of the ambulance next to Caterina. Christina followed him.

"Take care, Cat, I'll be back soon. Just watch your back okay?"

"Will do, but don't worry, Christina. I'm not going anywhere without you."

"You do what you have to do, Jimmy. Look after her," said Christina. She hoped that Jimmy would be mature enough to handle the situation. She didn't like the thought of leaving Caterina alone with him, but it was necessary. They were going to need all available hands getting the others back and Caterina couldn't drive.

Tom surveyed the interior of the ambulance. They had left the bags of provisions inside. They had no intention of staying on the Mount any longer than necessary and if the shit hit the fan at least, Caterina would have supplies to last her awhile.

He closed the doors and took stock. He was carrying a revolver and Jessica had the other. They only had two guns between them now, so it was the best they could do. Now that Caterina had the pistol, he decided he would take the automatic and he handed the revolver to Heidi. He knew Harry had been carrying two as well, so unless Lazarus had a fully stocked armoury up there, they were on equal footing.

Heidi tucked the gun in her pocket carefully and carried a large pair of loppers in her hands. She trudged after Tom and looked around at the group. Mac was carrying a sledgehammer and a mean look on his face. Christina had picked up a spade and had a large knife in her belt. Moira was wielding the long-handled shears and Jessica the bow-saw. All of them had pockets stuffed with small knives, pliers, cutters; anything that might come in useful. Heidi knew that she was going to have to stand up for herself, but was nervous all the same. She hadn't actually 'killed' anyone yet. She had seen plenty of killing, and plenty of dead bodies over the last few weeks, and she hoped that when the time came, she would have the strength to do it.

She wondered if her mother was safe and if she knew her father was dead. Heidi scurried up to walk beside Tom at the front of the pack as they walked across the sand. "You think we'll be all right, Tom?"

"Probably," he said, clearing his throat. "Sorry I can't be more positive than that, but we just have to wait and see. Look, at the base of the island there are some houses, just beyond the outer wall. We're going to have to be real careful. The island must be clear of zombies, but Lord knows who else is hiding in there. When we get there, I want you to stick to Moira like glue. She can handle herself and you're better off with her than being on your own."

"Why can't I stick with you?" she asked.

"I'll move faster on my own. I need to find Harry and Rosa. I need to find everyone and get them out of there. I'll be able to sneak around easier alone."

"Tom, there are more of them than us, what if you get cornered, what if you can't fight past them all? What if..?"

"Too late for ifs and buts," said Tom. "Doesn't matter if there are more of them, they'll be spread out trying to defend this place. Lazarus will have them all over the place. In twos or threes, we can take them on. That's why I want you with Moira. Go now, Heidi, please."

Tom looked at the Mount. They were going to have to navigate their way up the hill to the castle and Tom wasn't sure if there would be an easy way up. They were on a well-worn path now over the beach. It had been put down for tourists years ago and the thin path was leading them directly to the base of the Mount. On either side of the path were rock pools covered in seaweed from the receding tide. The ocean smelt fresh and strong. They would be at the Mount in minutes and still Tom saw no sign of life. He looked back over his shoulder to the beach where they left the ambulance. It was still there and he could vaguely see two faces looking back at him through the windscreen. Coming down the slip road were the first of the zombies, the ones who still had most of their bodies intact and fully operating legs. Tom knew they would follow them across the beach. He had no intention of leaving Lazarus behind up there to build another army once this was done.

"Mac, Jess, Christina, I want you all to stay together, okay? I'm going in first and I'll draw them out. I'm going to try to go ahead and find the others. Moira and Heidi will be right behind you. We don't have long. The dead are not far behind and we need to get back to Caterina soon as we can."

There were nods of agreement and Tom felt the ground underneath his feet change. They were on the Mount now. The ground had been concreted over and they were facing down a street lined with a few houses. There was an information booth to his right with a large signpost pointing the way to the steps up to the castle. He ran past the crumbling weathered houses, rotting bodies lining the street. Lazarus must have had his men take out all the zombies, but they had left them in the street where they had died. Was it a warning? Perhaps some found their way over here occasionally when the tide was out.

None of the bodies got up when Tom ran. Just when he thought he was going to make it to the steps a shot rang out and the tarmac in front of him cracked as a bullet tore its way into the road. Another shot was followed swiftly by another as he zigzagged his way through the estate. Two more shots flew past Tom before a door opened from a house to his left and a tall man ran out.

"Hey, you, stop!" The man fired again and Tom felt the bullet whistle past his ear.

Tom stopped running and turned around to face the man. He was tall with curly black hair and an even thicker beard. "I don't think so."

The tall man pointed the gun at Tom and fired. It clicked empty. Tom had counted the six bullets and knew the man was out of ammo. Before he had time to reload, Tom charged at him. He didn't want to waste his precious bullets at this point. The man was rooted to the spot as Tom flew at him with the pick-axe raised above his head. Tom brought it crashing down on the man and it landed in the man's shoulder.

Yelping in pain, the man tried to push Tom away, but Tom shoved the man back down to the ground, pulled the axe out, and thrust it into the man's shocked face. As Tom pulled the axe from the dead man, he heard more doors opening.

"Get them!"

Tom watched as eight men poured from the houses on either side of him. They left Tom alone though, as Mac, Jessica and Christina joined him on the street. Side-stepping the corpses, they fought the men who were armed with swords and knives. Tom watched briefly, reluctant to leave his friends, but aware he had to get moving onwards and upwards.

Mac dodged an old man who tried to run him through with a long sword and buried the sledgehammer in the man's skull. He whirled around and struck another man who was trying to stab Jessica. Christina was engaged in a battle with another man who was wielding a huge sword. She was keeping him at bay with her spade and Tom could hear the clashing of metal as they fought. He saw Heidi pull the pistol out of her pocket and shoot a man dead who was charging straight at her. Reassured, Tom got up and sprinted up the steps to the hilltop.

As Tom climbed higher, the slower he got. The uneven steps had been crudely carved into the hillside and he stumbled frequently in his rush to get to the top. Many of the granite steps were covered in slippery moss and algae. Thankfully, there was an iron handrail beside them and on more than one occasion, he had to grab it to stop himself from falling back down to a painful heap at the bottom. He could hear the shouting and crying from below intermingled with gunshots. He hoped the gunfire was only from Heidi.

Nearing the top of the steps, the castle began to come into view more. Tom paused to take a breath and an arrow suddenly landed beside him, thudding into the ground at his feet. Tom looked up and saw from one of the battlements a man with a crossbow. The man launched another arrow that flew over Tom's head. Tom pulled his gun out and took aim. His first shot missed, sending a plume of dust into the air as it hit the stone beneath the man. As he took aim again, he felt a pinching pain in his leg and looked down. An arrow had gone through his left leg and was sticking out with blood dripping down from the tip. He hadn't even noticed it and yanked on it to pull it out. It had snagged itself on his shinbone though and trying to remove it sent shockwaves of pain to his brain.

Tom ignored it and aimed the gun again, firing at the archer. Tom wanted to cheer when he saw the man topple over and fall sixty feet to the cobbles below. By chance, he had pulled off a head shot and the path to the castle was now clear. Trying to ignore the pain in his leg, he snapped the arrow's tip off leaving the main body embedded within his leg. He began to run across the courtyard to the castle door. Two men ran out in front of him and Tom stopped. One held a bayonet, the other a dagger. They slowly advanced upon Tom.

"Leave now and I'll let you live," said Tom.

"Ha, that's a good one, Ed," said the man holding the dagger.

"Sure is, mate." Ed began circling Tom. "You want to go first, Grayson?

The man with the dagger nodded and lunged at Tom. The dagger tore a hole in Tom's shirt as he danced to the left, narrowly dodging the sharp blade. Grayson turned around and lunged again, the dagger heading straight for Tom's chest. Tom swung the axe and as Grayson swung by him, the axe embedded itself in Grayson's back. The dagger clattered to the floor as Grayson fell, dead instantly. Tom tripped over, only just dodging the dagger once more.

"You fucking bastard, you killed Grayson!" Ed roared and charged the bayonet at Tom.

Tom saw Grayson and the axe lying a few feet away out of reach. The dagger was even further away and Ed was going to be on him in seconds. Tom pulled the gun out and rolled, firing as he did so. Ed fell to the ground, trying to stick Tom with the bayonet. Tom felt more pain as the sharp blade sliced through his arm. He rolled away and then felt nothing more. He expected to feel the full weight of this man on top of him and the bayonet sticking from his stomach, yet when he opened his eyes there was nothing but clear sky. Tom rolled over and Ed was lying next to him, lifeless eyes staring back. Tom had hit Ed in the face with a complete fluke. He had fired aimlessly, hoping to slow Ed down, but he had taken off half his skull.

With the two men dead, Tom stood up and felt his shoulder. The bayonet had sliced through his shirt, but the cut was not deep. Tom heaved the axe from Grayson's back and tucked the pistol back in his pocket. He headed for the small doorway to the castle that Ed and Grayson had come from. Tom kept the axe ready, prepared to slice and dice his way through whatever lay on the other side of the door.

* * * *

As Tom advanced onward, a figure from above watched. Walker saw Tom in the courtyard kill Ed and Grayson, and on the steps below came more of them, both men and women. Walker rushed down to Lazarus' room and barged in without even knocking.

"Are they dead yet?" said Lazarus from his desk, not even looking up when Walker barged in.

"No sir. They got past the men down at the base. I gave the gun to John as he said he had used one before. He was supposed to take them out, but…"

Lazarus slowly pushed his chair back, put the papers down, and stood up. "Are you telling me that they got past John? What about the other men you had down there? And Christopher? Ed?"

Walker shook his head. "They're dead, sir."

"Are you kidding?" shouted Lazarus. "Well, send everyone. Stop them!"

"The men are spread out around the island, sir, you wanted all angles guarded. Plus, it's early, some of the men aren't ready, they're still asleep. I can try, but we're pretty thinned out. You said the Mount had to be…"

Lazarus pushed Walker back and pinned him against the wall. "So help me God, Walker, you stop these people or I'll run you through myself."

"There's something else, sir," said Walker. "They brought the dead with them."

Lazarus let Walker go and turned to the window, puzzled. He threw the windows back and looked out across the causeway. Dozens and dozens of zombies were making their way across to the Mount. Some were already at the base of the hill and still more were cascading down the slip road at the coast's edge.

"You said you could contain this, Walker. Get out there and deal with them. Dead or alive, just fucking deal with them!"

Walker left quickly to gather more men, leaving Lazarus pondering his next move. He would be damned if he was going to let them come in here and take whatever they wanted. He slung his black coat on and stormed out of the room. He saw Walker in the main foyer to the castle talking to Norm. As he came down the stairs, they ran outside carrying hammers, blades and small swords. Lazarus ignored them and carried on toward the cells.

Laurent looked up as Lazarus strode down into the cells. He had fallen asleep. He looked over at Rosa's cell. She was still asleep too. Harry was nowhere around and neither was Norm. "What do you want?" he said as Lazarus stood outside Laurent's cell door.

Lazarus peered through the cold bars. "Your friends are here."

"I don't know what you mean. What friends?" Laurent knew it must be Tom. Harry said he'd come, but where was Harry now? He must've left in the night, but why wasn't he here now? Laurent could see Lazarus held a knife in his hand, but he had nothing to defend himself with.

"They're making a mistake, you know," said Lazarus. He was staring at Laurent like a hawk watches a mouse. "Your friends seem to think they can come here to the Mount and to *my* house, and just do what they like. You know they've already killed good men trying to get to you."

"Good men? Is that what you call your bunch of murderous bastards?" Laurent sat up. "You rape, you steal, you kill...and *we're* the bad guys? You are fucked up, Lazarus. Tom is going to kill your men and then he'll kill you."

Lazarus laughed and tossed the knife from hand to hand. "Really? You think he's going to do all that on his own?"

"No, not on his own, Harry will help him..." Laurent stopped, suddenly realising the mistake he had made.

"Harry? I suppose I should have expected it. A shame but I will just have to put him down like I did your other friends. Remember what I did to Lenny? Good times."

Laurent struggled to his feet and rushed at the cell door. He pushed his hands through the gaps in the bars and tried to grab Lazarus, but he was too slow. Lazarus backed away as Laurent raged.

"If Tom doesn't kill you, then I will. Unlock this door and we'll fight like men, like real men. Come on, Lazarus, prove you're a man." Lauren rattled the cell bars and Rosa stirred.

Lazarus smiled. "I'm afraid I don't have the keys, Mr Laurent. Oh well."

Lazarus pulled the gun from behind his back and shot Laurent at point blank range. Laurent was thrown back into the cell as his chest exploded. He was aware of the smell of burning flesh and he found himself back down on the floor of the cell. He put his hands to his chest and they found an empty cavity where his ribcage should be. He looked up at Lazarus, astonished. "But...but…"

Lazarus fired again and shot Laurent in the head. Laurent's head rocked back and his body collapsed as his brains flew out and splattered all over the cell walls. Lazarus walked across to Rosa's cell. The loud shots had awoken her and she had turned over just in time to see Laurent executed.

"What have you done?" she said choking back tears. "What have you done?"

"I truly had high hopes for you, Rosa," said Lazarus calmly. He looked at her battered and broken body. "Such a waste."

There were shouts and noises coming from outside, just above the cells in the courtyard. Through the small window in the cell walls he saw feet running past. Lazarus knew the others were getting close now. The fight would be inside the castle very soon. He raised the gun and pointed it at Rosa.

"I'm sorry, Rosa, I wish I had something pithy to say, some barbed witticism to impart, but I'm all out. Any last requests?" Lazarus held the gun pointed at her through the cell bars.

Rosa hugged her knees to her chest and cried. "Please don't, please...I just want to go home, back to my Jess." She pictured Jessica, her sweet face kissing hers, the way she brushed her hair behind her ears. She remembered lying with her in bed talking about the future, about what they were going to do. Rosa could still smell her, taste her, feel her warm arms wrapped around her. She closed her eyes and waited for the inevitable shot.

Lazarus looked at her for the final time. "You people are so fucking pathetic," he said squeezing the trigger.

CHAPTER NINETEEN

Harry held the sword with both hands and jumped off the last step into the cells beneath the castle. As Lazarus fired the gun at Rosa, Harry flew through the air and the sword sliced through Lazarus' midriff. Harry fell on top of him with the sword still held firmly in his grip. The gunshot echoed around the small dungeon and as it died away, Lazarus and Harry lay still.

"Rosa! Answer me, are you okay?" shouted Harry.

Lazarus was not moving and Harry got up, drawing the emerald encrusted sword out of the immobile body.

Rosa was crying, but unhurt. "Oh, Harry, get me out of here!"

"Are you hurt?" shouted Harry.

"No, he missed me when you jumped him. Is he dead?"

Harry kicked Lazarus's body. "I think so." Harry knelt down and felt in Lazarus' pockets for the keys to the cells, but found nothing but a knife. "Rosa, where are the keys, didn't he have them?"

"No. Laurent asked him to release us, but…"

Harry looked over into Laurent's cell. "Jesus Christ." Harry couldn't bear to look at Laurent's body. It was obvious he was dead. At least he wouldn't be coming back as one of the undead. Harry said a quiet prayer for his friend and then stood up. There was no time for grieving now. He rattled the cell door, but it was too strong to break down.

"Rosa, I'm going to have to go look for the keys. Here, take this in case anyone else comes down here." Harry kicked the gun Lazarus had been holding over to her and Rosa picked it up with trembling hands.

"Harry, what's going on?"

"We're getting out of here. All hell's broken loose out there. It's Tom. He's brought help. Look, Norm must have the keys. I've got to go find him. I'll come straight back for you."

Harry ran out of the dungeon leaving Rosa alone. She shuffled painfully to the door of her cell. She wondered if she should put a bullet into Lazarus, but then decided against it. Who knew who else might come down those steps? She would need every defence she had, so why waste bullets on the dead. Listening to the noises coming from outside, it was obvious something was happening. Harry had told her Tom had brought help. She wondered if Jess had come too. There was an aching in her heart when she thought about her. They had been together only a few weeks, but she loved her so much. Twenty four hours ago, Rosa had wanted to die. Now the thought that her friends and Jess were here gave her a new impetus for life. She had Harry's jacket on, the only thing she could use to cover herself up with. They had taken away the rest of her clothes long ago.

Suddenly, Lazarus coughed. He wasn't dead! Rosa recoiled into the far corner of her cell, away from him. She watched silently as he struggled to his feet. He stood in the shadows and she was unsure what was going on. He wasn't doing anything, not speaking, not moving; just standing there. Finally, he took a step forward and she saw his face. His hair seemed blacker than ever before now, dangling as it did by his pale face. He took another step forward and held onto her cell bars. He looked directly at her.

Rosa lifted the gun and pointed it at him. She was amazed he could stand at all. Harry had sliced the sword clean through him and blood still poured from his wounds down his legs. It was trickling down his trousers legs and out over his boots into her cell.

"I'm not dead yet, girly," Lazarus sneered.

With trembling hands, Rosa pulled the trigger and fired. The bullet ricocheted off a cell bar and whizzed past her into the mattress behind her head.

Lazarus laughed and pointed a crooked finger at her. "My men will win this war, you know. All of your friends are going to die here just like Laurent. Like Jackson. You know what I did with him? I chopped his diseased body up and threw him away with the rubbish. I hate people like you. My army will kill all of you defending this place."

"Really? I don't think so. You think your men will die for you? They're not an army, they're just rapists and murderers. They only hold allegiance to themselves. Trust me, they don't look up to you, they're afraid of you. When the first of your men falls to the ground dead, the rest will turn and flee. You're finished, Lazarus."

Lazarus cackled nervously. Rosa had been near death yesterday, but now she was full of fire. He spat on the floor. A disgusting great slop of brown and red blood splatted onto the stones at his feet. "I'll get you, Rosa. I will tear you in half and eat your damn heart."

He wandered out of the dungeons unsteadily, clutching his bleeding sides. Rosa pointed the gun at him again as he climbed the steps, but she knew she couldn't hit him. If she risked firing, the bullet could rebound and go anywhere. Frustrated, she sat in her cell, waiting for Harry to come back with the keys to her freedom.

* * * *

Out on the hillside, Harry didn't know where to turn first. The castle atrium had been empty, so he had run upstairs to see if Norm was up there with Walker. He searched all the rooms, but they were empty. He had gone into Lazarus' room too, but found no Norm and no keys. There had been some papers on Lazarus' desk and Harry stuffed them into his back pocket. They looked like they were important, perhaps something to do with the navy as he had begun to hear about the night before, and so kept them to read at a future date.

Harry went back out of the castle and surveyed the scene on the hillside before him. Norm could be anywhere. All around him mini-battles were going on. He saw Christina and Heidi fighting with two other men. Jessica was wielding a saw around, slicing apart anyone who was foolish enough to get in her path. All around them were more of the dead; many of Lazarus' men were preoccupied with them and Moira was running toward Harry up the path. Tom had brought more than just the group. He had brought a horde of zombies with him too. It was clever. Tom knew they were outnumbered and had brought reinforcements; an undead army to fight the living enemy.

"Harry!" Moira flung her arms around him.

Harry embraced her. "Moira, where's Tom? We have to hurry," he said.

"I don't know. He's around here somewhere. He was on his own."

"Listen, get the others and tell them to go down toward the pub. Get as many as you can and then go past the stocks and follow the path away from the castle. Follow it all the way to the cliff edge. There are some steps down to the ocean. It'll be the safest way off this island. Don't worry about Lazarus' men. They forgot all about their allegiance and duties the moment the bullets started flying. They're out to save their own skin now."

Moira ran, forcing her bloody shears into an approaching zombie as she did so. Its head slewed to one side and wobbled before falling off the zombie's decomposing shoulders. Harry looked around for Norm and finally spotted him hiding behind the well. His fat backside was sticking out and there was no doubting who it was. Harry ran over to him.

"Norm, give me the keys, now!"

"Go away, you'll give me away! Leave me alone, Harry. The zombies are...they're everywhere. What...what do you want the keys for anyway? Lazarus wouldn't…"

I haven't got time for this, thought Harry. He grabbed Norm and yanked the keyring off his belt.

"Hey, give that back," said Norm getting to his feet.

"Fuck you, you fat freak," said Harry pushing Norm back toward the well.

Harry had hoped that Norm would fall down the well and disappear, but his plan didn't quite work out as he had intended. He had given Norm a good shove and Norm, surprised, had indeed fallen over backwards into the well. Unfortunately, his obese frame was too big for the well's opening and he got stuck, arms and legs flailing uselessly making him look like a beetle on its back.

"Help! Help!" screamed Norm.

Harry ran as the nearest zombies turned toward the sound. He watched as three, four, and then five, descended on Norm and began to tuck into the feast laid on for them. They gnawed at Norm's limbs as he screamed in torment. Only when they had eviscerated all his limbs could Norm fit down the well and his screaming body fell to the bottom, finally stopping with a tremendous splash. When Norm's bloated huge body reanimated, it found itself with no legs or arms, unable to climb out of the well, trapped forever.

As Harry ran back to the castle, dodging the zombies who appeared to be increasing vastly in number, he was joined by Jessica.

"I told Moira to get you lot out of here!" shouted Harry as they ran up the hill.

"I'm not going anywhere without Rosa!" shouted Jessica back. Two zombies suddenly sprang toward her and Harry thrust the emerald encrusted sword at them. The blade swept viciously through the air and lopped the first zombie's head clean off its shoulders. The second zombie tripped on a rock and as it fell forward, the sword embedded itself in its chest. Harry left the zombie and the sword behind and ran behind Jessica toward the castle.

They reached the main doors to the castle and once inside the atrium, they stopped suddenly. Tom was stood facing Walker. Both were bloodied and bruised. Walker's sleeves were rolled up and it was clear they had given up on their weapons and descended into a fist fight. Tom's shirt had been ripped off and he had a nasty cut on his shoulder. Sweat dripped off his torso and every sinew, every muscle in his body was taut, pumping with adrenalin.

They watched as Tom aimed a blow at Walker who easily dodged it. Tom was tiring and still losing blood from his leg. Walker swung and landed a hard blow on Tom's temple. He fell to the floor and Walker picked him up in a stranglehold, his hands on Tom's throat as he tried to crush his windpipe.

Just as Harry was about to intervene, Tom reached around and grabbed Walker's arms. He rolled forward, throwing Walker over his back. Gasping for air, Tom quickly jumped and kicked Walker in the head. There was a shout of pain, but Walker was not down and out yet. He swivelled and kicked Tom's feet out from under him, and they both crumpled in a heap together.

"Tom!" shouted Heidi. She pushed past Harry and Jessica in the doorway and fired wildly.

Harry and Jessica ducked instinctively as Heidi fired three bullets at Walker. Tom rolled out of the way and Heidi stood over Walker firing the gun even though the chamber was empty.

Tom grabbed Heidi and took the gun off her. He looked down at Walker. Heidi had hit him in the stomach once, missing with the other two shots. Tom looked down at him.

"Go ahead, kill me," sputtered Walker. He held both hands over his stomach, but blood was pumping through his fingers furiously. Tom didn't need to kill him. He knew Walker would be dead in minutes anyway.

"Where are they, you piece of shit? Where are my friends?" Tom knelt over Walker, lifted his head, and slammed it back down on the stone floor. "What did you do to them? Jackson, Glenda, Lenny...where are they?"

Walker laughed and blood seeped from his mouth. "They're dead, all dead." He laughed again, louder. "You'll never get out of here. You'll die too."

Heidi let out a small cry. "Mum? Oh no, no." She began crying and Harry went to comfort her. He held her to him as she wept.

Tom decided maybe Walker was worth killing after all. He picked up his head, Tom's thick hands holding Walker's hair, and slammed his skull repeatedly onto the stone floor. After the third blow, Walker's skull cracked, and after the fifth, he was dead. He had no idea at what point Walker had lost consciousness, but Tom continued battering Walker's head onto the floor anyway until his head was nothing but mush and Tom's hands were covered in what was left of Walker's brains. He only stopped when Harry put a hand on his shoulder.

"Tom, come on, we have to go."

Tom stood and turned around. "What about Rosa, Laurent?"

"Follow me."

Tom picked up an axe and Harry led them down the steps to the dungeon. Heidi and Jessica followed.

"Harry, thank God. I thought..." Rosa dropped the gun when she saw Jessica.

Harry unlocked her cell, opened the door and Jessica barged past him into the cell.

"Rosa, oh Rosa, what have they done to you?" cried Jessica as she held Rosa.

Rosa couldn't answer. She was sobbing and had buried her face in Jessica's shoulder.

Harry gave them a moment then spoke. "We have to get moving. We can't stay here." Suddenly, he realised Lazarus was not in the dungeons. "Rosa, where's Lazarus?"

"He just got up and left. He wasn't dead, Harry. I tried to stop him, but I couldn't."

"Okay, look, the state he's in he won't get far. The rate he was losing blood I'd give him no more than a few minutes. He's dead meat. Let's go."

With Jessica supporting Rosa, they went back upstairs and out onto the hillside. Heidi was quiet, reflecting on the death of her mother. She had half expected the worst, but it was still a shock. She had lost both her parents in the last day and she was feeling shell-shocked.

"Harry, we need to get back to the causeway. Caterina's waiting there for us in the ambulance. We're going to use it to get to Penzance," said Tom absently wiping Walker's blood from his hands on his thighs.

"Um, Tom," said Harry, "where is it? Where's the ambulance?"

Tom looked across from the castle over to the beach, but the ambulance was gone. The slip road was empty and there was no sign of it or Caterina.

"I don't get it. We told her to wait. We told her to wait for us unless..."

"Unless what?" asked Harry.

Tom raced around the corner of the castle, almost straight into the arms of a waiting zombie. He felled the dead corpse swiftly, dropping it with one swing of the axe. He scanned the horizon, looking west in the direction of Penzance. The buildings of the town glistened in the sunlight, and across the water, Tom saw it. A huge naval ship was heading away from Penzance, out to see.

"No. Oh please, no, not yet," he said quietly as Harry came running around the corner after him. Heidi followed with Jessica and Rosa behind her. Jessica handed Heidi her saw and Heidi crushed the skull of an advancing zombie. Thankfully, most were drawn to the battles around the Mount. What few of Lazarus' men were left, were fighting and shouting, attracting the dead toward them.

"Harry, it's gone. It's too late," said Tom despondently. "The navy is leaving."

"They can't be going already," said Jessica. "Tom, what do we do now? If Caterina and Jimmy took off, how are we going to get to Penzance? Can we catch up to them?"

Tom threw his axe down in disgust. "It's too late. I was too slow."

"Could we stay here?" asked Heidi. "Make this place secure again?"

Tom shook his head. "No. If we stay on the Mount, we'd only end up getting attacked again, perhaps by someone with bigger guns or a bigger army. It's not safe here anymore. Besides, look around you, there are zombies pouring over the causeway to the Mount, dozens and dozens of them, far more than we have bullets for or can take care of.

"We're going to be surrounded by hundreds of the fuckers soon; snarling, drooling, infected festering corpses, just waiting to take a bite out of us. Fighting back through them will be dangerous. You try to do that all the way to Penzance and you may as well just jump off this cliff right now."

"The water supply is infected now too," said Harry thinking of the well and Norm. "There's still a chance we could make it though," said Harry "There's another way. I found a boat. I sent Moira there with Christina. It's not far, come on we can make it!"

Harry led them down the side of the hilltop, avoiding as many of the dead as they feasibly could, making as little noise as possible. The last thing they wanted to do was bring a hundred zombies with them to the boat. Harry noted that many of Lazarus' men had been overrun, unable to cope with the sheer numbers of the zombies on the island now. Some of them had been devoured, but some only partially before being infected, dying, and reanimating. Harry found the steps down the cliff side and ushered Jessica, Rosa and Heidi down.

"Harry, some of them are going to follow us, you know." Tom picked up a discarded dagger and thrust it into the forehead of a zombie that had tried following them. It dropped dead at his feet, the dagger sticking upright like a flagpole. The moaning sound of so many zombies close by was unsettling. Being out in the open was unsettling.

"I know, but this is the way, trust me. There's a boat down there. This is really the *only* way out of here, Tom."

As Harry reached the base of the cliff, he heard shouting. It was coming from inside the cave and he recognised Christina's voice.

"No, we have to go back!"

"Back? Did you see what was going on up there? There's no way we're going back now," said Moira. "We wait for Harry. He'll bring the others to us."

"I am *not* leaving Caterina alone with that kid. She needs me. She's six months pregnant, for Christ's sake, we can't abandon her."

Harry continued into the cave where he saw the boat was still tied up. Christina and Moira were standing on the rocks arguing and another man was sat at their feet, idly tapping a sledgehammer against a wet rock whilst the ocean threw spray over them.

"Moira, thank God, you found it, I was worried you wouldn't," said Harry embracing her.

She held onto him, unable to admit her feelings for Harry were growing stronger. She knew he was a good ten years older than her, but they had forged a strong bond over the last few weeks. She wasn't sure if he felt the same about her, but as long as he was alive, that was enough for her, for now.

"Christina wants to go back for Cat," said Moira, reluctantly letting Harry go.

Tom stepped forward. "Christina, she's gone. We need to use this boat to go too."

"What do you mean gone? We've only just got here, she can't have gone already."

"It's true," said Heidi. "That navy boat was there. Jimmy must've seen it too. We've no transport, so…"

Christina saw the looks on their faces and knew it was true. The navy had come already. So Caterina was alone with Jimmy? God help her if he didn't get them to Penzance harbour in time. Christina looked past Tom and Heidi, and saw Rosa.

"Oh Jesus, Rosa, what did they..?" Christina looked beyond her, but the steps were empty and she frowned. "What about Glenda? Lenny? Anyone?"

Tom shook his head.

"My friends too?" asked Mac. "Sally? Keisha? They didn't make it?"

"This is it," said Harry.

"Motherfucker. I hope you stuck it to the prick running this place."

"I did," said Harry. "He's long gone."

"Christina, we have to go, *now*," said Tom feeling queasy. The adrenalin was wearing off and he felt cold. "You know how to steer this thing, don't you, because none of us have a clue."

"Um, yeah, yeah, I have a yacht myself. *Had* a yacht. Not that I did much sailing myself. I always had someone else do it for me. I think I can figure something out. Yeah, okay." She turned to Moira. "I'm sorry, Moira, about earlier. I didn't mean anything, I was just upset."

"Don't worry," said Moira hugging Christina. "Now tell us what to do so we can get the hell off this place."

Christina got Moira and Mac to untie the boat as she jumped on board. Tom and Harry helped Rosa across, and Jessica and Heidi followed. Christina started the engine and everyone collapsed onto the deck, exhausted. Mac and Moira jumped aboard just as the first of the zombies came crawling around the steps to the cave. One saw the boat and reached for it futilely. The zombie tripped over the rocks and careered headlong into the shallow, choppy water. Behind it came more. Rotting bodies shuffled toward the boat searching for the living.

Christina slowly steered the small boat out of the cave, past the cliff to the deeper ocean. Looking around the boat, she saw a group of people who had nearly killed themselves. Tom, as usual, was cut and bleeding. He looked like he had been in a fight with a bear. Harry was comforting Heidi, and Moira was sitting quietly beside him. Christina realised that Heidi had just lost both her parents and her heart reached out to her. Jessica and Rosa were sitting on the deck leaning against the railings. Jessica found an old blanket on the deck and wrapped it around Rosa. She was whispering into her ear, stroking her hair, holding her close. Never again would she want Rosa to be out of her sight, even for a second.

Mac came and stood beside Christina. "That it?" he said pointing out to the ocean. There was a huge ship in the distance, a small grey spot on the horizon. "You think we can catch up with them?"

Christina turned the wheel, taking them away from the Mount toward the ship. "We have to. If we don't…"

"If we don't, then we'll figure it out. I've seen you with Cat. She's stronger than you think, you know. She won't take no shit from Jimmy." Mac dropped his sledgehammer onto the deck. "Guess I don't need this anymore."

"Look at that," said Christina. "They're everywhere."

Mac looked back at the Mount. It was eerie. The dead were crawling all over it, scores of them eating the flesh of Lazarus' men, tearing into the raw meat like starving dogs. The hillside was dotted with zombies amongst the rocks and the island resembled a giant ant hill. The morning was sunny, but the castle was dark, deserted and desolate. The castle was perched atop the hillside looking ominous, like a symbol of death. Mac shuddered. His friends Sally and Keisha had been brought here. He hoped they hadn't been infected. He didn't want to think of them walking around like that, like zombies.

"Can I help? You know what you're doing, right?" he asked Christina.

"Yeah I'm fine, thanks Mac. I've got the basics covered anyway." Christina looked around the boat. There was a small door to their side leading down into the cabin below deck. Apart from that the ship was empty. It looked like it had never been used. She sailed them away from the Mount and away from the mainland in pursuit of the naval ship. She hoped they would be able to catch it up, but in reality, she doubted it. If they wanted to, the navy could charge away in a heartbeat. Where would they be then? Where would Caterina be?

"At least we're safe," said Christina. "Sit down, get some rest. There's no rush now. When you're ready, maybe go down below and see if there's a radio? We could try to raise the navy on it. It's a long shot, but it's worth a go."

"Sure. I just want check on Tom first, he looks pretty beat up."

Mac wandered over to Tom and Harry whilst Christina steered the boat on, its small engine chugging away.

Jessica snuggled up closer to Rosa. Tears streaked their faces, but they were smiling.

"I don't know what I would do without you, Rosa." Jess planted a soft kiss on Rosa's lips.

Rosa winced slightly, but kissed her back. Her lips were cracked and swollen. "Those men, are they all dead?"

"Yep, all of them. You're safe now," said Jessica running her fingers through Rosa's hair.

"Good. After what they did to me I hope they rot in hell."

Jessica knew what they had done to Rosa. It was clear from the marks on her body how they had abused her. Harry had intimated as much to her, but it didn't need saying out loud. When Jessica thought about what they had subjected her to it made her feel sick and angry. Rosa was so naïve and innocent, she shouldn't be punished like that. What had she ever done to deserve being locked up with those animals?

"You know, Rosa, I think we're going to be okay." Jessica took Rosa's face and kissed her forehead. She looked directly into her eyes. "We'll find somewhere safe again, some place to call home. You're safe now. Nothing can keep us apart anymore."

They relaxed back against the ships railing as Christina drove the boat on, taking them away from the dangers of the land.

CHAPTER TWENTY

He could feel his life slipping away. He could no longer see, but he could *feel*. He could feel everything in excruciating detail. Below deck was dark and cramped. The boat only had two small cabins and he had locked himself away in one of them, closing the curtains before lying down on the single bed to die. He could tell they were at sea now. The boat was listing and he could hear the waves creaking against the hull. So someone had found his escape plan and used it for themselves. I hope it's Walker, thought Lazarus, and none of those deadweight losers from the mainland.

Lazarus was scared. He always thought it was his destiny to be a leader and something special. His father hadn't thought so, but his father had been wrong about a lot of things. Lazarus felt the twinge in his gut and knew the end would come soon. That devious traitor Harry had gutted him with his own sword. Now he was dying, alone.

Suddenly, his skin started bubbling and Lazarus gritted his teeth as the agony spread. From his roiling chest to his extremities, it felt like his blood was on fire. Is this what death felt like? No, something was wrong. This wasn't just the pain of death, this was something more. Was he infected? How?

Lazarus tried to sit up, but he was too weak. Is this what his father felt like when he was dying at home, spread-eagled on the floor? Lazarus tried to call out, but only managed to spew thick blood over the sheets. He opened his eyes, and saw nothing but blackness. Was he blind? He could hear faint noises from above: footsteps and talking. If they would only come down they could help him. Walker would help him.

Suddenly, Lazarus arched his back and he couldn't breathe. His muscles were collectively contracting and his lungs felt like lead. He opened his mouth, gasping for air like a stranded fish. He tried to grab hold of something, but only found the wooden walls of the cabin. His fingernails splintered off one by one as he pressed down on the walls, desperate for breath. Finally, his body relaxed and he drew in a huge gulp of air. Lazarus wished he was dead. He would rather die quickly than suffer this ignoble, painful death. Why could he not slip away quietly, why must he suffer these torments? His spine abruptly went into spasms, rippling up and down until it cracked. Lazarus fell onto the bed in acute pain, a pain so hot and overwhelming he had never known anything like it.

Shaking, Lazarus' body tensed again and abruptly his back split open. His spine careered upwards, bringing his skin with it. His blistered, blackened skin was now mottled with purples and bright greens, dark hairs growing rapidly from every pore. His spine, like a worm with a life of its own, ripped his shoulder sockets out and stretched his skin taut. Looking more like a giant bat, his head rolled forward and two antennae burst from his forehead, spraying the cabin with more blood. From between his legs tentacles slithered out from every orifice, slithering and sliding across the bed, entwining themselves together to form a long fleshy tail.

"And there were no more worlds to conquer," Lazarus said quietly, terrified. A single tear dripped from his eye and then his lungs expelled air for the last time. Lazarus' heart stopped beating and he died whilst his body kept moving; bones cracking, tissue and muscles shifting while the infection grew. His very DNA was being radicalised and redirected; restructured. Toxins and poisons ran through his veins. The next time Lazarus would open his eyes he would be able to see again. The next time he stood up he would be one of the undead, yet also something more. He would remember the man that used to be called Lazarus, but he would know his new name too.

* * * *

Harry pulled the bundle of papers out of his back pocket and began to read. He could see they were slipping further behind the naval ship, but nobody had said anything about it yet and he didn't want to be the first to broach the subject. It was still early in the day to have all your hopes crushed. Anyway, who knows, maybe Christina would be able to catch up with it.

"What's that?" said Tom. Heidi was trying to attend to the arrow still sticking in his leg but wasn't sure what was best to do.

"Tom, sit still, will you? The bleeding's stopped, but you need to elevate it. We need to get this thing out of you before it gets infected."

"I'll see if there's a first aid kit," said Mac, getting up and leaving them. "Hey, Moira, you wanna help me look?"

"It's a transcript," said Harry dryly. "Lazarus managed to get tuned into some military frequency or something. He heard more than that automated message we heard. It's a conversation between the British and US by the looks of it. I don't know what's on it but Lazarus thought it was important."

"Throw it overboard," said Heidi. "If that man thought it was important it's probably rubbish. Who needs it."

"No, go on, Harry. What does it say?" Tom sat up and let Heidi continue checking him over. It felt good. Her hands were soft and smooth. It felt good to have someone close to him. Jessica had Rosa, why shouldn't he have someone too?

"It says here that Samson is Captain of the USS Lincoln. From the childish scribble, I think it says the US Navy is based in the Caribbean. Then there's another note here, says he was talking to an Admiral McCulloch on HMS Daring. Oh shit, it's the Daring that was coming to Penzance, that's who we're following."

Tom studied Harry's face whilst he read. Harry started off with a furrowed brow of concentration which gradually receded into wonder and finally horror as he read.

"What does it say?" asked Tom.

Harry let the papers fall to his lap. "Well, at least we're not completely alone. The navy must've escaped the worst of the infection. I guess any ships out at sea would've escaped it. HMS Daring and HMS Illustrious made it, but the rest of the British navy haven't been heard of. On the American side, the USS Lincoln, the USS Wasp and the Gerald Ford made it. Both say that the administration's gone. There's no one in charge anymore. The world leaders, the UN, Europe, everything is all gone. The infection swept around the globe faster than a celebrity sex-video. That's why there was no firestorm. There's no one left to push the button."

"What else?" asked Tom. He knew from Harry's face he had read more than that.

"Samson says they picked up an alien in the US. They've been talking to it, actually *talking* to it."

"You're kidding," said Heidi. "An alien?"

Jessica was still comforting Rosa, but had heard them talking and her ears pricked up when she heard the word alien. She still found it hard to believe. Even after the two-headed dogs and the strange creature that had attacked her, it was difficult to accept without seeing it with her own eyes.

Harry continued. "Apparently, this alien was found somewhere in the South. They interrogated it."

"Tortured it, you mean," said Heidi.

Harry knew what interrogated meant too, but ignored Heidi. "Seems they managed to get it to talk in the end. At first, it was using a language they couldn't understand, but later, it changed to English. I don't know if this information is any good to us, but...this alien said some crazy stuff. Look here. It says, and I quote:

'We are not a technological race. We have made huge technological advances, but with the goal of expanding our race, nothing else. We are clearly superior to you humans and all the pathetic creatures that dwell on this backwater you call Earth. To us this is planet XY-77. We need to use your planet. That is why we are here. Humans are so arrogant. You think that we would waste vast amounts of time and effort just to conquer you? Our science helped us to develop biological warfare. There are others out there who wish to destroy us. To this end we have created a variety of biological creatures to attack our enemies. In order to test these, we needed a fertile testing ground, one rich in life, yet ignorant and dumb, retarded if you like, a race inferior to our own.

That is where your planet Earth comes in. Germs, viruses, plants, animals - twisting organisms at the very root of their DNA, manipulating them is what we do, and we do it well. They are better than bombs and guns because they can adapt, mutate, even self-reproduce on the battlefield. Biological weapons are immune to fatigue. We can use your planet to create the perfect invincible weapon to defeat our enemies.'"

"Or to put it another way," said Tom, "we're fucked."

Harry picked up the papers again. "It says here there will be schools of fish, hundreds upon hundreds of them, designed to look for meat that will scavenge our oceans for food. It says our skies will be filled with carnivores, larger than skyscrapers, and our land will be populated by the reanimated dead. They want to see how the creatures perform against us. Humans are just convenient test subjects for their new design of weapons.

"The alien says they sent a few test subjects full of toxins from the aliens' own race that they hope will combine with a human subject. It says both DNA will fuse to create the perfect killing machine. They launched one toxin over Northern Africa, one over the Eastern coast of the US, and one over Southern England. Apparently, they wanted to see how long it would take for the toxin to find the correct subject, and to see how long it would take to work in the field as it would only work with a rare blood type. The human who receives this toxin would have to have a unique genetic code. He would have to be strong too as the metamorphosis would inflict them with unimaginable pain. If successful, the new hybrid creature would serve the aliens and be pre-designed to have a hatred for humans.

"Huh, it says this killing machine will be able to reproduce at will, spawning a new generation to rule the Earth and guard their new testing planet, a race designed to live on Earth forever, wiping out any human resistance and protecting XY-77 indefinitely."

"You sure about this, Harry?" said Jessica. "What if this is some elaborate joke? Sounds a little off kilter to me."

"How will we know if it worked?" asked Heidi. "I've seen some bizarre things, but this sounds a bit crazy, if you ask me. Maybe the alien was just trying to scare them? Perhaps it was just bragging?"

"Sounds plausible from what I've seen," said Tom. "Back at the garden centre when you were all asleep, there were things in the sky: huge, amazing creatures. They weren't of this planet. I can tell you that for a fact. I've seen what this infection is doing to animals too."

Harry interjected. "The alien says here the new hybrid creature will be able to speak only its name to humans and all other communication will be in the alien's native tongue. It will be called Otaktay."

"What kind of name is that? If it is true, let's hope we never run into it," said Tom. "Anything else we need to know, Harry?"

"Not really. Unless you want to see some badly drawn doodles of zombies. Jesus, I wish I'd never picked this up now." Harry threw the papers over the side of the boat.

Mac and Moira stood in front of the cabin door beside Christina.

"There's nothing up here," said Mac. "I'll go down and see if I can find something." He tugged at the door handle, but it didn't budge. "It's stuck."

Moira pushed Mac aside. "Allow me." Moira began pulling on the door handle. "Hope there's a good book down there, because I left all mine behind."

Harry sat upright. If the alien had been telling the truth, then the toxin had been released somewhere potentially close by. What if it had been Laurent, Daniel or someone on the island? Surely something would have happened by now. Besides, Southern England was a large area, so the toxin could be anywhere. Jackson? No, Jackson was dead. Harry had put him out of his misery. That emerald-studded sword had seen to that.

As Harry thought more about it, there was something nagging at the back of his mind. He had used that sword once more, on Lazarus. Why did it matter? Lazarus was dead. The sword was long gone, left behind at the Mount. Harry had cut through Lazarus with it like a scythe slicing through hay. He was surprised when Rosa had said he had managed to get up and walk away, but stranger things than that had happened recently.

Harry watched Moira tugging on the door as Mac laughed at her, ribbing her for being a typical weak girl. Mac seemed comfortable with them. He would be a good addition to the group. Moira was laughing as Mac joined her in trying to get the cabin door open. Harry liked it when Moira laughed. It was rare that anyone laughed these days, but her childish giggle made him smile. He had seen the way she looked at him and he liked her too, but it was too early. His family was still fresh in his mind and any thoughts of Moira inevitably made him feel rueful. His wife and children were dead, but it was hard to move on. There had been no funeral or grieving period. Maybe one day, soon, he might be able to move on.

The alien's words would not leave Harry's mind and he found himself thinking about them. The dots were there, but he couldn't connect them. What was wrong with him? Why couldn't he forget it? Maybe the alien had been fucking with them all along.

The sword he had killed Jackson with, the same sword he had cut Lazarus with. The sword still had Jackson's blood on it, *infect*ed blood. Lazarus was a strong man, but strong enough to survive being run through with a sword? Harry's blood ran cold. This was Lazarus' boat. When he had left the dungeons, where had he gone? Not to the mainland. To crawl away in a corner and die somewhere? Not likely. What if he came here? What if he was infected? What if Lazarus was that one-in-a-million chance, the one subject the aliens needed? What if he had the rare blood type that the toxin needed to…

"Mac. Moira. Don't open that door!" Harry jumped up and shouted at them.

"What's up, Harry?" said Moira waving and smiling at him as she finally pulled the door open.

The deformed creature that used to be Lazarus flew out of the cabin and sliced clean through Moira, its wings cutting her in half. Mac was sprayed with crimson blood as Moira's lifeless body fell to the wooden deck. The flying creature's tail swung wildly and thudded into Mac sending him flying back into Christina. She screamed and let go of the wheel as Mac landed on top of her. Mac hit his head on the deck and was knocked out immediately. The boat, uncontrolled, lurched and Heidi fell over the railings into the ocean. The flying creature swooped up into the air and hovered above the boat.

"Moira!" shouted Harry in disbelief.

Tom could see she was dead before she had hit the deck. Bright red blood pooled from her body and sloshed across the wooden deck.

Harry looked up and saw the dead body of Lazarus silhouetted against the sun. He recognised the dark flowing hair and distorted facial features. Two antennae were sticking out of his skull and his eyes were dead, yet without a doubt, he could see. There was no doubt it was him either. Lazarus had somehow sprouted wings covered in matted black hair. His arms bled into them, leaving only short stumpy hands to protrude from his torso. His legs were the only part of him that still looked human, and where his genitals used to be there was now a long tail that lashed from side to side.

"Help Heidi!" yelled Tom to Christina.

She crawled over the deck and threw a lifesaver over the side of the boat. Jessica and Rosa got to their feet.

"Tom, what do we do, what do we do?" Jessica took her eyes off the abomination above them and looked at him imploringly.

"We don't have any guns left, we don't have anything. I…" Tom was dumbfounded.

Suddenly, the magnificent creature swooped down toward the boat again to attack. Harry roared as Tom ducked and Jessica tried to drag Rosa out of the way. Jessica slipped in Moira's blood as she felt the weight of the creature's wings flapping above her. The sunlight was obscured as Jessica was covered in a huge shadow. As she fell, she heard Rosa scream her name.

Turning over, she saw Rosa flying up into the air, the creature holding her tightly with its tail. Rosa was crying and beating on the tail, trying to force it to let go, but it held her firmly. The creature flapped its wings slowly, hovering about fifteen feet above the deck.

"Let her go!" shouted Harry. "Lazarus, let her go, take me!"

The abomination turned its head toward Harry slowly. It made a series of growling noises and clicks before it opened its jaw widely.

"O-tak-tay," it said slowly. "Otaktay," it repeated. The creature spat the words out rather than spoke. Its tail tightened around Rosa and she gasped as it began crushing her. Two of her ribs snapped as it slowly coiled more of its fleshy tail around her slender frame. Her eyes bulged as the tail squeezed harder and she could feel her bones breaking. A creamy substance oozed from the tip of the monster's tail, dribbling onto the deck far below.

"Rosa! Rosa!" screamed Jessica from below. She jumped up, trying to grab Rosa's feet, but she was too far away. Jessica was directly beneath her, but it was impossible to reach Rosa.

There was an audible pop when Rosa's spine came apart. As it splintered, Otaktay's tail sliced clean through Rosa's body, splitting her in half. With one last dying scream, Rosa was ripped apart. Her left side went one way and her right half went the other. A massive waterfall of blood cascaded down over Jessica, choking her as it filled her open screaming mouth. The ocean turned red as Otaktay threw Rosa's twitching decapitated body into it, discarding the useless flesh he had no desire to devour. He had pierced her head with the tip of his tail and he flicked it away, down onto the boat. Rosa's head skipped across the deck until it fell over the side and bounced one last time off the hull into the icy water. Jessica fainted, drenched in the blood of her dead lover.

Otaktay swooped high up into the sky and then plunged straight back down again towards the out of control boat. Christina was trying to haul Heidi up the side of the hull from the freezing cold water. Tom and Harry were frantically looking for a weapon to defend themselves with, so far unable to find anything.

"Look out!" shouted Tom too late.

Otaktay flew quickly above them and in an instant, Harry had been snatched up in its tail. Tom picked the sledgehammer up from next to the unconscious Mac. He took a swipe at the thing that used to be Lazarus and clipped a wing. Otaktay still managed to fly up out of reach of Tom and again hovered over them whilst Harry punched and kicked, desperate to release himself from the creature's hold.

"Harry, I can't reach you!" shouted Tom. "Fight it!"

Tom swung the sledgehammer wildly, but couldn't gain enough height. He felt useless, angry that they were going to be picked off like this, one by one, first Moira, then Rosa. Now Harry was going to be slaughtered whilst Tom could do nothing but watch on helplessly.

"Flare gun!" shouted Harry as he felt the tail tighten around him. He knew he only had a minute left before he was killed like Rosa.

Dropping the sledgehammer, Tom scrambled down into the cabin, praying he would find something. There, on the wall down below deck, was an emergency box. He pulled it open and was grateful to find it had not been used. He cast aside the torch, life-vests and whistles and finally pulled out a flare gun. Tom raced back upstairs while loading it. As he set foot back on the deck again, he looked up. He could see that Harry was in immense pain as Otaktay slowly squeezed his body, the tail crushing him like a python would a deer in the jungle.

Tom aimed and fired before the creature could react and the flare tore through a wing. Otaktay let out a howl of pain, but did not let go of Harry. The antennae on Otaktay's head suddenly went rigid and the monster flew away, up into the air with a burning hole in one wing, still holding onto Harry. Tom fired again but Otaktay was too far away, wings flapping relentlessly, and the red blossom of the flare harmlessly ignited the sky above them.

Tom watched as the creature flew away to the west, with Harry still kicking, until it was out of sight. Why had it not released Harry? If it just wanted to kill him, it could have done it easily by now. Tom looked across the deck. Jessica and Mac were unconscious, covered in Rosa's blood. Moira was dead, and Christina was hugging a wet, shivering Heidi. He walked over to them and picked up the sledgehammer.

"Oh Jesus, what now, Tom? What the hell do we do now? Where do we go?" asked Christina. She and Heidi began crying together.

Tom threw the flare gun to the side and weighed the sledgehammer in his hands. He looked upward into the sky and then back down to Christina and Heidi, who was looking up at him through teary eyes.

"We're going after it," snarled Tom, as anger coursed through him like fire. "I'm going to get Harry back. Then, by God, I'm going to fucking kill it."

THE END